Caribbean Moon

A Manny Williams Thriller

By
RICK MURCER

PUBLISHED BY:
Murcer Press, LLC

www.rickmurcer.com

Edited by
Jan Green - thewordverve.com

Interior book design by
Bob Houston eBook Formatting
http://about.me/BobHouston

ISBN:0615706770

Dedication

For my wife Carrie, who believed in me.

For JC, who loves me and keeps me on the path.

To Josh and Elizabeth, my favorites.

To Randy, my brother, for being my brother.

~~ Rick ~~

Caribbean Moon

A Novel

By
RICK MURCER

CHAPTER-1

"I'll need to see your ID, sir."

"What?" Manny Williams stared at the pretty, Latino barmaid. He must have looked like a deer in headlights because she started to grin, rescued her composure, and asked again.

"Uh, I'm thirty-eight years old. I don't . . ."

"Having trouble gettin' served, Williams?"

Glancing to his left he noticed Sophie Lee, his diminutive partner as she stood a few feet away wearing one of her famous *gotcha* grins.

"I should have known . . . and don't you have something else to do?"

"Why no, no I don't." Sophie sat down on the nearest bar stool and crossed her legs. "And you should have known what?"

"That you put the poor girl up to this. Does she know that even in Puerto Rico you can be arrested for messing with a cop?"

The barmaid's face raced from smiles to the south side of unsure.

"Don't listen to him. He has anger issues, plus he's a workaholic." Sophie lowered her voice to a whisper, drawing closer to the barmaid. "And well, among his other issues, he does the little blue pill thing."

The young woman's dark eyes grew large.

"Really? But he seems so . . . I mean, well, look at him."

"Blue pill thing?" said Manny, shaking his head.

Sophie ignored him. "I know. He's all blond and blue-eyed and hot. Sad, isn't it? You just can't tell these days."

"Ladies, I'm right here."

"Think of his poor wife."

"He's married with that . . . problem?" the barmaid said.

"Yep. It's like having the candy but you can't get the wrapper off, in more ways than one."

"Seriously, I haven't left."

"He's in denial, but he's starting to realize he has to talk about it, find out what's up, er, isn't," continued Sophie.

"You're right, it is sad. His wife must be miserable."

"Okay, I'm getting out the cuffs," said Manny.

"Wow. Does he like that kind of stuff?" asked the barmaid, now with a glint in her eyes.

Sophie nodded. "I think that's why he wanted to be a cop, you know?"

Manny reached into his tuxedo pocket and quickly slapped one cuff on Sophie's wrist, the other to the brass rod running under the teak wood bar.

His partner stared in disbelief at one hand, then the other. Her stunned look was worth a million dollars to him, and Manny couldn't remember the last time he'd seen her anywhere near speechless.

He turned back to the barmaid. "I'll take that pina colada now."

"Yes sir. On the house."

Manny didn't think he'd ever seen anyone mix a drink faster.

"Hey. Williams. Are you nuts? I mean you brought cuffs to a wedding reception?" marveled Sophie.

"You know me. I'm always prepared. And look at that, they came in handy."

He grabbed his drink and began to walk away.

"Manny! You can't leave me like this."

"I can. But say the magic word and you're free."

Letting out a breath, her pretty face displaying her Chinese-American heritage, Sophie answered. "No."

"Okay. I'll come get you in the morning, if I remember."

"Wait. Wait. Damn you. All right. *Please* let me out of these."

He tossed her the key. "Good girl. It's nice when people address me with manners."

"I got your manners right here . . . and this ain't over, Williams. Understand?"

Waving her off, he left the ball room and walked through the double doors of the reception room, his grin growing wider. "I still got it," he said out loud.

Continuing through the lobby, taking his drink with him, he was intent on harvesting his share of the fresh Caribbean air. He pulled open the crested glass door, strolled to the stucco patio, and leaned over the wall of the posh hotel on San Juan's Condado Strip. It was humid, and the damnable tuxedo upped his discomfort. Dots of perspiration multiplied above his lip. But that was okay. This was for Mike and Lexy's wedding, and he'd survive. Getting married in beautiful San

Juan, followed by an elaborate reception, was the wedding that dreams were made of. Not to mention the seven-day cruise that would start the next day. He hoped his fourteen-year-old daughter, Jennifer, would opt for something much less exotic when she tied the knot.

The full moon's pale reflection rippled across the waves as they tangoed toward shore and, ultimately, into the hotel's barrier rock wall. He'd seen a thousand full moons, but none matched this Caribbean version. Magnificent and serene. He felt some of his perpetual tension flow away.

Setting his drink on the ledge of the wall, he pulled out his wallet and touched his Lansing Police Department ID.

Manfred Robert Williams, Sergeant Detective, Lansing Police Department.

After eleven years, it still gave him a kick to see his title in print, almost as much as seeing his real name. His sometimes-eccentric father had pulled the name Manfred from *where-the- sun-don't-shine* because he had wanted his only son to be different.

Mission accomplished.

His strong fingers loosened the black bowtie, and he released a pent-up breath. It felt good to get away, but there were cases to solve. The thing is there would always be too many cases, too many sickos, and not enough hours. Walking hand-in-hand with that was the fact he had no real sense of when enough was enough. It all added up to a workaholic's perfect storm. Sophie had hit that nail on the head.

Complicating things even more were the results of his wife's last mammogram. There was something there, an anomaly that the doctor couldn't quite figure out. Louise had assured him it was nothing, that they would review the test results with the doc when they got home from this trip. But it didn't sound like "nothing."

Louise had insisted they not cancel this trip for a plethora of reasons, and she was right with most of them. Besides, his need to chill out had become as obvious as an elephant in the kitchen.

He sipped the drink—coconut aroma strong even if the drink was not—and tried to enjoy the scene in front of him. But his thoughts wandered again, this time to the job—what else—and his latest case. So much for relaxing.

"Good God, I've got the attention span of a two-year-old," he growled. But the grisly homicide involving the murdered wife of a prominent psychologist clung to his hip, refusing to let go. The details of the murder stormed his senses. He tried to shove them away, but they hung in there like a door-to-door environmental activist. Who knows? Maybe he didn't want to stop the thoughts from coming. He winced. Now *there's* a question for the department shrink.

Sylvia Martin's eyes—lifeless, posed in a glassy, haunting stare—were the picture the killer wanted no one to forget. Only the brutality of the attack matched its senselessness. The suspect had played out a host of sexual fantasies with her—postmortem, according to the CSU report. Not just sex either. He had lain waste to the corpse with such force that much of the upper torso had become a purple-and-black teething bar.

Alex Downs, the department's head Crime Scene Investigator, could only remember one case with similar brutality. Eleven years prior, a psycho named Robert Peppercorn had attacked four young women and had raped, beaten, and bitten them repeatedly, falling just short of killing the victims.

After he had acted out his malefic fantasies, Peppercorn had congenially handed each of his victims a long-stemmed, red rose and thanked them for a good time. Sylvia Martin's killer had left a black rose draped across her ravaged torso. Manny suspected it was no coincidence. The LPD wanted to talk to Peppercorn pronto. But he had been deemed cured by his psychological team and, after his release last year, had moved on. In fact, no one had heard from him since, not even his mother.

Manny rubbed his eyes with thumb and forefinger. There were differences. Men like Peppercorn were motivated and controlled by impulses, disorganized, but the killer in the Martin case was a cold, calculating psychopath. Alex and his Crime Scene Unit saw obvious similarities to Peppercorn's "work," but said forensic dentistry was just not that reliable, and there were only fragmented bite marks, not clean ones from which to make a partial mold. Alex said it was like the killer had varied his marks on purpose. And that was a detail Manny didn't think Peppercorn was capable of manipulating. He just wasn't that bright. Still, if they could locate him, Peppercorn would be a good place to start.

His thoughts ran deeper as he passed a hand through his hair, an old nervous habit from adolescence.

Was the whole world going crazy? What kind of animal does that to another human? It made Jack the Ripper seem like Captain Kangaroo.

It was more than a random act; he felt it in his

bones. The investigation could use him now, his intuition.

Let it go, man. The department can handle things for a week. You're on vacation. Louise needs you; concentrate on her for a change.

Again, he switched focus to the coconut delight in his hand while he tried to bum rush the overwhelming nuances of the job.

Sometimes these nuances loomed like unholy apparitions and hung on with a life of their own. He pushed again, and they scampered to some recluse corner of his head. No more work. Not here. Not now.

That's when the ear-splitting scream interrupted paradise.

CHAPTER-2

Eli Jenkins heard the shriek echo from somewhere beyond the pool, but didn't care. Hell, it might provide a small, well-timed diversion. He stayed focused on the newlyweds sauntering toward the shadowy northwest corner of the hotel's courtyard, their arms around each other's waists.

They giggled and bumped playfully as they moved near the wall, past the steamy, chlorine-filled Jacuzzi. Alone and in love.

Except they weren't alone.

Mike and Lexy Crosby were so absorbed with each other, and with the night, that it would have been impossible to notice the towering figure standing in the opaque shadows. Unless the couple had been looking for him. Really looking. Which they weren't.

Jenkins stood mere yards from their eventual destination, hands clenched in powerful fists. He could do it now. He could tear them apart, and no one would see.

With three long strides, he moved through the shadows and locked in on the newlyweds. He would destroy the groom and then help himself to the fine, young fruits that Crosby's new wife flaunted like a Las Vegas whore. Then he'd steal her soul, and if time allowed, he would make sure it happened with a slow, excruciating process. Anyone who hooked up with Crosby's ilk deserved that kind of communion with the Grim Reaper. He would make her dance an agonizing waltz with fear, turning her mind to Play-Doh. She would beg him to kill her. They all would.

His heart rate strutted with anticipation. He wanted to see her face as she checked out, as her life-light faded like a dying star. Then, at just the right moment, he would catch her soul and keep it for his own. She would be part of him forever, like the others in Michigan. Just like that. They were with him, even now. The more the merrier.

Migrating closer to the unmindful lovers, he could barely contain his thoughts. There was no rush like the hunt. Nothing compared to the thrill of the chase as unsuspecting prey, shadowed by a merciless predator, lived in ignorance regarding their advancing fate. It was how it should be.

Twenty feet. He could feel their insignificant lives being crushed and snatched from them by his greedy hands. The man-mountain was now completely out of the shadows.

One stride left.

Slowing, his dark eyes tracked the small beads of sweat that slid lazily down Lexy's neck toward her partially exposed cleavage. His nostrils flared with her scent.

He was judge, jury, and, of course, executioner—the very best part.

Abruptly, his anticipation turned to a limitless rage. It coursed through him as an endless resource, like black in outer space. The rage had been his constant companion, his life partner. Their mutual intimacy gave them purpose, like a symbiotic parasite and its helpless host. And now, they were both ready.

He returned his focus to the doomed bride and groom, taking one last, long stride that would ensure his immortality. This was it. All he had to do was reach out and they were his, eternally.

Until death do us part.

CHAPTER-3

The scream erupted again, to his left. Manny's insides leapt somewhere past his throat, as he whirled to locate the source of the raucous shriek, reaching for a weapon he'd left locked in the safe of his Lansing home.

He searched frantically through the dim glow of the courtyard. It took a minute, but it soon dawned on him that it hadn't been a scream of horror, or even alarm, but a piercing laugh coming from a boisterous, vacation-clad group of young women., The ladies were clearly enjoying the cash bar, though a little too loudly for him. Or maybe he was just wound too tight.

Imagine that.

One of the women stopped walking and turned to Manny. "Sorry if we startled you." She moved closer. "I think I could make it up to you if you wanted to come to my room."

"What a wonderful offer, but my wife wouldn't approve."

She grinned. "Lucky woman."

The young ladies continued to stampede past, and he realized they could probably teach him a thing or two. Living in the here-and-now wasn't a bad thing.

He ran his hand through his hair,

concentrating on bringing his heart rate down to 150 mph.

The word is "relax," Detective Williams.

Leaning against the railing, he looked past the two pools adorning the verdant courtyard and noticed the stars of the night, talking and laughing through the shadowy confines of the trees. This splendor was such a contrast to the gruesome, Hell-spawned scenes that he had become far too intimate with.

The bride and the groom stood in the shadow of the rock wall fifty yards away. She was still wearing the white, rhinestone-studded wedding dress that danced against the light whenever she moved. He guessed she wanted to wear it as long as she could.

Lexy had chosen wisely. Mike was a good man, strong, with a sense of purpose.

Manny had been a twenty-three-year-old rookie when he partnered up with Mike's dad, Gavin Crosby. Mike had been just twelve. Good kid then and a fine young man and excellent cop now, just like his dad.

Gavin had been a great mentor, a clever detective, and a perfect choice as Lansing's Police Chief. He had always been firm but fair, and Manny loved him like a big brother. To see Gavin's son marry a wonderful woman like Lexy Castro was truly a pleasure. He felt like a proud uncle.

The small, stone bridge that led across the waterway to San Juan's venerable old fort, San Cristobal, caught his eye, hovering above and beyond the bay. He followed the lit skyline to the cruise ship wharf where they would board the *Ocean Duchess* in the morning. Her lighted frame and distinctive exhaust stack towered above the pier district of San Juan, creating a striking silhouette, especially at night.

"Manny Williams. What are you doing out here alone? You could be accosted or something worse."

He looked to the sky and smiled. That voice was unmistakable. Liz Casnovsky, Lansing's accomplished DA, took a couple of awkward steps toward him and settled at his right. She was dressed in a silver, sequin-littered designer gown. Her black Prada heels and matching handbag topped off a sensational look.

She hooked her lean arm through his and gave him a peck on the cheek. Her breath was tinged with Kahlua, and her eyes held a slightly glazed quality.

"Well, if that happened, I guess I'd know who to hire to put the bad people away."

"Damn straight, you would. Besides, no one gets to accost you but me, got it?"

"Got it," he mused. "Where's Lynn? Did you ditch your devoted husband already?"

"Devoted my ass! Whatever," she slurred. "Do you know that he actually had the audacity to say I've had enough to drink and that I should go to bed before I hurt myself?" Liz straightened as to shuck away the words spoken by her husband, swaying a little too far to the left.

He steadied his good friend.

The tall woman peered into his face, "I have, haven't I?"

"I would say any more Black Russians would intensify the morning's headache."

"That's what I like about you detective; you never lie to me. Kind too. Not like other men."

"Shhh. You'll ruin that whole tough-guy rep

I've worked hard to acquire."

They gazed silently in the direction of the moving ocean, and he patted her arm. Manny knew that Lynn and Liz had had a problem or two, but it seemed they wanted to iron things out. He hoped they stuck with it because sometimes the castle in the sky can slip away like a dream at dawn.

Liz turned her head. "Do you think I'm pretty?"

"You're gorgeous. If I weren't happily married, wild horses couldn't keep me away."

Liz giggled. "You're such a smooth talker." She gave him another kiss on the cheek.

"Okay, I'm going to my room. Lynn was right . . . this time." Liz moved to the door, working hard to keep her balance.

"Do you want some help?"

"No, no, no, no. I'm fine. Thanks for asking." Liz hesitated and then switched her bag to the other hand. "I love you, you know."

"I know. I love you too, Liz. Now get your ass up to bed."

"Yes sir." The Lansing DA saluted with the wrong hand and disappeared inside the hotel.

Laughing out loud, he wondered about how much coffee she was going to need in the morning.

He finished his drink and stole one last look at the newlyweds standing in the shadowy courtyard.

Manny froze.

CHAPTER-4

Enormous hands extended toward Mike, then snapped back like a recoiling snake.

"Evening, folks," slipped from his mouth. "Sure is warm, isn't it?"

He watched as Mike and Lexy gasped in perfect accord, whirling to see who had spoken to them, who had interrupted their private kissy-face session, scaring the bejeebies out of them in the process.

Just your destiny.

The couple searched for his face. They had started a foot too low, but eventually found it. Their eyes widened in surprise. Jenkins was aware of how he looked, how intimidating. He would use it to his advantage.

All the better to kill you with.

Their undivided attention was all his. He smiled at the newlyweds with the disarming grin of a priest.

"Yes-s-s it is," Lexy stammered. "You scared the heck out of me, er, us."

"You're pretty light on your feet. We never heard you," said Mike.

"Aw, I think you were lost in love. I could have been a herd of runaway elephants, and you wouldn't have heard me."

The couple caught each other's wide-eyed looks and laughed.

"You got us there. Wedding night, you know," said Lexy.

"Well, I hope you don't typically wear what you're wearing on date night." He bent low and whispered. "People might think you're strange."

Mike smiled. "Got us again."

The conversation wound down as he asked the right questions about their special night, about them. They answered with gusto and naive honesty. He was so damn easy to talk to.

Besides, everyone loves to talk about themselves. Self-absorbed morons.

He could charm the habit off a nun, and he played it to the hilt. His amiable wit was infectious as his face animated with real warmth. It was easy for him to pretend to be the friendliest man on the island, and Mike and Lexy responded. They never suspected that he longed to tear them apart, to watch them die horribly painful deaths, begging for his mercy in pathetic whimpers. They would see the real him when he was ready, when his will said so.

The trio enjoyed a few more seconds of light conversation. Then he politely said his good nights and turned back toward the ten-story hotel. As he distanced himself from Mike and Lexy, a confident smirk spread across his sculpted face.

That's why I'm the master. Self-control. Discipline. This wasn't the right time. But soon. Justice is a bitch not to be crossed, especially mine.

The counterfeit grin disappeared like that of a kid whose candy had been stolen by the school bully. He was fully aware of ways to accomplish revenge. He had learned things in prison . . .

ways. He absolutely understood the old adage that there are worse things than death, far worse.

They would feel what he felt and that would be a special reward for them. It's always a treat to walk a mile in someone else's shoes.

He slowed his pace and raised his head to the sky. Memories of his punishment and seemingly endless sentence flooded his consciousness, threatening to overpower him. The imprisoned lunatics' oblivious, never-ending screams had attacked his sanity, his very soul. There had been times that he thought he would poke out his eardrums.

Vomit, week-old urine, and excrement had painted the concrete floors like some cage at the zoo. The mingled stench had been as repulsive as anything he'd ever endured—and that was just the beginning.

The oppressive guards had treated most of the inmates like garbage, less than caged animals. Except for him.

It had been his good fortune that much of the circumstances surrounding his captivity had been at least bearable. The guards would say little to him, preferring to keep their distance. The jerk-offs had been terrified of him. They'd been wise to be afraid. Very wise.

He glanced over his shoulder, targeting the couple one last time.

Bon voyage, bon voyage, my lovelies.

CHAPTER-5

Manny sprinted down the two flights of stairs, adrenaline rushing his heart, feeding like a hungry animal off his fear. That moving tree meant to hurt Mike and Lexy.

Halfway to the rock wall, he stole another panicked look in their direction, slowed his mad dash, and eventually stopped, staring intently in disbelief.

The threesome was no longer three, but two: Mike and Lexy. He scanned the yard, but the big man was nowhere to be found. It was like he had evaporated into thin air.

For the third time, Manny looked at Mike and Lexy and noticed how they stood so very close together, unconsciously swaying in perfect rhythm with the endless, cavorting waves. Not threatened, but in love.

His eyes dropped to his feet and then back to the animated duo. A full-throated laugh drifted through the Puerto Rican night. Mike had said something clever, something that belonged to just the two of them. He felt like some foolish eavesdropper.

Add busy-body grandmother to your repertoire.

Damn it. Would he always struggle with the never-ending process of unwinding? And this time, he came within a hair of looking like a complete idiot.

There is nothing worse than an overreacting cop.

But he could have sworn he saw a man behind his friends, arms raised and hands outstretched. Threatening. Menacing. Hadn't he? Manny threw his hands in the air.

Shadows can cozen the mind, even that of an experienced cop. But he wasn't in the habit of seeing things. Maybe it was the drink or the stress of worrying about Louise. Maybe he was rationalizing his slavery to his work, again.

This *always-on-duty* thing needed to stop before it killed him, or his marriage. Always on alert, on the watch. He was beginning to loathe that part of himself. The Guardian of the Universe—his daughter's favorite nickname for him—was on vacation, and he needed to act like it.

He walked back up the steps and stood over the iron guardrails spiraling from the balcony. He was facing the ocean, but barely saw the moonlit waves as his thoughts turned darker, inward, accommodating another self-evaluation session.

He was frustrated with his workaholic tendencies, but was almost helpless to change. It was easy to mask his compulsion with noble thoughts—like owing the good people of Lansing an appropriate return on their hard-earned tax dollars, or that he was merely being a good cop. But earning his paycheck wasn't the real reason, or at least wasn't the only one. Good cops don't let partners die, do they?

Harsh guilt welled up and attacked like a shark smelling blood. This was about Kyle Chavez, his second partner, his *dead* second partner. He closed his eyes. If Manny hadn't played in that damn golf tournament . . .

He had taken an afternoon off to tee it up, and a few hours later, Kyle had been shot at a domestic. Kyle had been just twenty-seven years old with a wonderful wife and two beautiful kids.

Manny fought hard to ward off the demons, but they had the key to the door and, for now, they were staying.

The news of Kyle's death had brought a suffocating weight to bear on Lucy Chavez, who had buckled helplessly to the hardwood floor of the couple's home. The memory of her anguish still caused the hair on his arms to stand. No one should have to tell another that the love of their life had just been used for target practice. Not even cops.

Responsible or not, he felt like he had let Kyle's family down, that he had donned the black executioner's hood himself and pulled the lever. The fact that Kyle had broken protocol and gone on the call alone brought no consolation.

The counseling sessions with the department shrink helped (not as much as the ones with Louise). Ultimately, he knew it wasn't really his fault. However, there are times when the mind understands, but the heart couldn't care less. It was a torturous, unforgiving ordeal, and he had sworn that it would never happen on his watch again.

The lobby door opened behind him, and the loud music brought him back.

Manny refocused on the view a bit longer before slinking back inside the hotel, grateful Mike and Lex hadn't seen him.

The rhythmic sound of the talented Latin band, playing across from the casino on the second floor, dominated the atmosphere inside. The lead singer was a tiny, energetic woman, whose throaty resonance soaked the room.

"Nothing like good music to soothe the head-case cop," he rued.

The escalator ended at the second floor, and he walked past the thriving casino toward the elevator. He stopped for a moment and took in the compelling sounds of electronic bells, bongs, and sirens emanating from the "sin pit."

Steely-gray smoke hovered above velvety gaming tables like it owned the place, and the pungent aroma of Cuban cigars and expensive cigarettes filtered to the lobby. Vegas had nothing up on this place.

Inside the elevator on his way to the fifth floor, he drifted back to the scene in the courtyard. Something wasn't right, but he couldn't put a finger on it. The sizable man with the deceptive demeanor had sparked a singular thought in his mind. *What if . . .?*

Manny bit his lip. Not tonight. Besides, he was tired, far too tired to make character evaluations that mattered.

Leaving the elevator, he shuffled to his room, stripped off the penguin suit, which stuck to him like a second skin, and crawled between the cool sheets next to his slumbering wife.

Closing his eyes, he felt his body begin to reject the tension.

Not tonight. Not this week. You're on vacation. Remember?

CHAPTER-6

Juanita Henkle was having a pisser of a night. She had lost a hundred bucks to those damn slot machines—mechanical, blood-sucking heifers. To add insult to injury, her friend, Sarah Cummings, who had brought her down to spend a week on the island, had disappeared with some local muchacho.

"He better be the real deal," she muttered.

It had only gotten better. Her luggage had arrived late to the hotel from the airport, and it was beat to hell. And some of her clothes were missing— her favorites, of course. Even though the airline promised to reimburse her for the trouble, where was she going to find an affordable clothing store on Sunday morning, particularly on San Juan's Condado Strip? After all, she was a twenty-eight-year-old working girl, and money didn't grow on trees, especially in Zanesville, Ohio.

Juanita lit a cancer stick. She wanted her old clothes back, her comfortable clothes, but she realized she was the only one who really cared.

The smoke dancing across her eyes caused her to squint. Shit happens, but it seemed like she was always out of toilet paper. Not to mention, she had been hit on by some of the most narcissistic drunks in Puerto Rico: Latin Don Juan wannabes who sought to "charm" her with stale beer breath, unfocused eyes, and dicks practically out of their pants. Soaking one's self in cologne must be the thing down here; they all wore enough to clear up any serious sinus affliction. She had turned them all down, flat. The big "L" was stamped on each of their foreheads. Maybe on their chests too. She didn't want to know.

The institution of marriage was gaining considerable creditability for her. She wanted someone to hold, and to be held. Someone to grow old with. To have babies with. To even fight and make up with. Especially the making up part.

But not just any man would do, not for Juanita Henkle. The predestined man of her dreams would ride in on his great white steed, or at least a Mercedes, and take her away from this bar- scene masquerade. Then they would live happily ever after.

She screwed her cigarette into the scarred ashtray and exhaled one last ring of gray haze. Her man didn't know her yet, but he would.

Someday my prince will come. Hurry up, boy. These drinks are gettin' expensive, and I'm not gettin' any younger.

Thank God the music was good. It was loud, but that chick could sing, and the band was tight. She had heard worse blaring from her car's radio.

Juanita drained the last of her drink, uncrossed her legs, and decided it was time to exit this fruitless revelry. She was sure Sarah wouldn't make it back to their room tonight, so she would get a little peace and quiet. Mama said a good night's rest always helped settle things down. Everyone knows that Mamas are always right.

"At least Sarah's having a good time," she

breathed to herself.

As Juanita got up, she caught her reflection in the wall mirror, bordered in Corona insignias. She was hot. Her flowing black hair, full cleavage, and shapely hips were more than a package, more like *The Package*. The red, low-cut Gucci dress (she had saved hard for it, and at least the airlines hadn't lost this one) accented her "attributes" just the right way.

Any woman who looks this good has the prerogative to be picky, right?

She was about to leave when she noticed the tall, well-built man at the end of the bar, sizing her up.

Hold the phone! Good God, look at that.

He was a little older, but wow. He had perfect hair, and he must be six-four or so. A slow grin crept across her face. She knew what tall meant.

The stranger got up and came straight toward her. "I'm Eli Jenkins. What might your name be, young goddess?"

Juanita felt electric heat radiate through her. *Hot and suave.*

What the hell. No reason to beat around the bush. He just might be the happy ending to the day that she needed.

"My name is Juanita. Are we going to cut through the bullshit and get to the point here? I don't need a drink or any more conversation. I'm in room 586, and I'll be there in about five minutes."

The band had begun an old Elvis tune, and she watched Eli flash a smile that would melt an ice witch's heart. This was going to be good, maybe better than good.

Without waiting for his response, she spun on

two-inch heels and walked across the glass-enclosed bridge that connected the two sides of the hotel.

****

Jenkins leaned back against his bar stool and scrutinized the waning bar crowd. No one seemed to take note of his encounter with Juanita.

He signaled the flabby bartender and ordered another bottle of water.

"She shut you down, compadre?" he asked. "Don't feel bad. She's sent everyone away from her all night. She is very picky, no?" He drew out "picky" in two long syllables.

The nosy peckerhead *had* noticed him and Juanita. Not what he'd hoped for, but fixable. "Shut down, yes, you are right, my friend. I never had a chance. But there is always another senorita, no?"

The bartender nodded an approving look. "Indeed, there is, especially for a man such as yourself."

"Hey, Miguel, more beer" echoed from the other end of the bar. The bartender raised his eyebrows and was off toward the pleading din.

Jenkins wondered if the simpleton would remember him. Even after he, and Juanita, shook this rich-prick hotel to the very foundation. It made no real difference. It would be too late anyway.

He finished his water and picked up his black-leather travel case, flinging it over his shoulder as he crossed the dance floor, happy to leave the sour tang of spilled beer and cheap perfume hanging in the air.

There wasn't a soul on the mullioned glass

bridge, leading to the south wing of the hotel, as he crossed it with seven long paces.

Exhilaration ruled his insides.

Juanita was fine, and she had never recognized him for what he was. Certainly not that twit. But she would be worthy of what he had planned for her, and of course, for him. He had found the perfect warm-up "playmate."

A roguish grin settled across his face as he knocked at room 586. He glanced to his left and saw no one in the semi-lit hallway. Perfect.

Juanita came to the door wearing only a short, red nightie and a mischievous gleam. "Don't you know that you shouldn't keep a lady waiting? It's a good thing my roommate's gone for the night," she teased.

"My apologies. Let me see if I can make it up to you," he replied in his most charismatic tone.

"I'm sure you can," she melted.

He slipped the Do Not Disturb sign on the outside of the door, dropping his travel case to the floor. The young woman moved close, pressing herself against him. He felt her excitement, her body heat. She kissed him with an eagerness that, for a split second, took him off his game. But only for a moment.

Juanita tilted back to look at her hot new lover, and he watched the eager smile evaporate from her face like rain on a desert road. She saw death smoldering from his face. Not just any death, but hers. Her one-night stand had become her last-night stand.

Her body trembled with a horror Jenkins knew she had never before felt. How could she have? She had never met *him* before. The woman's panicked reaction stoked his arousal.

He clutched her tighter.

"Oh my God," she whispered. "No. Please don't hurt me."

Jenkins knew paralyzing fear had gripped her. Her plea was all she could muster before the drug-soaked cloth covered her face.

Whatever dreams she may have possessed about meeting Mr. Right or having perfect babies were obliterated forever. But she was going to be his, and that was special. After all, she was going to be famous.

He watched as precious consciousness slipped from Juanita like a fast-setting sun. He sneered. "I'm your god now. Your soul belongs to me."

CHAPTER-7

Jenkins towered over Juanita's plundered body. He studied his grisly, but precise, handiwork. He was satisfied. She hadn't been the sport he had anticipated, not at first, so he had to "urge" her forward. She'd become responsive enough, though, as the drug wore off, and she'd understood her fate. But then again, they all responded like terrified animals when they realized dying was not just something that happened in the movies or on the six o'clock news.

Closing his eyes, he recalled the precise moment her soul had merged with his, at just the right time, at the instant *he'd* determined. He was in complete control. He was special. His evolution made him invincible.

Jenkins sponged blood from his mouth and chin with the back of his hand. He couldn't help himself. She'd looked so damn good. Good enough to eat.

A moment later, he gently placed a black rose across Juanita's body and then stripped the latex gloves from his hands, careful to avoid any contact with the bed sheet. He stood a long moment over Juanita before finally bending to her. Her expensive perfume, even as it mingled with drying blood, seemed to be everywhere.

He spoke in soft tones bankrupt of compassion, filled with only triumph. "You didn't think I could let you get away, did you? How could you believe that? You looked so good and, well, it was your time, our time." He whispered as if she would answer.

The room's balcony overlooked the wide lagoon on the south side of the hotel, and he went there. The Caribbean moon mirrored against rippling water and caused little spangles of light to dance like fairies in an enchanted forest. The breeze was sweet and clean, possessing an intoxicating quality. Not like Juanita had been, not that enthralling, but it worked.

The upcoming cruise and the carefully designed plan moved across his thoughts. It was time to take what was his and reward them with what they had earned. They were entitled to dine on what he had to serve, all of them.

His eyes reflected malicious contempt, his very soul embracing it. The hatred had boiled long enough. Too long. Juanita had been easy, and she had embodied the last trial he required.

"I'm ready for what's next, for my destiny," he said out loud.

What a kick it was to be able to combine his "hobby" with joyous purpose. Taking the souls of women, after they had served their function, of course, was the thrill he always knew it would be. Making the others suffer for their indiscretions would be an even more indescribable pleasure.

Jenkins reached into his back pocket and took out a worn newspaper clipping that he had carefully tucked away. It was creased and faded from years of use. He read each line again. Over and over. He wanted to absorb the faded script, to ensure that he never forgot what was written there or who had written it, that the details were always and forever the same. Though that part was not a problem. He had it memorized years ago, but having it in his hand made it real, fueling his purpose even more.

The fifth line of the article caused him pause while the veins at his temples throbbed.

How could they quote such drivel? Such dog shit.

The source of that citation would pay oh-so-dearly.

Hatred rose higher and higher, and he reveled in it, basked in its purity, its honesty. Why not? It made him feel even more alive, more impregnable. But the rage mustn't cloud his judgment. He must restrain the intensity of his emotions, or everything would be ruined. The process of learning that truth had been a hard lesson, but realized nonetheless.

Moving back into the air-conditioned room, he meticulously refolded the clipping and placed it safely in his pocket. He stepped closer to Juanita and slowly, like a tenderhearted lover, kissed her cooling, blue lips.

Then he walked out the door whistling a Three Dog Night tune.

Eli's coming! Eli's coming!

CHAPTER-8

"Hey, Sleeping Beauty. You gonna lay there all day or are you going to get your butt out of bed and take me on the most wonderful vacation of my life?"

Manny groaned and shaded his eyes from the bright, Caribbean sun that streamed through their room. The pesky clock radio blinked 7:15 a.m. Clocks and vacations were never intended to be friends.

Manny's eyes flickered back to his wife, catching a glimpse of Louise's face. It was all he needed to go from annoyed to a step above pleased.

"What are you talking about?" he said. "We're going home today."

"You can go if you want; I'll just find some hairy-chested local who wants to have a week of hot food, hot sun, and hot sex with a well-developed cougar." Her face was alive with anticipation.

"I have a hairy chest."

"Why yes, yes you do. You're a little older than I had in mind, but you might do. Want to be considered for the job?"

"Okay. How do I apply?"

Louise bent to Manny's face and kissed him

gently. She grinned. "Hold that thought. I need time to work out the rest of the interview process. But so far, so good."

"Great. I'm up for the rest of it . . . well, almost."

She looked to the ceiling. "I'm taking a shower."

Louise was truly excited about this trip. For his wife to outrace him to the shower was like a Republican voting for Barack Obama.

Swinging his legs to the floor, he thought again about Louise and her resolve. She was determined to enjoy this trip even though the specter of the mammogram results lingered in the back of their minds. She was one special woman. But he'd always known that.

Louise had started the coffeemaker, and the tantalizing aroma pulsed from the small in-room java machine, inviting him to fill his cup.

He pulled on clean, white briefs (always white because colored underwear wasn't manly) and started for the balcony. Parading out in his skivvies just might hand the beach joggers their first thrill of the day.

Moving past the full-length, oak-framed mirror, he hesitated and did a double take. Even though his face was scribbled with sleep lines and his hair mussed, he didn't look half bad for a cop pushing forty. It wouldn't last forever, but he would enjoy it while he could. He just might get that job Louise had open.

Manny continued his trek to the great outdoors, but a sudden, rapid pounding on the door said the balcony would have to wait. The knock echoed heavy and hard, like someone wielding a ten-pound sledgehammer, and for a moment, the heavy mahogany seemed ready to splinter into shards. Then silence. He threw on khaki shorts and hurried to see who had assaulted the peaceful beginnings to his morning.

He swung open the large, ornate door, panned one way then the other, seeing no one. The elevator was located twenty-five feet to his right and the stairs only about fifteen feet to his left. Whoever had battered their door was now long gone.

Frowning, he came back inside. That's when he noticed the white stationery lying on the floor with his name printed on the front. Manny unfolded the paper and read:

Bon Voyage, Detective, Bon Voyage. This will be a cruise that you will never forget.

His glower melted and was replaced with a perceptive smile. Sophie. Always the practical joker, and knowing her, she'd probably been thinking about the prank since last night. Retribution for the cuff thing.

Well, missy, two can play this game.

Putting the note on the dresser, he headed toward the balcony for the third time.

Manny opened the glass door, and the heat engulfed him like the smothering kiss from a worried mother. It felt wonderful. The Caribbean sun must be heaven sent, caressing like no other.

The sound of the ocean lollygagging toward the shore was therapeutic. This is where he belonged. Some mystic, all-knowing voice whispered to him that it was so, and everyone knows those internal gurus are never wrong. Michigan had its pluses, but what could match this? Besides, no one shoveled snow in the Caribbean.

****

Louise looked intently into the ornately trimmed mirror, wiping away the steam, and wondered how a woman her age could be concerned with the results of a mammogram. It didn't add up. She was in great shape, not that old, and had no history of any problems in her family.

The mirror spoke, and she moved a little closer, gathering more detail from the doppelganger in the looking glass. She had been a good person, a great mother, and maybe even a better wife. But that's how this beast howled.

Why would God allow this kind of situation in their lives? Then again, maybe God had nothing to do with it. Maybe there really is an unseen war between good and evil. Maybe humans were collateral damage and cancer was just one weapon that evil used to destroy the hope and peace God promised.

Louise fought the tears and glanced nervously at the unopened letter from her doctor. She began to slide a slender finger under the fold and then stopped. This wasn't the time. She grinned through her tears as she thought about breaking a nail—that wasn't going to happen before she got on the ship.

She took one last look, dried her eyes, and put on more eyeliner. Then she stuffed the letter back in her travel pouch. If the enigmatic dispatch was bad news, it would be bad news after the best vacation of her life.

****

Louise emerged from the bathroom wearing

only a black bra and lace panties, just as Manny sauntered back into the room. The coffee had helped, but the sight of his wife brought him fully awake.

They were to meet the rest of the Lansing crew in the lobby in about forty minutes and head over to a small, local breakfast nook, whose reputation for great food was next to none. But she looked so good, and he was feeling his oats.

"I think I'm ready for part two of that interview thing."

"Manny, I just took a shower, and we have to meet the group soon," Louise protested without conviction.

"Yeah, but we may never spend another day in San Juan," he said as he drew her into his arms. "When we get old, we can say we did it in Puerto Rico."

"True, unless you count next Sunday when we get back from the cruise. But you do seem like a good candidate."

She pressed closer, teasing him to an even harder state.

He flicked his fingers. Her bra went slack as he pulled it away from her with a sweep of his hand.

"You are good at that," she laughed. "I think the job's yours."

They fell back on the bed in the midst of a passionate kiss. In the enthralling ambiance of Puerto Rico, Manny and Louise Williams made love the way new lovers do.

CHAPTER-9

Fifty-six-year-old Gavin Crosby stood beside his wife Stella, shifting his considerable weight from left to right. He chanced a quick glance at his gold watch. Manny was late.

He couldn't remember the last time that had happened. But maybe it was a good thing. The boy just might be learning to lighten up.

The colorful tropical fish tank, part of the hotel lobby's wall, caught his attention. Blue angel fish trimmed in black circled with yellow-striped sergeant fish and narrow pipefish in an endless carousel of motion. He hoped to see some of that kind of wildlife when they snorkeled at Trunk Bay.

His eyes darted around the rest of the room, and he found himself doing a quick exercise observing human interaction.

Alex Downs and his wife Barbara stood near the concierge's desk carrying on a conversation with the newlyweds. Thinking of the day Alex was hired still made Gavin shake his head. Alex had just earned his PhD from the University of Michigan in criminology and forensic science. Bright man. However, he knew doodle squat about office politics and had gotten his proverbial tit in the ringer more than once. The CSI had come a long way, but kissing fanny was never going to be a long suit.

A short, balding man with an overlapping belly, Alex proved the notion that you can't judge a book by its cover. He hardly looked like an expert in his field. Hell, in any field. But he was one of the very best.

Alex's wife of twelve years looked like she belonged on the arm of a Hollywood movie star. Taller than Alex, she was slim with legs that went on forever. But her adoration for Alex was obvious: He was her one and only. Love indeed made strange bedfellows.

He switched focus to his son and new daughter-in-law, chuffing a sigh of relief. They had pulled it off. The newlyweds would never forget yesterday's ceremony. And that's what weddings were all about.

District Attorney Liz Casnovsky and her husband Lynn were engaged in a giddy conversation with Sophie Lee, Manny's partner, and Sophie's husband, Randy Mason. The group huddled near the glitzy, bronze-and-gold entrance of the hotel, smiling like Cheshire cats. Liz suddenly released an air-splitting laugh. Gavin cringed. Vintage Liz. She sounded like a mad dolphin, but it was always good to hear her laugh. Well, almost always.

The DA was a bulldog prosecutor, and with Lynn's investment company growing in leaps and bounds, they lived the life of flourishing professionals. Not to mention they looked like a tanned Ken and Barbie. Yet, there was a wisp of sadness that seemed to haunt Liz. He thought it had to do with the appointment with motherhood she never had time to keep.

Gavin rolled his eyes as he watched Sophie

interact with the others. She was always the comedian, the official smartass in the crowd. She was from the City, San Francisco, and the daughter of Chinese immigrants. Having moved east to marry the love of her life, the petite detective divorced him a year later after finding him "hanging out" with a couple of guys in a sleazy motel room on Cedar. She joked that she couldn't compete with the men. Bring on the women because she could, and would, do anything any woman could do. But men, that was incomprehensible to her. Sophie laughed about it, but the scars would never really go away, not completely.

She had met Randy a few years later. And even though she had fallen in love with him, Sophie had changed. She had kept her maiden name because it made her feel secure and independent. No man would take her dignity again, and Gavin applauded that.

He didn't care for Randy much. Maybe it was because Randy possessed the social skills of a doorjamb . . . or because Sophie's roly-poly husband, adorned with the red Afro, had never cared for anyone except himself, until Sophie.

The elevator bell rang, and mirrored doors parted like the red sea. Manny and Louise stepped energetically from the elevator. Manny was first, dressed in a loud blue tropical shirt and Ray-Ban sunglasses caught in the nest above his forehead. Louise followed, dressed in a straw hat; blue-and-white-striped midriff shirt; light-blue shorts; and white Tod sandals. They smiled like they had won the lotto.

"Where in hell have you been? You're four minutes late," said Gavin, tapping his watch. "And you look like a couple of damned tourists to boot."

By then, the rest of the couples had migrated to the elevator.

"What's that saying? You can dress 'em up, but you can't take 'em out," chimed in Sophie.

"Ahh, have you losers looked in the mirror?" Manny chided.

After a quiet moment, laughter rippled through the group. They *all* looked like tourists.

"Let's go eat, I'm starved," encouraged Stella.

****

No one noticed the big man leaning over the mahogany railing of the second floor balcony. He stared down to the lobby with black eyes and scorn to match. "This is going to be one hell of a vacation," he said, as he clenched his teeth. "At least for me."

CHAPTER-10

Sarah Cummings glanced nervously down the fifth-floor hallway. Oh man, she was in deep. Juanita was going to kick her ass up and down the steps of the hotel's marble stairs. Kick her ass? Juanita was going to kill her.

She had left Juanita sitting in the testosterone-infested bar. Despite Sarah's guilt and dread at facing her best friend this morning, she gave soul to a *no-regret-time-of-my-life* grin. Hector.

What a night.

A vision of Juanita's pissed countenance stabbed across her mind, and the grin disappeared momentarily.

Good going, Sarah. You left her alone the whole night and most of the morning.

Juanita's first night in San Juan, no less. "I'll make it up to you, Nita, I promise," she vowed, picking up the pace.

As she turned down the hall toward her room, the memory of her Latin lover's amazing performance caused her to stumble over her sandaled feet.

Maybe she was in love. Well, in lust, at the very least. It had been her first encounter with a Latin man, and her eyes must have looked like small breakfast saucers after he'd stripped out of his clothes. She put her hand to her mouth and giggled. She had certainly experienced the full extent of his offering, several times.

Vivid recall caused her temperature to rise. "Woooo! Down girl."

Then, for a second time, culpability for leaving her friend at the bar rose to the forefront of her mind. Juanita had told her to go ahead, that she would be fine. It's what most good friends would have said, even if your BFF didn't really want to be alone the rest of the night. Juanita and she had formed an unmatchable bond since third grade, right after the two girls had beat up that fourth-grade boy. There had never been any bullshit between them. They were like sisters and wanted each other to have a good time.

"Hey, you just got lucky first. My turn's coming. Don't worry, I'm a big girl," Juanita had said.

Sarah stopped moving along the burgundy carpet and searched for her room card in her large handbag, wondering if Hector really would call her. Sarah wanted to see him again. Maybe he was the one. He was definitely brighter than she had first imagined. He was on vacation before he went back to the University of Miami to finish his master's degree in environmental science. Hector wanted to save the world—well, at least Puerto Rico. It sounded so . . . noble.

The technical stuff that he chatted about had been fairly hard to understand. She had not followed his explanation of biodiversity or habitat restoration, nor had she really cared. Luckily, they hadn't talked that much. *Wooo!* Sarah cooled herself with an imaginary fan, feeling like she had spent hours in the warm sun.

She finally located the keycard just as she arrived at room 586.

"Maybe she's at the pool," she breathed. Her pulse was racing. If Juanita wasn't at the pool, maybe she was over to Max's Grill (the hotel's excellent restaurant) for brunch. But deep down she knew that Juanita would be inside, waiting like an old Jewish grandmother. Her shoulders slumped as she reconciled that she had it coming.

"Man, this is going to be ugly." She took a deep breath, fumbled with the keycard, and dropped it on the carpet. "Damn."

She retrieved the card and scowled at the Do Not Disturb sign dangling limply from the doorknob. She pushed the door and crept into the darkened room. The door caught on the plush throw rug causing it to hang open.

A timely breeze moved the patio door's blind back and forth, offering the only light source. Her eyes were adjusting to the shadow-infested surroundings when she noticed the smell. She put her hand over her nose to block the sweet, coppery scent. Out of the corner of her eye, she noticed movement. Sarah spun toward the source, held her breath, and waited.

The crimson numbers on the clock radio had changed, and she put her hand on her chest, swearing at the clock. The late night horror flicks might have to go.

Then she saw Juanita. Her unmoving form lay sprawled near the head of the farthest bed.

Moving closer, she found herself wishing Juanita was screaming at her. Her pulse raced faster. Maybe the girl was sick. She took another step, and the smell intensified.

Her ears pounded like a bass drum. She bent with caution, moving closer. Something was wrong, very wrong.

"Juanita? Honey, are you feeling okay? I'm so sorr—" She stopped in her tracks, then quickly tore open the drapes.

She lost all ability to speak or move. Her French-manicured hands clenched and unclenched with unconscious rhythm. The sight of her friend's ravished body wrenched away Sarah's grasp on reality. Bloody rivulets meandered down tattered breasts, and Juanita's plundered neck was caked with maroon patches, her once-beautiful face bitten too many times to count. Her eyes were set with an unearthly, eternal stare that seemed to ask why Sarah had let this happen to her, why had she left her alone.

Sarah's eyes darted to the solitary black rose cradled across her friend's chest, briefly noting its contradiction to the horrific portrait in front of her. That was the end of Sarah's sane observations. Her psyche could handle no more, and her screams erupted like lava spewing from a volcano. One after another. She felt madness drape its welcome arms around her and hold on tight.

****

Carlos Rivera, the newly hired room steward for the fifth floor, exited the suite across the hall, quite pleased with the white-glove cleaning he had administered, when the screams incited his scrotum to tighten like hard rubber. He rushed to the semi-open door of room 586, swung it open, and hurried inside—a move he would regret forever. One glance at the bloody scene framed on the bed sent him stumbling for the door.

"Dios mio! Dios mio! Dios mio!" rattled from Carlos's tremulous throat.

Running down the hall, he suddenly stopped, and his breakfast wretched from his gut, splattering on the expensive hallway carpet.

Sarah was still screaming, but Carlos was oblivious to any single thing other than getting the manager up to the Room from Hell, pronto. It was a lurid second, and final, day on the job.

CHAPTER-11

The Lansing party arrived at an oblong, slightly tattered building displaying a small, yellow-and-red sign hanging—barely—above the stucco patio.

"HACIENDAS."

Manny watched uneasy looks bank through the group.

"Uh, well. So this is it, eh?" asked Liz.

"Way to go, Williams. You bring us to a place that's guaranteed to have us spending the next two days in the john," whined Sophie.

"This place has a great rep with the locals," said Manny.

"Who told you that, the owner's mom?"

"The concierge. And I thought you were a cop? We don't judge a book by its cover."

"Maybe you don't, but this looks like salmonella heaven to me," said Sophie.

"Oh come on, take a chance. If you get sick, I'll buy you dinner on the ship."

"Oh how kind, given that dinner is included in the cruise."

Manny grinned. "But my heart's in the right place."

Just then a round woman with a wide, pleasant smile joined them. "You eat with us today, yes? Best breakfast on whole island. Come. Come," she encouraged in a thick, homey Latin accent. "I show you it."

Rosalina (her name according to the tag on her uniform) grabbed Manny's arm and ushered them in. The aroma was just short of amazing. They quickly put two tables together. Manny and Louise faced the north end of the eatery, which opened to the ocean, windows cranked wide. Green-blue waves rhythmically rushed the rocks, tossing foamy spray to the morning air and creating prismatic rainbows suspended in mid-air. They got up to take a closer look.

"Okay, big boy, now I know why you brought me here. This is awesome and relaxing, and you know how I am when I'm relaxed," said Louise.

"How is that, honey?'

"Great . . . some cop. I have to explain it to you? Let's just say you're going to have a heck of a week," she finished.

"Well, if it's going to be anything like the last day and a half, maybe we should move here."

"I don't think you could take it."

"Maybe not, but I can't think of a better way to go."

She squeezed his arm, and they went back to the table.

They sat down to eggs, crisp bacon, stacks of pancakes, and steaming coffee. Frothy orange juice and ruby-red strawberries topped off the meal.

Thirty minutes later, Gavin stood up. "Damn, that was good. You all ready to go?" Manny saw the partially hidden eagerness in his eyes. Even cynical old cops like Gavin could get excited about what was coming next.

"You bet your ass, Chief," cheered Sophie. "Let's go cruisin'."

While everyone voiced their approval, Manny reached into his pocket and pulled out the note that had been pushed under his hotel room door, holding it high.

"We'll go . . . right as soon as one of you smartasses 'fesses up to sliding this note under our door this morning. I don't recognize the handwriting, but you are a clever bunch, even with hangovers. So who did it?"

He glanced around the Lansing contingency without detecting a trace of mischief from anyone. Even Sophie looked innocent.

"What note?" gruffed Gavin.

Manny handed it to the chief, who read it out loud: "Bon Voyage, Detective, Bon Voyage. This will be a cruise that you will never forget."

Gavin looked at Manny with narrowed eyes. "You complaining about someone wishing you a good time?"

"Nope. Just trying to avoid a *pay-back-is-a-bitch* situation," informed Manny.

"No one's going to step to the plate? Sophie?" asked Gavin.

"Not me, I was, ahh, busy."

There was a group groan and someone mentioned "too much information," as Sophie's face turned red, a rarity to be sure.

No one stepped forward and owned up to authoring the note, and for a brief, ominous moment, he wondered if anyone in this group had performed the prank.

If not one of them, then who?

He chased the doubt away. Someone from this crowd was guilty, and he would find out. "Okay, you've all been warned. It's on."

Louise grabbed Manny's arm, "You're the crack detective here, so you can figure it out on your own time, but I'm ready to go."

It was apparent by the stampede for the door that everyone felt the same way. Still, Manny's sense of uneasiness returned, hanging in there like a summer cold. Something was off the mark, but he would be strung up from the rafters if he said so. He stuffed the note back in his pocket.

Liz and Lynn had picked up the tab without protest from the rest, as the group exited the restaurant. Louise pointed to the massive cruise ship, *Ocean Duchess,* glimmering in the distance. "These things look more like floating castles than ships."

"It makes you wonder how they float," Liz commented.

"Well, it has to do with ballast and the physics of distribution—" began Randy.

"Not now, sweetie," Sophie interrupted. "You can explain it over dinner some night. But I want to get my butt in that taxi and onto my boat, er, ship. Whatever. I'm ready to go, now."

"Okay, okay. But I think it's fascinating stuff," Randy responded with a hint of dejection.

Thirty minutes later, the Lansing crew had assembled and was roaring to go.

"It feels like Christmas morning," prattled Sophie. "Let's get this show on the road."

Just as Manny and Louise jumped into the last cab with Sophie and Randy, high-pitched police sirens screeched into earshot. The squat taxi driver, singing loudly, closed the van's wide door and started down the driveway as three black-and-whites, lights flashing, pulled under the verandah of the Condado Wyndham. Three uniformed officers and two in suits ran into the hotel.

"I wonder what that's about?" asked Randy.

Sophie and Manny exchanged uncomfortable glances. They knew what it was about. Whenever that many suits accompanied the blues, it was serious, probably a homicide. It was about the only reason detectives showed up at a crime scene in the first wave.

"The police radio said there was a woman found dead in her room about ten minutes ago," said the driver in almost perfect English. "There may have been foul play. That's what my cousin Enrique said. He is the dispatcher who took the call."

"How awful," said Louise.

Manny grasped his wife's hand as the van-cab bounced over the old, stone bridge and journeyed to the pier and the cruise ship that would be their home-away-from-home for the next seven days. He tried to hide from Louise just how far his cop persona had forced its way in—even as his mind screamed this wasn't his problem.

Sun. Food. Casino. Exotic islands. Blue ocean. Sandy beaches. Skimpy bikinis. He was on vacation.

Not my problem.

Still, he couldn't shake the foreboding feeling that placed its familiar hand on his shoulder, causing him to finger the mysterious note in his pocket.

CHAPTER-12

The cab lurched to a halt in front of the brightly painted pier.

"'Demonic speed freak' must be part of the job qualifications for taxi drivers," said Louise, clutching her chest.

Manny smiled. "But we got here fast."

Louise gave him a less-than-approving look.

After the persistent baggage handlers had loaded the group's luggage and received their tips, the excited cruisers stood in a line, staring in awe-inspired silence at the *Ocean Duchess*.

According to Randy, she was 1,015-feet long and 122-feet across, weighed 124 tons, and only needed a 29-foot draft to sail. Teal borders ran horizontally the full length of the fourteen-story ship that was less than a year old. She sparkled like a white diamond in the brilliant, noontime sun.

"I've not seen one like this," exclaimed Liz. "This wench is humungous. That means bars and shops and restaurants, oh my! You did good, Gavin."

Gavin nodded. "Well, I aim to please." He pointed to the very top of the ship, where the wide smokestack was shaped like a traditional-style kite and painted with curvaceous blue, teal, and white letters: CAROUSEL.

"See where the smoke stack comes up? Right below it, on that deck level, is the nude sunbathing area. That's where I'll be, if any of you women are interested," deadpanned Gavin, sucking in his belly.

Stella's soda sprayed from her lips. "How did you know that?" she choked.

He thumped her on the back. "I read it in the brochure, honey."

"Sure you did," said Manny.

Gavin gave him the family look. "Thanks, Williams."

"No offense, Chief, but let me tell you where I *won't* be sunning myself," giggled Sophie.

"In my office, first thing next week," he teased.

"Yes sir," she saluted. "I'll keep that in mind, sir."

Manny grinned at the exchange between his partner and Gavin. Always a show.

Louise, Stella, and Barbara started toward the pier's gigantic restroom for a quick freshening-up session. "Sophie, you coming?" asked Louise.

"Naw. I don't need to freshen up. I'm plenty hot already, and I'm too excited to pee anyway."

Manny couldn't remember laughing this much in a long time. It was starting out to be the trip he needed it to be.

Out of the corner of his eye, bright, whirling, red lights caught his attention. Manny's newly formed joy disappeared like chips in a casino. An ambulance was headed toward the hotel.

He was back on edge.

Since he heard no siren splitting the air, he knew there was no emergency—or perhaps the ambulance and crew were on a training run. But his instincts told him this was no training exercise. Somehow he knew the EMS crew was going to pick up a body at the hotel they'd just left. The CSU would need time to process the scene, so it made sense that the body couldn't be moved until the forensics squad was ready to let it go to the medical examiner's office. That could take hours, if they did it right. The ambulance crew might be in for a long wait.

The edge grew more intense when he recalled what the cab driver had said.

"There may have been foul play."

Had the local detectives gone from room-to-room? He would have. His frown deepened, running his hand through his hair. A room-to-room search would be tough because so many people had already left the property. San Juan is a tourist town, so he guessed things like murder in a swank hotel would be held far under the radar.

It could have been a domestic thing? What if—?

"Hey, get rid of that working face, we're on vacation," growled Alex. "Your wife will castrate you if she sees that look."

"I know. Once a cop, always a cop." Manny confessed.

"For some of us. I saw the officers at the hotel and the ambulance too. But it's not our problem, your problem, and we're on vacation. Did I say that already?"

"Yep, you did and you're right. As of right now, I'm out of work mode."

Alex gave him the evil eye.

"I promise."

The CSI slapped him on the back. "That's more like it, but I don't believe a damn word that just came out of your mouth."

"Cross my heart."

Alex looked at Manny. "Okay. I still think you're lying."

The ladies returned just as the gate swung back, allowing the line of passengers to begin the embarkation process.

After getting their Fun and Sun ID cards, the rest of the embarkation process took about an hour, most of it waiting in line for the housecleaning crew to ready the cabins.

Finally, after what seemed an eternity, Manny and Louise entered their 208-square-foot balcony cabin on the sixth deck, cabin 6224. Tossing their carry-on bags to the bed, they did what every first-time cruiser does—rushed out to the balcony to take in the view.

They were on the port side of the ship facing the harbor. The turquoise water was an expanse of glittering gems in the sunlight. Breathtaking.

Manny cleared his throat and leaned over the railing.

Louise looked at him, horrified. "You are not going to spit from this balcony, Manfred Robert Williams."

He pointed to his mouth, indicating he couldn't answer with a full mouth.

"Manny! Don't you dare. What if you hit someone?"

He smiled, drew back his head and let it fly, leaning even farther to watch his loogie descend to worlds unknown. "Oh. That was awesome. Always wanted to do that."

"You are a sick puppy. You know that, right?"

"Maybe, but you love me just the same."

"It's my lot in life. Did you hit anyone?"

"Nope. Straight to the water. You should try it."

"I'm a lady. That's not going to happen."

He drew her close. "Yes, you are. And I'm glad."

"This is going to be amazing." Louise gave him a warm hug.

She was right, but his mind turned back to what he thought was happening at the hotel and then to the letter burning a hole in his pocket. Alex's voice slapped him across the face.

We're on vacation.

He wondered how he was going to slay the dragon.

CHAPTER-13

The killer sat naked on the edge of his bed, the worn newspaper article resting gently in powerful fingers. The faded clipping could have been a trembling bird or a tattered piece of ancient parchment revealing the eleventh commandment. It was inconceivable that hands and fingers such as his could possess an unobtrusive touch. But he thought himself filled with such paradoxes.

The quiet whine of the air conditioning unit was steady and maybe even a little curative. He had closed the pale blinds hiding the balcony's door to keep the curious light from inspecting his cabin, inspecting him. Instead, a minute corona seeped through the window dressing. Not quite dark, but close enough for one who preferred the company of shadows.

His luggage—a single bag—sat on the small, leather loveseat like a silent sentinel. A bottle of Brut champagne chilled in the polished pail near the vanity table—compliments of his travel agent for booking his second cruise in six months. His first one, a recon cruise. It was amazing what could be accomplished in just one seven-day sprint to the Caribbean.

A single drop of perspiration fell to the carpet, unnoticed. None of his surroundings mattered.

Not right now. Not this moment. Not even the nosy, old broad across the hall. He was lost in deep, intricate thought, reflecting on the complicated journey that had begun fourteen long months before.

****

After his prison release, Robert Peppercorn had been deemed cured from the multiple personality and duality shit that the doctor and his staff had diagnosed. He had certainly changed—more accurately, evolved.

Dr. Fredrick Argyle had spouted on and on that, supposedly, a person could hide in his own mind, become another person with a different personality, and not be aware of his actions. They called it Dissociative Identity Disorder (DID). Argyle said it could have been brought on by certain traumatic experiences during childhood.

Would wonders never cease? The messed-up quack had finally got one right. The cords tightened in his thick neck.

What the hell did they know about traumatic experiences?

Robert Peppercorn had been released from the prison, but Eli Jenkins was the one who was now truly free. He had promptly taken over the simpleton's mind and body, as was his right. He'd loathed his imprisonment, both physical and mental, but now he was in charge. This was Eli's time.

He took the waiting cab to the halfway house on Maple Avenue in downtown Lansing. The one assigned by the parole board. He checked in, went to his room, and tossed his meager belongings on the U-shaped bed.

No one noticed that he had changed. That he was different. That Eli Jenkins was in control. And why would they? None of these people had ever met him. The hypocrites didn't care anyway. Even Peppercorn's parole officer wouldn't notice. The system didn't give a rat's ass about ex-cons, no one did.

The room was simple and clean. A three-drawer dresser supported an old twenty-inch TV. To the left of the bed was a diminutive oak nightstand that supported a simple brass lamp with a lavender-flowered shade. A small two-paned window faced west. The sun had set, and slow-dancing pixels of pink and purple layered the spring sky. But what was around him was secondary to what he had been planning. His plan was his motive for living. His purpose.

He reached into his left front pocket and removed a small, yellow piece of paper with the name and address of the man he was to meet tomorrow. His face broadened into a full smirk. Some visits were better than others.

The bulge in his jean pocket disappeared when he pulled out the wad of cash. The $1,245 was all the money he had. But it would be enough for what was planned for the next day, more than enough.

He stretched his huge frame out on the bed, and rusty bed springs creaked tired resistance as hate-filled eyes stared at the water-stained ceiling.

Tomorrow it starts. The beginning was just on the horizon. No more waiting. No more hiding.

Jenkins finally drifted toward a keyed-up slumber.

It was going to be a wondrous visit.

CHAPTER-14

The next morning, Jenkins fulfilled Peppercorn's legal obligations, including a quick call to his parole officer, and then took a cab to the address written on the small piece of paper. The house was in the middle of Lansing's seediest area, and the taxi driver made a hasty exit after dropping off his larger-than-life fare.

Jenkins knocked on the door of the run-down brick ranch and, after a short wait, watched it crack open with the thick safety chain pulled taut.

"What do ya want?"

"Are you Fixer Holmes?"

"Who wants ta know?"

"I got out yesterday. Sly Fredrick said you could help me."

"Sly, huh? Not that I give a flyin' shit, but how's that old black bastard doing?"

Jenkins smirked. "You know he ain't black. He's almost as white as me. Are you screwing with me? 'Cause if you can't help me, I got another name . . ."

He waited, knowing that Fixer was mulling over whether he was on the level or not. No problem. Patience was a close friend of his. Finally the faded door closed, and Jenkins heard the rattle of chain against wood. The door creaked open leisurely, like some melodramatic scene in a grade B horror film.

The small, wiry man, with a wad of snuff bulging from his right cheek, sized him up. Fixer stood in the semi-lit opening that led toward steep basement steps, not really hiding the long switchblade clenched in his bony fingers.

"What are you gonna do with that? Give me an enema?"

"Maybe. If'n I had to." Fixer continued to look him over. "You're a big mother huncher, aren't ya? If I had a mind to do it, I guess I might need help with that there enema."

"Would a sloppy-ass kiss come with that butt-reamin'?" he charmed.

Fixer snorted a laugh and spit tobacco juice a few inches from his foot.

"You a cop?"

"Do I look like a cop?"

"No, I'm guessin' you don't. Just covering my ass. You got money?"

He pulled the roll of cash from his pocket. "This enough?"

"It'll do. Come on down."

They emerged from the bottom of the narrow stairs and entered what appeared to be a photo studio with lights and blue-dappled backdrops. There was also an old print press, two hi-tech copiers, two computers, and reams of colored paper stacked five boxes across and four deep. The basement reeked of musty Michigan cellar and harsh chemicals.

"Well, what do you need? I don't have all damn day."

"I need everything. Driver's license, birth certificate, passport, social security card, the works."

Fixer looked at him with rat-like eyes, "You sure you got twelve hundred in that wad?"

"You want to count it, dickface?"

The forger spit another glob of tobacco juice on the concrete floor and motioned Jenkins over to the tripod and camera. Fixer then put his magic machinery in motion. Two hours later, all of the paperwork Jenkins would ever need to travel, get a job, or move to another country was completed. He could do whatever he wanted to do. Fixer was a genius, just like old Sly had said.

"This looks real good, real good," said Jenkins.

The smallish man shrugged his shoulders as if to say *what did you expect?*

Fixer handed him a wrap-around file folder containing the counterfeit documents and held out his hand. Jenkins counted out the money and gave it to him.

"You can let yourself out," he said. Then Fixer Holmes made the last mistake of his life. He turned his back and headed for the half-open Keystone safe hidden behind the printing press.

"And you can kiss your ass goodbye," sneered Jenkins.

The forger tried to move, get out of the ex-con's way, but it wasn't in the cards.

The killer lifted the small man by his head and neck and twisted violently. Fixer convulsed as his third and fourth vertebrae were reduced to shattered bits of calcium. Jenkins had wrenched Fixer's head with such force that they were virtually eye-to-eye when he dropped the lifeless forger to the stained floor. Small runnels of tobacco juice mingled with scarlet trickled down Fixer's unshaven chin and stained the back of his shirt.

After giving his handiwork a curious look, Jenkins strode over to the steel safe and pulled out all of the stashed money. He stared at the pile of dead presidents, and they stared back. Almost twenty-two thousand dollars in all. Jenkins laughed. Old Sly had told the truth about the money too. Fixer had never trusted banks. He should have.

Jenkins would have to send the old lifer a thank-you note someday—if gratitude ever seeped into his consciousness, that is.

He put most of the cash in his folder, some in his pocket, and started up the stairs. He hit the first step, paused, then stopped. Her stare was hot, full of reproach.

Fixer's wife stood halfway down the steps and was looking at him with eyes the size of tires. "My God! What did you do?" she cried.

Her expression prompted him to flash a wide smile. "Well, darling," he said, putting his foot on the second step. "What does it look like I did? And too bad you saw it."

Jenkins saw revulsion turn to panic. She scrambled up the four remaining stairs, but leaned too far at the last one and stumbled, skidding to her chubby knees. Crying and cursing, she hurried to get up and had almost made it when Jenkins reached her. He unceremoniously jerked her to her feet. Spinning her around, their eyes met, and he knew she was mesmerized like a bird captured by a cobra's stare.

What could match this feeling? He held sway over the woman's most precious commodity, the gift above all gifts. He laughed again, only harder.

She screamed, but he clamped her mouth

shut with his right hand so nothing more came out. And nothing would again.

The folder fell from his grasp, and he clutched her white throat with his powerful left hand, squeezing with all of his strength. Ninety seconds later, she let out a soughed breath and left this world, windpipe crushed like a twig in a vice. He threw her plump, lifeless body down the steps, reuniting her with her husband.

How poetic.

Jenkins grabbed his folder, locked up the house, and walked to the nearest bus stop. He took the next white-and-blue downtown to the Washington Avenue hub, then a cab to the train station in East Lansing. An hour later, he boarded the train that would sweep him away from Michigan, at least for now.

As the locomotive rolled away, his thoughts turned to the future, both immediate and distant. He had work to do, preparations to make, a body to change. There were months of research to do. He needed time and a place to be as inconspicuous as someone his size could be. Jenkins would be a white rabbit for the next year. Then all hell would break loose.

****

The blaring announcement concerning the evening's lifeboat drill filled the cabin and began to bring Jenkins out of his trance. Lucidity replaced reflection as he traveled back to the here and now.

It was really happening. The time had come. No more lying awake at night in some flea-bitten hotel waiting for this day.

He flipped the newspaper clipping around and around with his strong fingers. The motion became more energetic, more truculent as the paper became a hypnotic blur. Suddenly, he stopped the mind-boggling spin and placed his black-and-white treasure on the small table.

Jenkins was in complete control, and he always won, always.

CHAPTER-15

Sophie rested tanned, wiry arms on the wooden rail that ran the length of the room's verandah. It was impossible to not be geeked about her first trip to sunny paradise, not to mention her first cruise.

She watched in childlike wonder as a dark patch of thunder clouds loped over the ocean toward Puerto Rico's highest point. Seemingly with a mind of their own, the clouds settled on the mountaintop that housed one of the Caribbean's largest rain forests, El Yunque, and loosed their moist cargo. Minutes later, as the Puerto Rican breeze freshened, she could smell the rain as it prattled against the mountain, transforming the summit into a hazy shadow.

Within a few seconds, a vivid, amorphous rainbow dominated the skyscape. She recalled from Sunday school class that rainbows were proof of God's promise to never destroy mankind with water again. (She smiled at remembering *something* from Bible lessons.) It was a striking symbol and an even greater promise.

"Good call, God," she whispered.

As she shifted position, searing pain shot from her hip and throbbed at her tailbone. She bit her lip until the ache dimmed to a dull roar. The source of her hurting—two deep, purple contusions shaped like whips—were strategically hidden by her red-flowered, one-piece swimsuit.

Tears slipped down her face. Not because of the pain, but because of her shame . . . and what she had gotten herself into, especially with him.

How could I be so stupid? Why was I drawn to these men? It can be fixed in a New York minute; I'm a cop, for God's sake. I'd helped plenty of women in this same situation, although mine is a little more complicated, maybe.

Physician, heal thyself.

Randy was belting out a love song—in a key that Bach wouldn't recognize—while he showered, causing her to laugh in spite of everything. He wasn't the type of man most people thought she would marry, but he loved her beyond reproof, and she was lucky to have landed him. His sun rose and set with her. Randy said as much. And he made her laugh. Really laugh.

After the divorce, she never thought that would be possible: to laugh, to love again. She supposed most people felt it inconceivable for broken-hearted pain to ever truly be vanquished. But new love proved to be a special kind of medicine, nectar in which she had desperately imbibed. How could she have betrayed that? She wiped away a fresh gush of tears.

It was becoming harder and harder to hide the marks. But what could she do? Maybe she could tell Manny. He was a good listener, but he would be pissed that she hadn't told him sooner. He might even go after him.

What of poor Randy? What would he do? How could she tell him that she was having an affair? Let alone with a sadist prick. How could Randy's "faithful" wife tell him she didn't have the strength to end the affair? That she wasn't even sure she wanted to. That part of her even liked it?

Randy emerged from the bathroom looking like a soaked Buddha. "I'll be ready in a few, baby. I want to see the ship. Just you and me. Okay?"

"Whatever you want, honey. I'm up for anything. But I think you'll have to get dressed first . . . they have *some* rules here."

"Deal." He dropped his towel. "Once the women on this cruise got a load of this, they'd divorce their men on the spot."

"What if they were lesbians?"

"They'd give it up, return to the land of boy-toy wonders. I have that kind of thing going on."

"Just remember who brought you, boy toy."

He grinned and stepped back into the bathroom.

Sophie turned back to the balcony and looked at her hands without seeing them. She hated herself for the game she was playing, the liar she had become. But the time was approaching to come clean, to get real. Soon, maybe sooner than she imagined. Lies always take on a life of their own. That made them harder to kill and impossible to forget.

There were ways to run and hide. And right now, all of them seemed better alternatives than facing this truth.

CHAPTER-16

All she had wanted was some help with her bag. It was so heavy, and the last heart attack had robbed her of more strength than she wanted to admit, if the truth be known.

The whole truth, so help me God.

How ironic was that? God wasn't going to help her here, not this time. He had bailed her out often, maybe more than she had coming, but she had made one mistake too many. The very last in a long line of misjudgments, ill-advised trusts, and displaced compassion that had caused her life to be tougher than it should have been.

But this one mistake topped all the rest.

The man across the hall was a big one, but had seemed nice and his smile was . . . sexy, even to an eighty-two-year-old woman. So asking him for help wasn't a problem, but rather enjoyable. Didn't cruise ships thrive on friendly?

How could she have known what she would smell when he opened his door? Her forty-five years as a nurse had always been a good thing, but not today. Today it was a curse. Most people wouldn't recognize the odor of chloroform, faint or otherwise. Not only that, she saw the twelve-ounce bottle resting on the dresser. No one would bring that on a cruise unless they were up to something,

something no good.

If only she had left then . . .

He had been so fast, and she had been so slow to react. She hadn't been able to get her door shut in time. Forget about screaming, not with that big mitt over her mouth.

Now Rose Charles lay on her bed, his hand snug around her throat, and wondered what he was waiting for. But she thought she knew. This needed to look like a natural thing, or at worst, an accident.

Was that a smile?

Evil was relative, but she thought that smile the most unholy thing she had ever seen.

With no wasted motion, he reached for the cushion from the loveseat and pressed it to her face.

That's when the first pain hit, like an elephant stomping on her chest. She hardly felt the second one. This was the big man's lucky day. Her exhausted ticker was going to take care of his dilemma.

CHAPTER-17

It was almost time to head to the Lido Deck for the Sail Away Party, and Manny was ready. Louise primped inside the tiny bathroom, putting on her final touches of makeup. As if she needed to. She was even more attractive approaching forty than at thirty. He was indeed a very fortunate man.

What a day today had been. Lingering thoughts of how he and Louise had investigated the *Ocean Duchess*, deck by deck, came back to him with amazing clarity. With first-time cruiser enthusiasm, they had entered every brightly colored bar and dazzling public room. Most ships have a particular theme, and the *Ocean Duchess* decor represented royalty from every major country.

Manny had taken special note of the jazz bar called the Sapphire Room. Nothing like jazz to get the juices flowing. He might actually relax in that kind of a venue.

The couple had browsed every shop window of the ship's surprisingly complete mall. Fine clothes and stylish, expensive gems from every persuasion called to them.

They'd sat in the thick velour chairs of the Palace Theater and Lounge and wondered what would be the night's main attraction. The stage was shrouded with a purple rhinestone-studded design that resembled the Taj Mahal.

They'd checked out the brightly lit Las Vegas-style casino on Deck Five where one-armed bandits and a dozen or so gaming tables waited like sophisticated muggers. But like the shops, the Casino of Kings remained closed while the ship was in port.

At the ship's tuxedo shop, they had picked up his rental tuxedo, which he would wear on both formal nights. Two times in a tuxedo in less than a week? Not good. Cops from towns like Lansing didn't don tuxedos. It was a serious dichotomy. Like the Detroit Lions and winning football games.

Louise had also wanted to check out the photo lounge and the two main dining rooms located at the rear of the ship. When they'd reached the restaurants, wonder escalated to a new level. The Atrium spiraled upward through four decks with a royal blue décor, trimmed in awesome hues of gold and silver. Manny had reached out to feel the ornate light fixture at the left of the elevator.

"Hey, don't touch that stuff. If you break it, the price goes right onto the room's bill."

He'd responded with running his hand over her hip. "Really? How about if I touch this?"

"Manny! There are people everywhere. Control yourself."

"What's the fun in that?"

"I'll show you fun, just not in the Atrium." The look in her eye had more than offset her feigned look of mortification.

"Chicken."

"Nope. Just being proper."

All of their exploring had been accomplished

with the Drink of the Day, a strong rum punch, clutched in their hands. Louise had wanted one so she could keep the "expensive" plastic tumblers. He couldn't let her drink alone. Besides, the drinks came with cute little umbrellas.

When finally back at the cabin, after an unbelievable meal of glazed chicken and rib eye steak, they sat on the balcony and experienced the incredible Puerto Rican sunset. It was like every postcard Manny had ever seen.

Louise stood up. "I'm ready to go to my first Sail Away Party, big boy."

"Works for me."

"By the way, don't think I didn't see your face when those cops showed up at the hotel. For a minute, I thought you were going to get out of the cab."

"What? I would never do that. At least not on vacation."

"Just remember, we're not in Lansing, and the world will survive without your crime-solving talent. Got it?"

"No problem. I just didn't like how the scene at the hotel was going down. It *felt* bad."

She put her arms around his neck, "Manfred Robert Williams, the only feelings you are allowed on this holiday have to do with my ass and a great time."

Manny laughed and promised, again, to do as he was told.

He held the door and followed Louise out. He knew she wanted it to be that easy, and he would try. But he didn't always know when to quit. A trait he loved and hated about himself.

CHAPTER-18

The Crosby wedding group agreed to meet on the crowded, festive Lido Deck at 10:15 p.m. sharp. Manny, Louise, Gavin, and Stella waited for the others, marveling at how the Sail Away Party had begun to take on a life of its own.

Loud island music engulfed the crowd of a thousand or so diverse cruisers with its mesmerizing cadence. And who doesn't like party music?

Manny watched as cruisers sang with the band and danced with freedom and gyrations that would embarrass them to a bright red if their coworkers and family could observe their "vacation" behavior. But the atmosphere was spellbinding. It reminded him of the National Geographic documentaries. An indigenous tribe in some third-world country would dance to a traditional, centuries-old drumbeat, celebrating a wedding or important festival. Primitive, yet exotic and riveting. He had never seen traditional native dancers with rainbow umbrella drinks and silver cans of beer clamped to their hands in any of those documentaries, however. Maybe someday recordings of cruise-ship behavior would be studied to see how *this* primitive culture celebrated.

At that point, the others arrived, minus Lynn and Liz. The couple was probably "enjoying" the new surroundings and would be here soon enough.

The ship released a deep bellow, and Manny watched as dark smoke rolled from the unique stack as the vessel began to shimmy and move away from the pier. She swung left and headed toward the narrow canal that would set her free to roam the Caribbean Sea and its wondrous islands. The group pushed to the railings and watched San Juan slip away into the dark, humid evening, waving at imaginary well-wishers, laughing at the gesture.

After moving away from the railing, the group waited another fifteen minutes for Liz and Lynn to show, but they didn't. The young natives in the group were getting restless.

Finally, Gavin released the newlyweds with an impatient wave of his hand. "I don't know what on earth I was thinking. Why would they want to hang out with us?"

"Hey, hey. Speak for yourself. I'm not that old. I could hang with them," Alex said.

"Maybe you don't remember that little nap I just woke you up from, party boy," ribbed his wife Barb.

"Oh yeah, that," Alex grinned.

"You too?" asked Gavin.

"What is this, an old fogy's cruise?" said Sophie, shaking her head.

"Nope. Just conserving energy for the rest of the week," answered Gavin.

"I don't know where Liz and Lynn are, but let's grab a place to sit. They can find us when they get here," suggested Stella.

"Good idea." Manny moved to claim two empty deck tables and promptly plowed into an older, corpulent woman. She would have hit the deck with authority if he hadn't reached to steady her. He winced as her piña colada tumbled to the deck, splattering in a hundred directions.

The woman was dressed in a pair of faded jeans and a blue flannel shirt. Her thin, white hair was mostly covered with an experienced straw hat. Her black-rimmed glasses were fogged over from the humidity.

"I'm so sorry. I didn't see you. Are you all right?"

"I'm okay. It's these damn glasses. They steam up out here. I probably walked right in your way. Blind old woman, I am," she rasped. She had "that sound," like she had been sucking on cigarettes the majority of her life.

"I'm sure it was my fault. I get in a hurry. Let me make it up to you and replace your drink," Manny said. Without giving her a chance to respond, he called over one of the many willing waiters and ordered a fresh drink.

The old woman strained at Manny through her glasses, looking like an owl in some long-forgotten cartoon.

"It wasn't necessary, but thanks."

Manny started to reply and stopped in mid-sentence, looking at her intently; like he should know her or that he had been in this scene before.

"What is it, young man?" grated the old woman.

"Nothing. Just a little *déjà vu.* Are you sure you're okay?"

The woman said she was and waddled away toward the buffet.

"What the hell was that?" asked Sophie.

"Like I said, just a little *déjà vu.* Almost like I knew her."

"Do you?" asked Louise.

He thought for a moment. "No. Just that weird feeling thing, I'm sure." Except he wasn't sure. There was something about her. Another place in time?

"Okay then." Louise grabbed his arm and bum-rushed him to the dance floor. "We're going to shake our booties."

Between the music, dancing, and a few drinks, Manny forgot the incident with the old lady, eventually plopping down in his chair, perspiring heavily from the impromptu Dance Night.

Two hours later, the crowd had thinned and the atmosphere had settled to a dull roar. Alex commented that Liz and Lynn had never put in an appearance, suggesting he should go roust them out of bed.

"No need to harass them tonight. Maybe they needed the rest. They'll be on the excursion to Trunk Bay in the morning. We can give them a hard time then," said Manny.

The group talked awhile longer, and Manny and Louise got up to go to their cabin. As they walked past one of the occupied deck chairs, he noticed the old woman he had bumped into sleeping hard, her slack mouth half open, breathing heavily. A partially consumed drink rested on the deck near her hand. Perhaps she had enjoyed the evening a little too much. Her wayward hat revealed more of her thin, white hair, which made Manny think of someone recovering from chemotherapy.

The same odd sense of *déjà vu* returned. He

wasn't sure what that meant, but it would come to him, if it needed to.

CHAPTER-19

The loud knock at the door woke Lynn Casnovsky from his sound slumber, forcing him to a shaky sitting position. He rubbed one eye and blinked around the cabin, attempting to gather his wits. The brass reading lamp pushed out a soft funnel of light that spilled over his shoulder, giving that side of the room an unnatural, faded glow. His eyes glanced down at his Rolex, and he moaned. They had missed the Sail Away Party. Liz and he made it a practice to never be late—for anything—and especially with these guys. The ribbing would be relentless. The last thing he remembered was booking two island excursions and scheduling Liz's full-body massage. It was marvelous that you could book any activity on and off the ship by just following the prompted menus on the TV screen. He looked at the remote control resting on the ruffled bed comforter.

Another magnificent use for the all-powerful Excalibur.

He was glad he had checked out Carousel's stock situation because it could end up being one profitable investment.

Standing on the small balcony, Liz had been taking in the incandescent sunset, right after they'd returned from the perfunctory lifeboat drill.

He'd meant to join her, but never made it. He must have lain back on the bed. Liz had let him sleep.

The knock came again. Liz was bustling around in the tiny bathroom with the hair dryer going full bore. She obviously didn't hear the door. It seemed an appropriate metaphor for how things had been going for the last few months. She talked. He pretended like he didn't hear her or acted like she'd meant something else.

His wife, the attorney. She knew he was whoring around with his current fling, and the last thing he wanted to do was get anywhere near the subject. Not now. Maybe not ever.

The rap was louder this time, more persistent. It was probably the Purser's Desk with the bottle of champagne he'd ordered. But it could be their room steward, checking with them to see if they needed anything else for the evening.

"Hold your horses." He crawled off the front of the bed and shuffled to the veneer-covered door.

Maybe it was the pervasive sense of comfort that had wrapped itself around Lynn like a warm blanket on a cold Michigan night, but it never occurred to him to peer through the security hole in the door. He should have.

Lynn pulled open the door and was sent crashing toward the queen-sized bed by a powerful right hand that instantly shattered his jaw in four places. Amazingly, he hung on to a groggy consciousness. The room was spinning as he heard the towering figure shut and lock the door.

The intruder jerked him from the floor and turned him around so that Lynn's face was pointed away from him. The man possessed the strength of the damned. Lynn knew what was next. His training in the Marines opened that hideous door of enlightenment.

Why?

His arms wouldn't move, and he was helpless to stop the attacker. He wanted to scream for Liz to lock the bathroom door. To save herself. Pain seared his mouth as he sought to move a jaw that had already swollen to twice its normal size.

Lynn caught the reflection of his attacker shining in the terrace window, and confusion assailed his senses. He recognized the tall man behind him. What was he doing here? Why would *he* want to kill *him*?

The large, strong hands positioned themselves on each side of his chin. Regret raised its ugly head, and fear held his hand. He wasn't ready to die.

A revolting sound of breaking bones disrupted his thoughts as several of Lynn's vertebrae shattered like moldered cement. He was dead before he hit the floor.

****

The visitor pulled Lynn's limp body onto the bed and positioned him in a fetal position, as if an innocent, slumbering child. Then he sat on the edge of the bed and waited.

Tall, shapely Liz Casnovsky would exit the bathroom in a few minutes. He would greet her his way. She would be confused, shocked, maybe even drop her mouth open. Not only because someone else was in their cabin, but because it was *him.*

What could be better than this?

A moment later, Liz emerged from the tiny bathroom. "I'm ready for dinner, L—" the rest of her statement stuck in her throat.

"Hi, Liz."

He watched her try to regain some of her lost composure, "What are *you* doing in here?"

"Anything I want, DA Casnovsky. Anything I want."

He saw alarm steal over her. She swung her hand at him, and he easily caught the blow. He trapped her eyes with his own and read them like a familiar book. She was thinking that this sort of thing just doesn't happen, at least not to folks like her. This scene, this invasion, was only played out in a horror movie or a Dean Koontz novel.

It wouldn't do to let her scream. Not when he was this close. With incredible quickness, he covered her face with the chloroform-laced rag, forcing the sickening fumes into her nose and mouth.

A few seconds later, her lithe body relaxed completely. "Now the real party can begin," he uttered as he carefully laid Liz beside her dead husband.

His eyelids fluttered in ecstasy while he anticipated what would happen next. She was quite attractive, and he would enjoy this one. Paybacks are sweeter when one can orchestrate the exact set of circumstances.

He slowly began to unbuckle his belt.

CHAPTER-20

Captain Vicente Serafini stared at the taunting piece of paper in front of him—even after he'd read it a third time. The words reached out and grabbed him by the front of his uniform and demanded attention he took no pleasure in giving.

It was early on Monday, and they had just docked in St. Thomas, when his first officer brought the disturbing fax to his office. He had never gotten one quite like this, not in his fourteen years as a cruise ship captain.

He gazed around his opulent office and fixated on the plaques and black-framed certificates of achievement hanging neatly on the wall. They reminded him of what his hard-driving ego could accomplish, and he liked them. Why shouldn't he?

He'd worked with uncompromising effort to learn the intricacies of being a ship's captain in Italy, his homeland. Those years of commitment and sacrifice had been rewarded when Carousel Cruise Lines hired him and two years later gave him his own ship. The appointment of his first captainship rivaled the births of his two sons, and his wedding day, as the most special events in his life.

Standing, he gazed out the small porthole behind his desk. It was another day in paradise, and that's just what he and Carousel sold: paradise. Lavish green, riveting blue, charming native cultures, and colorful umbrella drinks for those who would part with their hard-earned money. He rubbed his chin. There was no room in paradise for messages like the one laying spread-eagle on his desk. None.

The captain turned back toward his chair and caught his reflection in the mirror-like polished chrome that encircled the window. Even though his hairline had receded over the last couple of years, he was still good-looking in a distinguished sort of way. But the crow's feet were gathering, and mornings like this accelerated the process. They made him feel older than his forty-six years.

The fax begged him to read it again.

Dear Captain Serafini,

We regret the necessity of sending this communication, but we deem it essential to alert you and your officers of potential danger to your passengers and crew.

Yesterday morning, at approximately 11:55, we discovered the brutally murdered body of a young woman at the Condado Wyndham Hotel. We have reason to believe that the murderer may be a passenger on one of the three cruise ships that sailed from San Juan last evening. We emphasize *may*. We are still conducting our investigation and will advise if anything pertinent arises to the contrary.

If you or your crew witness anything unusual with any of your passengers or uncover any information that would assist in this investigation, please contact me at once.

Again, the purpose of this communication is to simply request that you alert your security staff and senior officers of the potential risk. We do not wish to cause widespread panic aboard your ship, but every precaution should be exercised, given the level of the disturbing attack administered against the young victim.

Thank you for your cooperation.
Detective C. Perez, San Juan Police Department

The Captain rolled his eyes“. . . *anything unusual with any of your passengers . . .*”? He wondered if the good detective had ever been on a cruise.

If he and his officers reported everything cruise ship passengers did that fell into the vague category of “unusual,” he would have to add a dozen staff members just to review the hundreds of generated reports. Many behaviors marched to the beat of “unusual.” It ranked right up there with “we were just having fun.”

What did the police think he would do: send out a message on the PA system for people to be on the lookout for a dangerous murderer? And oh, by the way, we don’t know what he looks like or if he is truly on board. Or even if the killer is a he.

He shook his head. This is a cruise ship, not some damned City Hall.

Still, he would bring it up in the senior staff meeting later in the morning, time permitting.

The paper burned a hole in his hand, and he wished he had never received it. Better yet, that it had never been sent. He tried to convince himself that it was just another item on the long list of situations that can arise when running a cruise ship.

It would be a long day, and he had more important things to concern himself with.

The captain folded the communication and tossed it into the shallow drawer of his desk.

CHAPTER-21

"Please leave a message, and I'll get back with you . . . if I feel like it," recited the response from Liz's cell phone.

"Liz, this is Manny again. Are you guys coming to Trunk Bay? Call me or get your asses down here."

He stopped pacing, clicked off the cell, and glared toward the ship's gangplank. He adjusted his well-worn Detroit Tigers hat with the raised Old English "D" and pulled at the left shoulder of his bright-green palm-tree shirt, pacing like a caged panther.

"Good God, man, will you settle down?" said Gavin.

"I know, I know, but they're never late, and this is the second straight get-together they've missed. I know they *really* wanted to snorkel at Trunk Bay. That's all they talked about on the flight down."

"They have ten minutes before the tender pulls out. They'll be here."

Manny didn't think so. Something was haywire. His instincts told him so. It wasn't customary for Liz and Lynn to be late for anything. In fact, he couldn't remember a time when they had been. He was going to knock on their door on the way back from breakfast, but there was a Do Not Disturb sign hanging from the knob. He had raised his right arm to knock anyway, but then at the last second, dropped it back to his side. Maybe they just wanted to be left alone. Maybe they were just tired. Not everyone vacationed the same way, especially on a cruise ship.

He drew in a deep breath of ocean air and gazed out to the Pillsbury Sound inlet. It looked like they could be touring the set of the Love Boat. Large, white yachts rocked gently in the aqua water while anchored sailboats of every size and color dotted the brilliant, early-morning seascape.

Here he was, in the middle of his first Caribbean port of call, all this beauty, and he couldn't get Liz and Lynn's no-show out of his mind.

There was only one way to alleviate the gnawing tension in his gut. "I'm going to go get them. I'll be right back."

"Oooo, this could be good," giggled Sophie as she stepped away from Manny and Louise.

Manny gave her a sour look.

"You just called them for the third time, and besides, you don't have time, honey," said Louise. "You don't want to miss this trip to St. John, do you? Besides, maybe they signed up for the afternoon excursion. I think there is one at 12:30."

There was a building edge in Louise's voice. Manny knew what that meant, only too well. He had no desire to tangle with her, or the persona that voice characterized, at least over this. Talk about Jekyll and Hyde.

In spite of Louise's subtle warning of future hell to pay, the urge to bolt the pier and find Liz and Lynn was overpowering. His senses were tingling all over. His cop senses. At times like these, he was virtually helpless to stop it. He had been trying hard to tame the workaholic brute on this trip, bury it deep, but the beast wasn't cooperating.

Damn. Think about it. What could go wrong on a cruise ship anyway?

"Everyone aboard the boat that's going to Trunk Bay, we be leaving shortly, mon," blared the voice from the double-decked shuttle boat's PA system.

Manny hesitated, weighing how long he could handle Louise being pissed off at him. No brainer.

"All right. Let's go. They must have signed up for the second one. I'm still going to chew ass when I get back. They could have at least told someone."

"Don't worry. We'll see them tonight, and you can chew all the ass you want," chided Alex.

"Better get your wife's permission. About the chewing thing, I mean," prodded Sophie.

"Hey. I do have input into your work review," Manny pointed out.

"That's better, O Guardian of the Universe," Sophie snickered.

They boarded and found seats on the lower deck, port side. The *Sunkist* pulled away from the dock and swung east, entering Pillsbury Sound toward St. John and beautiful Trunk Bay.

The shuttle cruised past several smaller, quaint islands including one that Kevin Costner had owned and then sold after a major hurricane hammered the area. He had unloaded his Caribbean sanctuary for a paltry fourteen million.

The more the tour guide spoke, the more enamored Manny was with the enchantment of his surroundings. Concern for Liz and Lynn was replaced by prospects for the upcoming excursion. He had never snorkeled before, and he was catching up with the rest of the group's heightening anticipation.

"So that's what you do with that kind of money—buy an island in the Caribbean," cracked Sophie. "Just once. That's all I ask. Just once."

"You're going to need a big-time raise or win the lotto. And I don't think there's any money in the budget for a raise," Gavin jabbed.

Sophie grabbed Randy's face. "We're buying lotto tickets when we get back."

"Good idea. I could get used to this."

Looking toward St. John, Manny noticed the flags flying high over one of the pointed gables of the Governor's Mansion and wondered how much Liz knew about the mansion's architecture because she loved that stuff. She'd be giving the group every detail and date.

He stole a quick glance to the west side of the sound, trying to combat the voice of trouble that wouldn't be silenced. He had never wanted to see Liz and Lynn as much as he did at that moment.

Louise grabbed his hand and flashed him a radiant smile. He reached for her hand. He wasn't going to spoil this trip for her. He owed her that. She was working hard trying not to think about the mammogram, so at least the Guardian of the Universe could do his part.

Besides, just think about it. What could go wrong on a cruise ship?

CHAPTER-22

Jenkins spread out leisurely on a red-cushioned bench located on the upper tier of the *Sunkist.* The *Ocean Duchess* faded from sight as the shuttle bore steadily en route for St. John and Trunk Bay. His mind wasn't swimming with possibilities (there was no room). Only unrelenting execution of his will controlled his thoughts. No time to indulge in frivolous perceptions of pleasure.

A regal lion couldn't have carried itself with any more confidence as he stretched, then rose from his seat, tilting his long body over the edge of the railing.

He watched the group from Lansing gesture with animated hands and heard their tittering laughter. He felt like a Master looking down on his slaves. Why not? It fit.

Stupid-ass, first-time tourists.

Once the tour started, he would make sure that today would be a day that St. John would never forget, ever. And of course, when the time was right to reveal himself, they would forever remember him.

Jenkins, the first passenger off the ocean shuttle, climbed into one of the colorful, floral-painted tour buses that awaited the *Sunkist* passengers. He flashed a compelling grin at the overweight driver and asked if it was all right to sit in the passenger's seat because he got cramped in the smaller benches in the back.

"No problem, mon," responded the driver, presenting a well-practiced greeting of his own.

Once everyone was aboard the three buses, they began the fifteen-minute trip to the bay. Each vehicle eased on to the road and veered to the left side of the narrow asphalt.

After eight minutes of twisting, turning travel, the driver swung off at a sandy, well-worn turnout area so that passengers could take pictures of Hawksnest Bay and the thriving surroundings of Caneel Bay.

The stop only served to intensify the impatient expectation knocking at his door. But there was a schedule to adhere to, and he would adhere to it.

Every fiber in his body screamed for action because he longed to show the world his strength. *His* way.

His smile, laced with friendliness, caused the driver to comment how happy the big man seemed. The island chauffer could not know how good a thespian Jenkins was, because his expression was the exact antithesis of his being. *Patience, she'll be there. Where else did she have to go?*

Finally, the caravan arrived at the welcome center of Trunk Bay Beach, and folks of all ages and sizes adorned in bright beach attire headed for the sand. To him, they scurried like lost peacocks just escaping their cages. Fools.

Once most of the tourists had left the dirt parking lot, he hooked his bag over his shoulder and headed for the small group of gray-brown buildings that extended back into the sprawling brush some forty yards. He strolled past the small souvenir shop and made brief eye contact with the overweight, already-glowing woman behind the counter.

Damn, eat a salad once in a while.

He continued past the slightly larger, bamboo-sided grill where the smell of coffee and cooking ham had already infiltrated the warm breeze. He bent to fidget with his sandal, making sure no one was eyeing him. Once satisfied, he headed deeper into the thick trees. Working his way along the path, he reached the last building of the sun-faded trio and stopped, reading the neatly carved, wooden, three-by-three sign out loud:

US VIRGIN ISLANDS NATIONAL PARK,
TRUNK BAY
RANGER ON DUTY, DOROTHY MAXWELL

Hello, Ranger Maxwell.

The corners of his mouth jerked into a satisfied simper. She was where she was supposed to be—and now he was where he was supposed to be.

He knocked on the door of the squat building and waited. The door groaned open and a tall, thirtyish woman with mousey-brown hair tied back in a ponytail leaned partway out of the screen door.

Dot Maxwell was average-looking and the Kelly-green park ranger uniform did little to flatter her unusually thin body. She hadn't changed. Her commitment to a vegetarian lifestyle made her appear gaunt and almost sickly. Her white skin reflected none of the color that her sun- soaked environment could coax out of the palest of pales.

Playing on the beach or basking in the sun didn't seem to be part of Dot's agenda. He wondered if that was why she got the job that most sun-worshippers would kill for. She was about the work, not the surroundings. But she would play soon enough. And only for him.

He suspected most people, seeing her for the first time, would assume that Dot would retire an old spinster. There was also an almost daunting sadness about her that sent off melancholy vibrations. Some people were just downers.

"Can I help you?"

"I was wondering if you had a bandage. I stepped on one of those darn Starvation Fruits and put a hole in my foot."

The ranger's answer halted before it began. He felt her study his face. He sensed her heart skipping beats as harsh recognition overcame any denial.

Dot's face contorted with terror, paralyzing fright that wouldn't allow her to utter a sound, let alone a scream. He'd seen it before.

He shoved the ranger with a powerful straight arm, and the thin woman flew some eight feet through the air, sprawling helplessly on the wooden floor.

The park ranger lay there, trying to gather her shaken senses. He reached down with cable-taut arms and lifted her from the floor like a rag doll, her feet dangling a foot off the surface.

"Why again, why?" she choked.

As the cloth pressed against her nose and mouth, he supposed she at least deserved an answer. "Because we didn't finish the last time, my love. I'm your fate, Dot. No one escapes their fate."

He placed her tenderly on the floor, closed the opaque shades resting over the tired wooden windows, and locked the door.

The short-sleeved blouse tore easily, as did the rest of her uniform.

He had waited long enough. Too long. It was time for these festivities to renew, and renew they would.

CHAPTER-23

"Manny, can we talk about a little problem I have, or maybe had? Hell, I don't know," said Sophie.

"I don't care what your bra size is."

"No. Not that—Really? You don't care? You haven't thought of me in that way? Are you lying?"

"Soph, I'd never lie to you."

"You ever heard of a woman scorned?"

"You ever seen Louise pissed off?"

"Good point. But seriously, I need to talk."

Manny had been waiting for this conversation, and it was about time. He hoped she hadn't waited too long, that things weren't too crazy.

The rest of the group snorkeled near the small, rocky island that sat smack in the middle of pristine Trunk Bay waters, oblivious to Sophie and Manny coming in to take a break.

The island climbed out of the water about fifty yards away from the beach. Manny had just had first-hand communion with black-tipped angelfish; yellow-and black-striped sergeant fish; long, narrow pipefish; and rainbow-tinted parrotfish.

"Sure, Sophie. What's up?"

Sophie moved her small foot back and forth in the fine white sand as her downcast eyes watched, but never really focused. She finally looked up, tears trickling down her cheeks.

"I'm having an affair. Or maybe was having an affair is the right thing to say. I'm not sure it's over. I don't know how to explain it."

It was Manny's turn to watch his feet in the sand. "I know. I don't know with whom, but I know."

Sophie looked at him with stunned surprise. Her mouth moved like a fish out of water, but nothing came out. The second time on this trip his loquacious partner had been rendered speechless. He could get used to this.

He took her left hand into his right. "Listen. We're friends. Partners. Cops. You think I don't see things about you that others can't? I could tell you were seeing someone. You laughed a little too loud on the phone when you weren't talking with Randy. You were constantly messing with your hair and putting on fresh makeup. You sometimes left work acting like a giddy, seventeen-year-old schoolgirl, even after we put in tough, ten-hour days. Sorry, Sophie; those kinds of things don't go unnoticed by a workaholic detective."

"How come you never said anything?" she asked, shoulders slumping lower.

Manny looked at his hand around hers and then back to her. "Remember when we had that miscarriage a few years back? I sat at my desk and drew those little pictures of the baby's face and wondered how close to right I'd been. If the baby's eyes would have been blue or if he would have had blond hair. You were the only one to ever ask about them. But when I told you who they were, you just gave me a hug and never mentioned it again. You knew I had to work it out myself."

"So you think I have to work this out for myself?"

"I could tell you how wrong it is. What it would do to Randy if he found out. But I think you already know."

Sophie's brown eyes moistened, then ran unchecked.

"He hurts me. At first I thought it was, like, rough sex. Just a little kinky, you know. The last time he bruised me up pretty good. I told him it was over."

Manny gritted his teeth and dug his feet deeper into the sand. He had seen too many bruised faces, battered and scarred bodies. Pain inflicted in the name of love, whatever that twisted bullshit meant.

"I have two questions. Is it over, and who is it?"

His partner looked out to the island as the others were working their way back to the beach.

"He hasn't called in two weeks, and I . . . I . . . damn, I sort of miss him. But I think I'm past the hard part." Sophie nodded slowly. "Yeah. It's over." She grabbed one of the blue beach towels and dabbed her eyes and face.

"You have to promise to keep it to yourself and not confront him if I answer your second question. You have that damn *save-the-damsel-in-distress* thing going on, and you can't give in to it."

After a long moment, he sighed. "Okay. For you, I'll do my best. But no promises."

Just then, Sophie's chubby husband emerged from the clear water with his fluorescent-green snorkel dangling from his hand.

He shook water on the two detectives like some oversized, shaggy dog trying to dry off from the rain. Randy laughed like a mischievous ten-year-old and sat down to take off the matching flippers.

"Saved by the bell. I'll tell you later, I promise," she whispered.

"Deal."

CHAPTER-24

When the departure time neared, the Lansing contingent packed up their multicolored beach bags and headed for the changing rooms to shower and put on dry clothes. The tour buses would pull out at noon. No questions asked.

"No island time on this trip," stated the tour guide.

"That's fine with me," joked Alex. "I swallowed enough salt water to lower the ocean's level an inch or two."

"You can die from that," answered Sophie.

"Then bury my fat ass right here."

"Well, you're right about one thing."

"What?" asked Alex.

"Let's just say we can't bury you here," she grinned.

"Funny. Bad things happen to smartasses."

"Too late. I'm already a cop."

"Who says there's no karma?"

"Do I have to separate you two?" asked Manny.

"No, Dad," said Sophie.

The return trip to the *Sunkist* went quickly despite the driver making an unexpected stop at the turnout. It seemed that two of the passengers finally figured out the operation of their digital cameras and wanted to arrest some once-in-a-lifetime memories.

While they waited, Manny's mind turned again to the Casnovskys and why they hadn't made this excursion. Did they have a fight? Over what? Were they seasick? Not an uncommon occurrence for sure. Maybe they were—

"Penny for your thoughts?" asked Louise.

"Just getting hungry and can't wait to get back to the ship to eat," he lied.

"We'll be back soon. I'm getting hungry myself."

Louise nudged him to look at the pictures on their digital camera. He shifted his attention to his wife and the pictures.

They pulled away from the scenic turn out and ten minutes later boarded the *Sunkist.* Manny and Louise walked up to the front of the boat to watch the *Ocean Duchess* grow bigger as they approached St. Thomas. Then Louise went below deck to sit with Stella because the stiff breeze was blowing her hair into snarls and the hot sun was too much.

While Manny took in the approaching St. Thomas, Sophie shuffled up to his side and leaned over the railing. Mellow island music blared from the shuttle's speakers as the roiling smell of burning diesel from the *Ocean Duchess*'s colorful smoke stack became ever-more intense.

Sophie gripped the railing. "Lynn Casnovsky. My affair was with Lynn Casnovsky," she breathed.

CHAPTER-25

Sally May Thompson was glad this Monday was over. Today had been especially busy because two cruise ships had steamed into Charlotte-Amalie. She didn't care for the busy days. It was too hot to work that hard.

"Dees people bought everything from logo golf balls to cheap tee shirts dat wouldn't last da year. Fools dey were, no doubt," she marveled.

The faded numbers on the yellowed clock were barely visible. But she didn't have to see the digits to know when it was quittin' time. She had worked the tourist shop at Trunk Bay for almost thirteen years, and there were no surprises. She could feel when it was time to finish the day's work.

"SSDD. Same Shit, Different Day," she rued.

The job paid the bills, and she was grateful, but there had to be more to life than listening to starry-eyed tourists dressed like clowns ramble on about how beautiful Trunk Bay was.

Her pointed thoughts caused her to look toward the almost deserted beach. "Well, dey got dat part right, at least. But dey still damn fools for telling O' Sally 'bout it all day."

Sally May turned off the latest Bob Marley tune bawling from the old radio and reached an ebony hand underneath the warped bamboo counter. She located her secret mini-cubby and brought out a pint of the island's best homemade, 70-proof rum.

Once uncorked, she swung the clear bottle to her nose and inhaled with zest. "Mercy. What rum! It not only clears de troat but clears de sinuses, too." She purged a full belly laugh. "But I tink I like de troat clearing better, don't ya know."

Following two long draws, Sally May snorted her appreciation and stashed the bottle back under the counter, wiping away a couple of stray drops that had fallen on her flowered frock. That was enough for now. It wouldn't do for the wife of a Baptist preacher, a Southern Baptist preacher no less, to come home three-sheets to the breeze. She laughed again.

If God didn't want us to have de rum, why would He make it, I wonder?

Still, she had to keep up appearances. What would people say?

My, doz people would talk, dey would.

With a weary grunt, Sally May raised up from her stool, restocked the quaint little shop, then switched to the paperwork for the day's sales. Balancing the receipts had never been a problem. She had always been good with numbers even though she only possessed a tenth-grade education. After she had gotten herself pregnant with Cedric, her first of three children, going back to school was never really on her agenda. Besides, there was no reason for her to go back; she needed no more education.

Sally May finished up, balanced to the penny, as usual, and bundled up the cash and credit card worksheets for the auditor who marched in every morning to check her work.

Talk bout a mon that needed a shot of de rum. He don't trus nobody, not even his Mama.

The anal mannerisms of the government auditor caused her to wonder about his childhood. Sally May had no idea why he, or others, flew that way. It didn't jibe with island culture. Not a bad looking fellow, though.

She reached for the black strongbox to lock up the money and noticed the tightly wrapped package that had come for Dot Maxwell. She could see it was from the ranger's family on the mainland. It may very well be the package that girl had been asking about for the last week. Dot was so excited with the prospects of getting it; her eyes would sparkle when she asked if it had arrived. She wouldn't tell her what it was, but wanted to show Old Sally.

Odd, now that she thought about it, she hadn't seen Dot since early morning. Sometimes the girl would go out into the brush and take pictures of the wild donkeys, crested hummingbirds, or a basking iguana. Dot loved wildlife photography and wanted someday to try making a living at it. Sally May thought she spent more time out there since that "incident" about six months ago. Dot hadn't told her everything—just that she wasn't really raped, more like terrorized. Anyway, since then, every once in a while, Dot simply lost track of time and would come back late, but usually not this late.

"Maybe she had one of dem stuffy meetings at de Govnar's house," she mumbled to herself.

The ocean breeze stiffened into a comfortable gust, and Sally May closed her eyes and basked in its coolness. When "her" ocean decided to cuddle like this, she could stand in it all day. Eventually, the kissing ended, and she spun back to reality.

The oblong package called her name, and she reflected how thrilled Dot would be to get it. And maybe she would show Sally May what was in the damn thing.

I guess supper can be a tiny bit late; we'll all survive, I tink.

With the strongbox locked, she bent over to place it into the thousand-pound safe buried in the ground, slammed the door, and spun the combination dial four times. She straightened up with a wince and rubbed her considerable back. "Dis getting old shit is fo de birds, fo sho," she groaned out loud.

Once the shop was secured and the alarm set, she firmly placed the brown paper package in her meaty hand and headed for the ranger's cottage. Dot was scheduled to work until 5 p.m. so she had hopes of catching her. She could at least drop off the package inside the screen door.

She plodded down the sandy path and ambled toward the steps of the weather-worn porch. Her breathing became labored, like she'd been running a 5K race. She swore she was going to lose the extra weight. This time for sure.

Reaching the foot of the stoop, she crutched her hand on a round knee and looked upward to the stand of trees. Usually there were sounds of agitated or singing birds filling the air, but there was no noise echoing from the mahogany trees lining the path. Strange. She dismissed the thought and remembered why she had come to Dot's hut.

The top step moaned in protest as she scuffled up the steps and raised a hand to knock, but the inside door was already open an inch. A twinge of uneasiness pulled at her. Dot wouldn't leave the office without locking the door. She was too methodical to make that kind of mistake, and that computer was worth some money.

"Dot, girl is you dere? Dot? I got dat package from home. "No response from Dot caused her nervousness to escalate. She looked to her right and noticed that the shade was drawn on the front window. She didn't recall that being closed. Ever.

Senses on full alert, she gently leaned the package against the hut and clutched the worn out door handle, finally working up sufficient courage to pull open the rusty screen door, slowly pushing the inside door with her free hand. It swung open and then abruptly stopped as something blocked its path.

An unfamiliar odor prompted Sally May to wrinkle her nose. "What de hell is dat?"

The metallic scent hung in the air like a helium balloon. Her body tensed even more, and her eyes grew wider as she poked her head through the partially opened door.

"Dot? Dot, do ya hear me, woman?"

No response came from the darkened room. The thumping in her head grew louder. The quiet inside the small cabin was as unnerving as the stillness surrounding it. She moved a little farther through the entrance. Just as her hand slid up the door's smooth wood, movement trapped the corner of her eye.

"MEEOOOWWWW" split the humid air as Scully, Dot's big tiger cat, raced through the doors in a frenzied rush, brushing past Sally May's sizeable calf. The cat scampered toward places unknown.

Sally May screamed. Her arms launched into

the air causing her to twist off balance and slam flush into the inside door. The door gave way, and she tumbled backwards. Her world spun in slow motion as she plummeted out of control. There was a resounding thump as she landed full on her backside.

"Damn o' cat! What you tryin' to do, kill ol' Sally?" she yelled.

The preacher's wife closed her eyes for a moment and concentrated on steadying her frazzled nerves. She took a deep breath and looked around the shadowy room. She could make out the dark shape of the computer desk and realized that the window facing the south had the shade drawn too. In fact, all four shades were pulled. The sickly odor was so intense she could taste it. She placed her right hand behind her to brace herself. Something cold and sticky clung to her palm, and she pulled it away like she had just touched the burner of a hot stovetop.

"What in God's name?" She rolled over to her hands and knees, pushed herself up, and hurried to open the blinds.

Her eyes grew large as she saw the blood on her hand. Her gaze moved past her hand and rested on Dot Maxwell. The park ranger's unseeing eyes stared at the dark ceiling. Dot had been stripped of her clothes. Her throat and breasts looked like they had been served to barracudas for lunch. There were dark bruises tattooed about her face and neck. Large chunks of flesh were missing from her left thigh. A solitary black rose rested across her torso.

As reality caught up with the incomprehensible, she screamed, again.

Then Sally May was overcome by the strongest

of all instincts, and she scrambled out of the cabin, moving with unexpected speed for a woman her size, toward the shop and the phone, all along speaking prayers to God to keep her safe from the demon who had murdered her friend.

She dialed the police. Waiting for a response, she was struck with an odd thought. Dot would never get to see what was in that package. She would never tell Sally May what she'd been so excited to share. She didn't know why, but that seemed important.

The dispatcher came on line, and Sally May quickly reported what she had seen, maintaining a surprisingly poised manner.

After she hung up, all of the emotion building from the previous ten minutes erupted like a broken water pipe. Her ebony body heaved with hysterical sobs. She wept for Dot, but for herself too. Sally May would never be the same. How could she be? The devil had just shown her his work up close and personal.

CHAPTER-26

Lynn Casnovsky? His partner cheating with his good friend's husband? It seemed crazy, made up.

To top it off, Lynn had a sadistic and domineering itch that Sophie was scratching? They had both walked a dangerous line and were lucky they hadn't been caught.

Once Sophie had confessed her lover's name, she'd hurried back to one of the padded benches, away from her friends, away from him. She'd plopped down and hung her head. Her contrite action could have been convicting shame or sheer relief. Manny thought a little of both. It had taken courage to go this far down the road to confession. He respected Sophie for that, but he wondered if some things could ever be fixed, really recovered from. He didn't have to dig too deep to find the answer.

There would be time to talk later. For now, the truth would have to do. He ran his fingers through his hair and realized that was the first step to figuring out this mess.

After the *Sunkist* dropped its passengers back in St. Thomas, Louise wanted to go shopping at the strip mall right at the pier where the *Ocean Duchess* was docked.

"Come, on. Every woman wants to shop in St. Thomas," she begged.

He never could say no to her.

"Tell you what, let's go eat, change into something other than these beach clothes and then I'll go shopping with you. Deal?"

"Good idea. I guess that's why you make the big bucks, huh?"

"Yeah, and don't forget it." He forgave her fist to his shoulder.

The others decided to head to the mall first; they would catch up with Manny and Louise at dinner.

Manny watched as Randy and Sophie strolled hand-in-hand toward the pier's shopping sharks. As the couple grew smaller in his sight, a helpless sigh escaped his mouth. His partner and her mate were an odd couple, no debating that, but he thought they could hold it together. He'd seen worse marriages survive more apocalyptic circumstances, and he hoped he would be right on this one.

Louise hurried him across the shaky gangplank, and they rushed into the elevator to the bistro-lined Lido Deck.

Cruise ships are notorious for the mountains of food served daily and, today, Manny and Louise claimed their share of the mother lode.

The Mexican buffet—complete with the familiar smell of warm cheese, spicy chicken and beef, and cilantro-laced salsa—was almost more than Manny could take. He chased it all down with the vanilla-and-chocolate-swirled ice cream cones. Manny devoured three as Louise looked on.

"You're going to the gym after we get back from shopping, right?" she teased.

"I think it would be better if you worked it off me when we get back to the cabin."

"You do, do you? That could be arranged, if you're a good boy," she said, running her hand slowly through the hair of his forearm.

"I'm always a good boy."

She laughed and they left, Manny leading the way to their stateroom.

He shut the cabin door and before Louise could walk out of arm's reach, he cradled her and brought her close, nuzzling the back of her neck, something that always got her attention.

"Not fair," she giggled. Louise turned and kissed him with surprising hunger.

"Wow. What they say about these cruises being an aphrodisiac could be true," he said.

Louise stepped away from him and in one motion, removed the top of her bathing suit. "Then what do *these* do for you?"

Manny swooped up his wife and headed for the bed. "Let me show you."

Their lips came together again with mutual tenderness. Manny kissed her eyes, her ears; gently he teased the soft underside of her throat. She ran her hands over his back and cradled his head as she kissed him. Fire swirled from her lips. The heat of their breathing increased, like a hot, Caribbean wind. They moved closer, and Manny felt her soft breasts press against his chest. She felt wonderful.

His hand ran along the curve of her hip, and he pulled her closer. Not in a heated lust, but with gentle, loving response to each other. Two people in love, making love.

Afterwards, she grabbed his face with her hands and moved slowly to his side. "I love you,

Manny Williams."

He kissed her face and pulled her close to him. "I love you too, baby."

Fifteen minutes later, Manny and Louise showered, then rambled for the shops of St. Thomas. As they worked their way through the forward hall of the ship, Manny noticed the Do Not Disturb sign still hanging on the Casnovsky's room. The sign refused to mask its taunting leer.

Louise glanced at the sign. "Liz never called you back, did she?"

"No, she didn't."

"Okay. Maybe this *is* a little weird. They could be seasick though. Didn't they say it happened to them on the last cruise they took?"

Without answering, he knocked on the door. They waited. He knocked again. No one answered. Manny raised his arm to hammer the door again when Louise stopped him.

"Whatever they're doing, let them do it. It's their trip, and if they want to spend it in the cabin, it's fine. Besides, there's a million other places they could be, yes?"

"Could be, but it doesn't feel right. Maybe something's wrong."

"Like what? What could be wrong? It's a cruise ship. How much safer could it be?"

She was right, but he couldn't shake the nagging feeling of doubt. Especially since Liz hadn't returned his calls.

His right hand glided through his hair—the old habit resurrected in times of stress—and he pressed his lips into a straight line.

Liz would have contacted someone if they had changed their minds about the excursion. It was how the woman operated.

"This is what we'll do; if this sign isn't gone by the time we get back, we'll have the room steward open the door. Okay?" Louise said.

He nodded. "All right. That works for me."

****

The couple continued down the hall toward the elevator, holding hands. The door four rooms down from the Casnovsky's opened to a narrow slit. The big man watched the detective and his wife turn the corner and entertained a toxic smile.

Think about it. What could go wrong on a cruise ship?

CHAPTER-27

Standing on the breezy balcony, after he had wrangled into the black tux, Manny watched the foamy wake of the big ship as it headed out to open water and the island of Dominica. (Pronounced Dom-a-neeka.)

The shopping in St. Thomas had been great for Louise, and Manny appreciated the alone time they had enjoyed. Added to that, Louise had found the perfect necklace. An emerald-studded pendant, shaped like a teardrop. It hung from a thin, white-gold chain. Manny had to admit it looked like it belonged around her neck.

He grinned when he thought of the shell-shocked clerk. By the time Louise had concluded her bargaining, the clerk had gone from "how I can help you" to "get this daughter of Satan away from me." But Louise had saved hundreds, and *that* was a good thing.

He left the balcony as she stepped from the bathroom. He nearly fell over.

She was wearing a strapless, jade gown with shimmering white rhinestones trailing across the front and down pleated sides. The new necklace completed the stunning look. "Well?"

He whistled in a low tone. "You're going to turn every head on the ship. Just don't forget who you're married to."

"I won't, babycakes. Now let's go." She grabbed her wrap and proceeded to the door.

When he stepped into the hall, Manny remembered that he was going to stop by Liz and Lynn's room, but in the rush to get ready, it had slipped his mind.

"This will only take a minute," he said.

A small, dark-complexioned room steward named Usman, from Indonesia, exited the room directly across the hall at the same time Manny reached the Casnovsky's cabin.

The insidious Do Not Disturb sign still hung from the door. Manny quickly explained the problem, and Usman verified that he hadn't been in the room since the night before because he had to honor the sign. The steward said he couldn't open the door without his supervisor and left to find her. He came back less than a minute later with Raduca, his Romanian boss, a large woman with bright-blue eyes, who had good English skills and a pleasant personality.

"You think they are sleeping?" she asked.

"I don't know. We haven't seen them since yesterday afternoon. I just want to make sure they're all right."

By then, Louise had made the trek down the hall and was standing beside Manny.

After knocking a few more times, Raduca nodded and pulled out the master key from her pocket. She turned the knob slowly and motioned for Manny to go in. He pushed it open and stepped inside with Louise at his heels.

Their room was fairly bright because the terrace curtain was wide open, bathing the cabin with gentle, setting-sun light. To his immediate left, the bathroom door was open and the light over the medicine cabinet gave off a portentous glow.

Manny's heart rate quickened while he did a quick scan of the main cabin and balcony. He stopped cold at the bed.

The blue-and-pink comforter lay undisturbed. Some of their suitcases were stacked near the foot of the bed, but it looked as if no one had slept or even sat on it.

Another fast glance around the room, and his stomach dropped to his toes. The room was empty.

CHAPTER-28

"I don't get this. Where are they?" puzzled Louise. Manny heard the thick tension in her voice. He didn't have an answer for her, but agreed: this didn't add up.

He moved farther into the cabin and walked over to the balcony. The only things on the sunlit veranda were white deck chairs and a matching table that teased him with knowledge Manny didn't have.

Once outside, his heightened senses took in the ocean's heady fragrance accompanied by the reek of cigar smoke swaggering from the next balcony. The smooth sound of Mindy Abair's tenor sax echoed through the ship's speakers. Still no Liz or Lynn.

Bending over the railing, he inspected the row of orange, tarp-covered lifeboats playing follow-the-leader some fifteen feet below. Beneath them swam nothing but blue ocean.

Sometimes, simply because of the surrounding circumstances, he'd get an idea or some vibe about what had transpired at a particular scene. This time, however, nothing came to him except more conviction that Liz and Lynn were in trouble.

Finally he came back into the cabin and dropped to his knee, searching under the bed. Red

Gucci suitcases stared back at him. He pulled open the two closet doors: nothing but expensive shirts, dresses, and shorts hanging undisturbed.

Both of the couple's Sun and Fun cards rested on the beige vanity, along with Lynn's leather wallet and both of their smartphones. He chewed the inside of his cheek. The presence of the two cells could be the biggest tell-tale sign of trouble because Manny had never seen Liz or Lynn without them. Their phones were, more often than not, stuck to the sides of their heads.

Raduca stepped into the cabin looking at Manny with a strange curiosity. "What were you looking for?"

"I'm sorry. I'm a cop and I acted like one. Habit. I just wanted to make sure everything was all right with our friends." He showed her his badge.

Raduca nodded slowly. "Maybe they are on their way to dinner, no?"

The Sun and Fun cards and the phones winking at him from the vanity top said otherwise, but he didn't want to worry either of the women.

"I'm sure you're right. I'm sorry for any inconvenience."

He turned for one more look, took Louise's hand, and exited the room, moving in the direction of the elevators.

"Just like that? You're going to leave that room, just like that? Are you not feeling okay? There is something wrong there. Even I figured that out."

"Now who's being paranoid?" he asked. "But you might be right. We need to go to dinner and see if Liz and Lynn are there. Maybe Raduca is spot on. Maybe everyone's already at the table, drinking wine and waiting for us."

"But you don't really think—"

"Honey, I don't know. It doesn't feel right, but we've both been wrong before. Let's just go to dinner and find out."

She gave him a solemn stare. "Okay. But what if they're not at dinner? Then what?"

"We go to the Purser's Desk and have them paged. If that doesn't work, we find the head of security and ask for help to search the ship. They have to be here somewhere." Manny shrugged and adjusted his bow tie. "Maybe they don't want to be found, you know? This could be a time for them to talk life over, to sort some things out."

Louise helped him with the tie. "Okay. You're right. That paranoia thing's what I get for being married to a cop."

The elevator arrived, and Manny and Louise traveled in silence.

Wishing to alleviate her concerns and, to some degree, his own, he wrapped his arm around her waist.

"You look amazing. Did I tell you that?"

"Yeah, but you can say it again."

"You look amazing."

"You're such a charming man."

He winked. "You ain't seen nothing, yet."

"Oh my. What do you have in mind?"

"Stuff."

She laughed, and Manny enjoyed every bit of it.

The Paupers restaurant was beautifully designed and gave the feel and aroma of the most elite Detroit eatery. A hostess greeted them and led Louise and Manny to their assigned table, where they were greeted by Gavin and Stella, Alex and Barb, and Sophie and Randy.

Manny's heart sank deeper. The troublesome sense of trepidation became a full-blown siren. Liz and Lynn were nowhere to be seen.

A table host pulled Louise's chair out for her. After Manny had taken his own seat, he related to the others how they had just left the Casnovsky's cabin and there was no trace of their friends.

"Nothing?" asked Alex.

"Nothing," responded Manny. He stared at his plate and ran his hand through his hair. "We haven't seen them in twenty-eight hours, and I don't like it. We need to find them."

The group nodded in unison. He laid out his plan to have the Casnovskys paged and search the ship, if necessary. The others agreed.

"I just don't get it. How do you vanish on a cruise ship?" said Sophie. "Of course, unless you wanted to."

No one responded, but increasing uneasiness hung over the table, like a sinister, black cloud.

"Let's go have them paged. I don't like this either," urged Gavin.

They left the table together, the Purser's Desk their only goal.

The feeling of desperation, like searching for a lost child in a giant department store, stuck to Manny's ribs. He suspected everyone felt the same; you'd have to be dead not to.

They hurried toward the elevators and to the third deck, to the Purser's Desk. Manny realized that they could be in for a godforsaken journey that would only end in some horrible way. But they had run out of options.

He wanted to be wrong, but wanting and getting are two different things.

CHAPTER-29

"Would Mr. and Mrs. Lynn and Elizabeth Casnovsky please report to the Purser's Desk, deck three, immediately," echoed the powerful PA system for the third time in ten minutes. The Purser, Richard Smith from Liverpool, England, didn't require a twist of his thin arm to make the announcements, especially after Manny relayed the circumstances surrounding the last day and a half.

After he had spoken to the Purser, the rest of the Lansing party left the third floor and hustled back to their rooms to change. Everyone was to meet back with Manny to see if Liz and Lynn had responded to the page. If not, they were to start a deck-by-deck search with four members of the security staff assisting them. Manny was elected to stay at the desk and be there when, and if, Liz and Lynn responded to the PA's request.

Craig Richardson, the ship's security chief, stood by the desk, hands on his hips. The retired detective from New York City stood well over six feet, with white, close-cropped hair on his oval head. His beady, dark eyes peered from the permanent frown of his ruddy features.

A flowering look of skepticism had blossomed on Richardson's face when Manny first approached him about the missing couple. His guise didn't change an iota, even after he listened to Manny's account of the day ending with the empty cabin and the no-show for dinner. Richardson's doubtful expression progressed to impatience and did little to inspire confidence in the ship's top cop. Manny tried to hide his immediate dislike for Richardson, but it was like trying to stop the sun from rising.

The head of security didn't display any sense of urgency and harbored an irritating attitude of *don't-screw-up-my-dinner-time-with-something-so-trivial.* Manny didn't do well with nonchalant; it only pissed him off. Plus Richardson's quick assessment of the situation was wrong. That pissed him off too.

"You're a cop, Mr. Williams. You know how this stuff works. Sometimes people don't want to be found, and it happens far more on cruise ships than you would think."

Sophie, standing to Manny's left, scrunched up her nose. "You don't believe what just came out of your mouth, do you?"

"No reason to get excited."

"No reason, huh? No wonder New York is so screwed up. Do you take drugs? No, I know, you're drunk." She stepped closer. "Manny, I'm going to kick his ass, hold my purse."

"Easy. I'll handle this. Go hold Randy's hand."

She pointed at Richardson. "Your lucky day, punk."

Richardson grunted and smiled. But his eyes grew colder. Richardson didn't seem to do well with confrontation, especially with a small, Asian woman cop. Could it be he didn't play well with others?

It was time for a "talk." Manny drew close to Richardson, eyes on fire.

"Listen to me, asshole." His voice smooth as silk. "I know my friends. I know missing person situations, and I know the difference between trouble and habits. You help us with this search, or I'll have every senior officer on board up your ass with a microscope. Got it?" His teeth clenched together on "got it."

Richardson took a small step back and stared at the shorter detective, but squinting eyes and frowning face never changed expression. Manny thought Chief Richardson was doing a marvelous job of controlling his temper. He was also pretty confident that hitting a guest was a surefire way of getting a one-way ticket home.

Finally, the taller ex-detective answered Manny with a thin smile. "I'm sure your friends are fine, but this is what we'll do. Let's break up into four groups. Groups one and two search the even numbered decks, one group on each side of the ship. Groups three and four do the same for the odd numbered decks. Okay?"

"Thank you."

Richardson's reaction didn't reflect "you're welcome," more like "eat shit and die." At least he had displayed some emotion, and Manny didn't think that could hurt.

It took a minute to form the groups so that someone in each search party would recognize the Casnovskys on sight. Manny felt better; doing something was always better.

As Richardson led his group past Manny, he stopped and bent to his ear. "Don't ever threaten me again," he rasped.

The security chief disappeared inside the

elevator, and Manny smiled. There was more than one way to skin a cat.

He quietly panned the formally dressed crowd of cruisers moving past the long, mahogany reception desk. Who knows? Maybe he would see Liz and Lynn before they saw him. That would be a sight for sore eyes.

Ten minutes passed, and he caught himself staring at the wall, pondering Sophie's surprising confession and, in the next overloaded thought, wondering how he would react when he saw Lynn. He told himself that wasn't important, yet. First things first.

Waiting wasn't one of his strong suits, and if he were a smoker, he would have chained half a pack.

Whew. Slow down, boy. You're going to pop a blood vessel.

He continued scanning the people, hoping for a glimpse of Liz or Lynn that would send his angst packing.

Down the hall to the left were several picture-taking stations, and the lines were long. Vanity or remnants of the trip of a lifetime? It didn't really matter. The ship's guests were having a great time. Even under these circumstances, the thought of Liz brought a smile to his face, a painful one, but a smile just the same. She lived for this kind of thing. She was attractive and very photogenic, and he knew part of her wanted the world to see how lucky Lynn was to have her. She especially wanted Lynn to feel that way.

The sterling silver clock hanging above the counter read 8:32 and still no sign of the Casnovskys, in spite of several more pages. The search parties agreed to convene at 9 p.m.in front of the casino, located on deck five near the middle of the ship. The seconds continued to tick away and each stroke of the red second hand seemed like an hour. With each passing moment, his faith sank lower, if that were possible.

Fifteen minutes later, it became clear that Liz and Lynn weren't coming to the Purser's Desk. Fearfully clear. It was time to check in with the others.

Each step toward the casino brought more dread than hope, and he had a harder time controlling his imagination.

What the hell had happened? Did they fall off the balcony? Foul play? Who? Why? Lynn's wallet still sat on the vanity bench with hundreds of dollars folded inside, so it couldn't have been robbery. How would someone get into their cabin?

All thoughts of turning off the Guardian of the Universe's work mode were now gone like bad bets at a blackjack table. There were times when this *once-a-cop-always-a-cop* persona could be a real pain. But this wasn't one of those times.

The sudden scream that punctured the busy deck brought him to a swift halt. For the second time on this trip, he reached for the gun that wasn't there. Old habits. The first scream had not stopped reverberating when a second hysterical wail began: an awful two-part harmony.

Manny did a one-eighty just in time to see three young ladies, dressed in full formal attire, sprinting on the black, marble floor directly toward him. Their heels clacked in wild rhythm to their flailing arms.

"Oh my God! Oh my God!" sobbed the middle girl. "Help! Help! Oh my God!"

When he met the trio, the young woman on his

left grabbed his arm. Long, trembling fingers with painted-red nails dug into his skin.

"Calm down. Calm down." But there was no calming the panicked women.

"What's wrong? What did you see?" Manny tried to get the girls to answer, even though he knew this wasn't going to be good.

All three began talking at once. Finally, the young lady with the vice-like grip on his arm spoke through streaming tears, this time clear enough for him to understand.

"There's a wom—woman's arm hanging out from one of the boats. It has blood on it. I think she's dead." The young lady pointed at the starboard side of the ship, toward the lifeboats.

Manny's heart turned cold as he took off. He prayed that the girls were wrong. It could be some sort of silly prank, but deep down, he knew it wasn't.

Once to the lifeboat, breathing hard and lungs begging for more air, he wiped away the sweat running down his temples and pushed through the small crowd gathered on deck five near lifeboat sixteen. The now-multiplying circle of rubberneckers caused him to become instantly angry. People were willing to get a glimpse of anything and then wish they hadn't.

The boat's orange tarp had been pulled away just enough to display the slender, tanned arm hanging limply. There were several runnels of dried blood tracking down to her wrist. Manny could see the outline of the rest of the body, clearly visible under the sweating canvas and knew, right away, that this was more than a murder.

The killer had staged this. He wanted everyone

to see his version of a three-ring circus.

A stout, black-haired woman standing just behind Manny, dressed in a glittering, purple, formal gown, ejected her recent dinner, splattering on the deck with conviction. The stench filtered over the crowd and triggered several other guests to follow suit. Vomit plastered all over the deck was not in the cruise line's brochure.

Just then, Richardson chugged up beside him. He was out of breath and clutching his chest. His wheezing gasps caught in his jowled throat when he saw the arm.

Manny took a step closer, and the weight of the world dropped on his shoulders.

Any remaining hope that Manny held of finding Liz alive had vanished. He recognized the large diamond ring and polished gold wedding band attached to her unmoving ring finger.

It had belonged to Liz's mother, who had been married with the ring and had wanted her only daughter to have the same experience.

Liz Casnovsky's cruise was officially over.

CHAPTER-30

The dismal silence thrumming through the sterile, impersonal waiting room of the ship's infirmary, where Manny and Alex sat, did little to alter Manny's mood. The aroma of rubbing alcohol jitterbugged through the air, reminding him of every doctor's office he had ever been in.

Manny scanned the textured floor, knowing they were both walking through various stages of denial, trying to deal with the murder of their friend.

The others had decided to wait in Gavin and Stella's suite until Manny and Alex returned. None of the rest really wanted this duty call anyway. Not tonight, not this one, not Liz.

Mixed emotions strolled into Manny's mind like they owned the place, and in a sad way, they did. He had sworn this wouldn't happen on his watch, like the murder of his partner those years ago, yet it had. He knew he hadn't been on duty, but pensive, nefarious guilt said that he was partly to blame.

"Stop it," interrupted Alex. "This isn't your fault, and it's not about you, got it?"

Denying where his thoughts were running, especially to Alex, was like suggesting water wasn't wet. He looked back to his good friend. "I know. I'm working through it."

Alex sighed. "Yeah, me too."

The joy rising from a Caribbean cruise should go hand-in-hand with simply boarding the ship. Cruise was synonymous with a great time. But not this one. Instead, it had become a harbinger of dread and sadness, and for good measure, guilt.

How did this happen? It was a wedding celebration and a Caribbean cruise. It doesn't get much more harmless than that.

The ship's security staff had taken over the murder scene and cleared the deck so they could process the area and move Liz's body to the infirmary. Richardson made it quite clear that cops from Lansing would be treated no differently from the rest of the guests, and he would call them when he needed them to identify the body. Manny started to argue, but thought better of it. Richardson was an ass, but even more so, a fool if he thought Manny wasn't going to be a part of this investigation—with or without the security chief's pointless approval. No one was going to put him, or the rest of the Lansing contingent, on the sidelines.

He studied his hands, but didn't really see them. He'd never been in this situation before. Far from home, no jurisdictional rights, and in unfamiliar surroundings: the trifecta.

Nothing about any murder case on a cruise ship could be considered routine, especially given the emotional investment they all had with Liz. There were too many people with too many opportunities to contaminate evidence, and a clever killer would find it relatively easy to hide in a population of 5,300 people. Particularly when the ship's senior staff wanted to keep a lid on things. It wasn't a sound business practice to have dead bodies hanging out of lifeboats.

Nothing like shoveling shit against the tide.

He funneled a glance toward Alex. He was glad he had brought the chubby CSI to the morgue. Maybe Alex could see something that the ship's staff wouldn't or hadn't. He had a feeling that crime-scene processing was rare on a cruise ship, and the people doing it weren't that talented. At least not like Alex. To top things off, there had been no sign of Lynn anywhere. Where in hell was he?

Over ninety percent of spousal deaths and assaults were committed or conspired by the other spouse, so that made Lynn a natural place to start the questioning, but they had to find him first.

Manny's thoughts churned over what Sophie had told him earlier—that Lynn was involved in an affair. How he took pleasure in getting his rocks off imitating the Count De Sade. Manny wanted to find Lynn first.

If Lynn did this, then where is he now? Maybe he jumped ship after he killed Liz. But he has no money or ID. Is this an elaborate scheme to get rid of Liz and start over?

What if it isn't Lynn? Is he in a lifeboat too? How did Liz get into the boat without detection?

The questions bombarded him like some frantic finale from *Lord of the Dance*.

Dr. Simon Kristoff—from Kazakhstan, according to his worn name tag— entered the tiny waiting room, and Manny and Alex rose and shook his hand. The doctor's round face was ashen and drawn. His already thin lips were mere lines grooved across his face. The doctor's eyes were glazed over like he had seen the impossible or something close to it.

"Are you all right?" asked Manny.

Kristoff stuck his hands in his pockets.

"No, I think not. In all of my years of training and studying medicine, I have never seen anything like this." The doctor had a thick, Russian accent. "It is beyond vicious."

"What did you see?" quizzed Alex. "It can't be that bad."

Manny thought maybe it could.

Dr. Kristoff stared at the men and, without another word, motioned for them to follow as he turned back toward the examination rooms.

They walked through whitewashed rooms with black, padded patient tables tilted on forty-five-degree angles. Several instrument cabinets housing medical paraphernalia eyed them as they moved past.

The doctor led them through another door on the other end of the hospital, and Manny was surprised at the sign above the entrance. MORGUE.

He looked at Alex. "Morgue? On a cruise ship?"

Alex nodded. "It makes sense. I read somewhere that as many as a hundred people a year pass away while cruising. Usually older folks with health problems."

"Not something they put in the commercials," said Manny.

Alex smiled a tired smile. "Not good for their image."

As they walked through the last door, Manny noticed four brushed-steel, rectangular doors about the size of a dormitory refrigerator on the right, kitty corner from the entrance. He looked closer and saw a name on one: Rose Charles. He wondered what had happened to poor Rose.

To the left were two stainless steel tables situated about eight feet apart. Each one had a large umbrella light hovering above it. The lamp on the second table spotlighted a sheet-covered body.

The doctor strode to the second table and grabbed the white, bloodstained sheet, then hesitated. "Are you ready for this?" Without waiting for an answer, he rolled the sheet down to the victim's waist.

Hot, stinging silence raced up and down Manny's body as the two friends took in the sight of Liz Casnovsky's body. Manny swallowed hard. He heard Alex catch his breath.

Angry tears of frustration and sorrow burned a path down Manny's cheeks. He just wanted to leave his body and come back when things were normal, when God had restored sanity to the unholy portrait in front of him. Maybe then.

Liz's neck and chest were ransacked. Shreds of skin and muscle were tangled everywhere. Bite marks riddled both sides of her once pretty face. There was a small section of orbital bone bulging under her left eye. She barely resembled the hard-charging attorney that he'd grown to love.

Some things never leave you. A good song. Your first kiss. A religious experience. The first time you make love. The birth of your first child. Your first car. But nothing could attach itself to a man like a violent crime scene. Its memory, forever blistered into one's psyche, could eviscerate wonderful recollections and render one sleepless for nights without end.

It seemed impossible that he would ever see anything like this again. Even the textbooks said so. But the textbooks were wrong. All that was pure screamed that such a depraved scene couldn't exist again. Not in a million years, not on a cruise ship, and especially not to his friend. But here it was.

Kristoff reached over to a small, steel table and picked up an object. It was wrapped in a plastic evidence bag, but still easy to recognize. Resting in the bag was a black rose with bloodstains running down the length of its foot-long stem.

"We found it underneath the body."

Manny heard Alex mumble something under his breath. Then, as if he realized he hadn't spoken clearly, he said it again. "Sylvia Martin's killer."

CHAPTER-31

Liz's killer stood on his private balcony, basking in the sultry, late-night air, draped in his arrogance. The full Caribbean moon's cloying light adorned his huge body. He hardly looked human.

The train was in motion and picking up steam. His plan had begun to unwind just as he hoped it would. Even better. The ship's security staff consisted of inbred misfits, especially their fearless leader, Craig Richardson, and wouldn't be any challenge.

A sneer enveloped the killer's smooth-shaven face as he thought about the New York cop. The incompetent dick never had expected to be in the middle of a grandiose crime scene like this one. He was probably in his room right now playing kissy face with a bottle of rum hoping this would all be gone in the morning.

He laughed. *I'm not going anywhere.*

The FBI would be brought in, and Williams could be a problem, but that only made the plan more of a challenge, better. For him, at least.

Feds or otherwise, none of them would ever suspect what was coming next.

His concentration slithered back to his years at the godforsaken prison. It was where he'd developed, where he'd figured out life—and death.

No one should have to be exposed to what he had seen and heard. But for him, there had been a spiritual teacher, a reciprocal lover, and an opportunity to be reborn, instead of the hopeless resignation that usually accompanied prison life. He had risen from the ashes, like the mythical Phoenix. That shithole had been the equivalent of elemental soup, where some scientists said life developed. Order from chaos.

There were so many truths learned by immersing one's self in full-bore survival mode. He had fooled them all, and had more than survived. He had become.

He'd mimicked all the right responses and avoided the wrong, playing their game and winning.

Not one single degrading thing he had been subjected to would control him again. He had made that promise to himself and intended to keep it.

Turning from the past, the killer's thoughts skipped to his next "assignment." This one would be better. Not that making sure the Casnovskys were taken care of hadn't been a real pleasure. But this one would be . . . mindboggling.

The more he thought about the next day, the more his body stirred. His thighs began to twitch, and he had become aroused to a steel-hard state. Blood vibrated through his veins. He could not contain himself any longer. Visions of her spun in his mind.

It will be so good.

He closed his eyes and concentrated on *the plan.* He had to stay clear, unattached, unemotional, setting aside any desire he might possess—because the only thing that mattered was completion of the goal.

He slowed his breathing until it became shallow and controlled. His muscles, his entire system, bridled down enough so that he could get dressed for dinner. A meal with all the trimmings was just what the doctor ordered.

As he left the room, his contemplation was about the island of Dominica and her trimmings. How he'd collect them. Make them his own.

What a stop it would be. Not just for him, no, but also for the sweet object of his affections, his new woman, particularly for her.

CHAPTER-32

"You can't be serious. I don't need any help with this investigation," fumed Richardson. "Carousel hired me to handle these things, especially situations like this. These people are from Podunk, Michigan, for God's sake. How in blazes do you think *they* can help *me*?"

Captain Serafini's black eyes simmered as he addressed the ship's security chief. They snapped across the great expanse of his desk as the captain struggled to stay his infamous temper.

The large, leather chair shifted under his weight. He had never really cared for Richardson. He found it difficult to respect a man who wouldn't look him in the eye. His father had always told him it was a way to judge a man's character. Papa was right.

He knew Richardson's drinking was worse than the chief let on, much worse. If he pushed the issue, he supposed he could have him removed, but the position wasn't high profile. Until now, that is.

There were the usual drunken guest scenarios, an occasional assault, even accusations that guests were cheating in the casino—all needing to be discreetly investigated. But that was the problem with Richardson, wasn't it? Discretion was not his typical *modus operandi*. The man probably couldn't even spell the term. He'd upset more than one innocent guest with false accusations. Throw in a drinking problem, and there could be real trouble.

The captain shifted to the opposite side of the chair and drank a mouthful of his gourmet coffee. There had never been anything like this on any of his ships: a murdered woman for the whole ship to see and a missing husband who had vanished in the tropical breeze. Damn it. Guests on a cruise ship weren't supposed to see ungodly things like that. It was bad for business and bad for *him*.

He needed Richardson functioning at full capacity, whatever that may be for him.

"Mr. Richardson. How much are you drinking these days?"

The chief's eyes darted to his sandals and then spiked contempt toward the captain.

"I don't see what that has to do with anything."

"You don't? Well, I do. Let me spell it out for you. If you're drunk or even under the influence a tiny bit, you could miss something important." Serafini leaned over his desk. "Now, please answer the damned question."

"I had three beers Sunday night and nothing last night," he said.

The captain knew better. "No more. Not another drop until this is over. Do you understand me?"

Richardson bit his lip, holding back words that would most certainly cost him his job, and then seemed to have a change of heart. "I won't. Does that make you feel better?"

"Do I look like I feel better?" He hoped Richardson was telling the truth, but he knew he had to play the hand he was dealt, even if it was most assuredly going to cost him. Maybe dearly. He had, at least, made his point.

"I talked to Dr. Kristoff last night," Serafini said, "and he told me what the Lansing officers said about the woman's injuries, what they had seen before—which you, by the way, never bothered to share with me."

"Captain, I think they're blowing smoke up my ass with a peace pipe. I don't think they have ever seen anything like that before. My professional opinion is that when we find the husband, we find the killer. There is no psycho lunatic running around on this ship ripping out women's throats. Especially a killer that followed them down here." A defiant tone rose in his voice. "I know what the hell I'm talking about."

Without speaking, the captain yanked open the top, right-hand drawer of his immaculate desk and pulled out two documents, sliding them across the polished finish.

"I received the first one from the San Juan PD yesterday morning. I got the second one about an hour ago. It's from the authorities in the Virgin Islands. Read them, and then tell me you still know 'what the hell you're talking about.'"

The chief picked up the papers and gave the captain an uneasy glance. He read both faxes. His eyes widened, quickly looking back to the captain. "Is this shit for real?"

"Oh, I assure you, my fine chief, it's for real. That's three murders in less than forty-eight hours, and it would appear that the sick maniac is on this ship. My ship."

Serafini swiveled in his chair and looked out his window, intently focusing on the lush, green, island landscape.

The ship's crew had done its best, with fair success, to minimize the traumatic effect of last night's incident. The rumor mill, fueled by the crew at his orders, depicted an awful suicide by an unhappy woman. If word got out that this was the third incident in three days, it wouldn't take a genius to figure out the killer was cruising on the *Ocean Duchess*.

He desperately needed to keep a lid on this. It was hard to accept that Richardson was his best shot at doing that. His security officer may be as sloppy as the killer was clever. They needed real help.

He curved his chair back to face Richardson. "In an hour, Detective Perez from the San Juan Police, FBI Agent Josh Corner, his associate, and four members of the Lansing Police, to whom I have extended invitations, will meet with our staff to discuss this situation. If the people from Lansing think they have information that can help and are willing to assist us, we are going to accept that assistance. Is that clear?"

Richardson slapped the two documents on the desk. "Perfectly." He lifted his large frame as the chair squeaked in protest. "I hope you know what you're doing."

After the chief slammed the door, Serafini let out a long breath. "So do I. So do I."

CHAPTER-33

Gavin, Alex, Sophie, and Manny sat around the white deck table. The half-eaten breakfast and barely sipped coffee bore witness that Liz's death weighed heavy on their hearts.

The Tuesday morning sun spilled its rays over the deck, hypnotic in a cloudless sky. The smell of coconut mixed with banana came from the fruit bar to their left, while festive tin-drum music flowed from hidden speakers, striving to lift its listeners to no-worry mode. A perfect morning in paradise—*except it isn't*, Gavin thought. He had witnessed a thing or two during his tenure in law enforcement, ugly things. Too many times he'd knocked on the door of a slain officer's family. And each time he'd walked away from those families swearing *never again*. But nothing had prepared him for the death of a close colleague, particularly *that way*. He was glad he hadn't had to ID the body. That was an assignment ordered for younger men like Manny and Alex. They seemed to rebound better than him, especially these days.

Manny and Alex had spent the last forty-five minutes bringing him and Sophie up to speed with what they had seen in the morgue. Gavin didn't like what he heard.

"Could it be Peppercorn?" Sophie asked. "I

mean we put him away for ten years for those assaults, then his doctor said he was cured and no threat to society. In fact, the warden vouched for it. But then he disappeared right after he was released, what, fifteen months ago? Like the day after." Emotion seeped into her voice. "I know we want to talk to him about the Martin case, but we don't even know if he was near Lansing in May, and now we're supposed to make the leap that he could be here, on this ship? To what end?" She tasted her tea. "I'm just not buying it, I can't."

"I don't know, but I have to agree with Sophie on this one," Gavin said. "Why would he suddenly show up in the Caribbean? Furthermore, how? It's not like the guy was returning to a lifestyle of the rich and famous."

Manny put his hands on the table. "We saw what we saw. I know it seems crazy, but he is the only one we've seen do anything remotely close to this. Just because we couldn't locate him to talk about Sylvia Martin's murder doesn't mean he's farming peacefully in Montana. He could have been in Lansing." Manny lifted his fork from the table. "Listen. Peppercorn used the same *rose-as-a-gift* setup—except the roses were red—on his four victims. Whoever killed Silvia Martin left a black rose, and now one shows up next to Liz's body. What happened to . . . to Liz and the Martin woman is disturbingly similar. Does anyone think that's a coincidence?"

Manny picked at his eggs and then finished his thought. "Sophie just said it. He disappeared and hasn't been seen since his release, the consummate white rabbit. Of course, having said what I just said, it doesn't figure that a man with his limited intellect could get this done."

"He couldn't, unless . . . well . . . unless there is something more to that whole Dissociative Identity Disorder thing than we gave credence. I mean, Peppercorn's stepdad was no saint, and what he did to him and his sister could cause serious psychological damage," said Gavin.

Sophie sat a little straighter in her chair. "Okay, say Peppercorn really did develop a dual personality, and somehow it, him, her . . . hell, I don't know . . . took over. It sounds crazy, but it wouldn't be the first time for this kind of thing."

"Peppercorn had claimed he didn't remember attacking those girls and that we had the wrong guy. I did some research and even talked with Sylvia Martin's husband about it once. Doctor Martin said it could happen to almost anyone, but the trauma would have to be so intense that facing it would be like putting a gun in your mouth," Manny pointed out.

Gavin stroked his mustache as the others grew silent. No one wanted to think about a mind that had been altered that much.

Finally, Alex stopped making love to his mocha latte and broke the silence.

"I need to get a closer look at the body. The neck injuries were consistent with what we saw on Peppercorn's victims. If it wasn't him, it was an adept copycat. After the Martin murder, I researched case history files in all of the law enforcement databases, including VICAP, NCIS, even Interpol—things we didn't have years ago. I cross-referenced murderers, rapists, kidnappers, and every other conceivable pervert, trying to get a match with his particular MO and psychological profile, but I didn't really see anything on the level with what that sad prick Peppercorn did. Tearing victims up with his teeth, I mean." Alex pushed his cup away. "This could be him."

"Peppercorn never killed before, though. He raped and disfigured those young ladies, but always stopped short of killing them," observed Sophie.

"That's true. But we all know the profiles of these psychos. Their games almost always escalate to more aggressive behavior, and eventually killing is the only thing that gets them off," said Manny.

Gavin raised his hand in the universal stop motion. "We'll have plenty of time to discuss theories with the rest of the people at the nine o'clock."

He looked around the table and exhaled. "None of you have to do this. It's your vacation. I don't expect you to spend it working, particularly on a cruise ship in the Caribbean. You have family here, and you should be relaxing with them."

"Relax? What are you talking about? That would be a trick now, wouldn't it? One of our own is lying in the morgue. Her husband has disappeared, and there is some nut case who may have committed murder in Lansing and then decided to follow us down here for God knows what reason. Hell yeah, I'm all set to take it easy," boomed Manny.

Sophie hit Manny's arm. "Way to put a lighter slant on things, Williams."

Everyone laughed.

Gavin knew laughter could be pure medicine, but little by little, its effect faded as realization brought a grim quiet.

They were wrestling with his words, and who could blame them. Hell, so was he. But more importantly, Liz's death was against all his people stood for, particularly Manny. He knew their hearts before they did.

"I'm in. Barb wouldn't want it any other way," said Alex.

"Me too," agreed Sophie.

"That makes three," stated Manny.

"I've been out of the investigation frontlines for a while, but I'll do whatever I can to help," Gavin said, looking at each one of his crew.

An efficient busboy approached the table wearing a burgundy-and-gold paisley vest, flashed a courteous smile, and asked if they were finished with their breakfasts.

They were, except for the java.

"Now what?" asked Sophie.

"Well, I know I won't be able to look closer at the body until at least after the meeting this morning, maybe not even then because they may not let us help with the investigation. In fact, if it's Richardson's call, I know we won't be able to get involved," stated Alex. "The next best thing would be to process Liz and Lynn's room. But I'm sure that's just as far out of the question."

"Maybe not," said Manny.

Gavin shot his best detective a look. "What do you mean? I don't think you're going to be able to get the supervisor to open the room again, especially now."

Manny's blue eyes glinted like a kid at the toy store with birthday money burning a hole in his billfold.

Reaching into the pocket of his shorts, Manny tossed a rectangular object on the table. Gavin and the other two leaned over in unison to get a better look. Liz Casnovsky's Fun and Sun card stared up at them from the table.

"How did you pilfer that?" asked Sophie in amazement.

"I slipped it into my pocket when Louise and I were leaving the room. I thought it might come in handy."

"You'd make a great thief," marveled Sophie.

"Thief? More like tampering with evidence at a crime scene," snorted Gavin.

"What crime scene? We don't know if anything happened in there, right? Besides, Liz was our friend, and she deserves better. I'll be damned if I'm going to leave this up to that screw-up Richardson and his staff to handle."

Gavin's rubbed his chin, making little scratchy sounds with his stubble. He leaned toward his long-time friend, fixing Manny's gaze to his own. He felt his best detective recording his countenance like a video camera. He knew that even the crow's feet resting at the corner of his eyes were etched in Manny's brain. Manny remembered everything. Gavin also knew that look. The one that said: *I've just read your mind, Gavin, so there is no use in continuing the facade.*

The Lansing police chief felt every one of his fifty-six years this morning, and that might have weighed in on his decision, but one thing was sure—this investigation needed his people, particularly Manny.

"We'll share anything we find with the rest of the ship's task force," Manny said quietly, "or whatever it's called. But I just want to make sure they don't miss anything. Alex is better than anything they have, and Sophie and I aren't chopped liver either."

Gavin nodded. "Do it quietly, and do it right."

CHAPTER-34

The black, Samsonite backpack slung loosely over his back contained everything he would need for the trip. Excitement danced through his veins. Some days were better than others, and this was one of those. Nothing would disrupt what he had planned, except an act of God, and there was no God.

The big man wiped the leg of his shorts with a sinewy hand. Perspiration, inspired by the hot, humid air surrounding Dominica, had started to build on his palms, and he didn't like how it felt. He only wanted things in his hands that he put there, things he controlled.

Clearing his mind, he focused on his playmate for the day. He had waited months to turn the cog in this wheel, and he was going to enjoy every delicious moment. He could almost taste her.

Hiding behind dark glasses, he watched the gathering crowd of cruisers congregate on the pier in Roseau, the island's capitol. They lived in a fantasy world, one that Carousel sold, but reality would catch up with them today. They would receive a lesson from a class they never knew existed. Death 101.

"Excuse me. Is this the line for the rain forest and Emerald Pool tour?"

He looked down at the portly, young woman smiling like an imbecile. Her yellow-blond hair was pulled back into a short ponytail, and she was dressed in a tank top, white shorts, and pink ASICS cross trainers. A swatch of sunblock crossed her wide nose.

"Yes it is. You're right on time."

She hesitated, but he saw the appreciation in her eyes, and there was more. She wanted to say something else, to engage him, maybe even charm him, but the woman turned away and moved to another part of the pier. Good thing for her. It wouldn't bode well for her to remember him, his face.

The time was quickly approaching to board the red tour buses. He shifted focus to the group of indigenous tour guides, clad in pale-green uniform tops and baggy shorts, as they emerged from one of the idling vehicles.

His heart skipped a beat. There she was. Rebecca Tillerman, the woman who would help him to ascend another step from hell to glorious bliss, his magnificent heaven.

The sun shone on her light-brown skin, and small trails of her bleached dreadlocks escaped from underneath her khaki cap, scaling down her shoulders. Her full breasts rippled seductively as she laughed at one of her peer's comments. But he knew it was just for him. The little slut wanted him to notice her, and he did. He could be plenty attentive, as she would soon discover.

Did she sense today was her day? He thought maybe she did. He was sure that somewhere deep down she knew, that she felt her providence.

Rebecca boarded her thirty-passenger bus, and Jenkins followed.

"You're a tall one, mon," she mused.

He returned her smile with an enchanting display of his own, but said nothing. He would introduce himself later. Like the first time with the park ranger in St. John, only better.

Hello, said the spider to the fly.

The convoy of buses finally pulled away from the cement pier and the shadow of the *Ocean Duchess*, heading up the mountain road toward the thriving rain forest some 3,800 feet above sea level.

Jenkins endured the thirty-minute trip in silence while the bus wound up spiraling hillsides covered with dense vegetation and orange-flowered trees. They meandered past the island's famous Botanical Gardens, but he barely moved his head.

Rebecca spoke through the bus's PA system and related some of the history of the island, its Caribe Indian population, and the tribe's almost complete extinction. She addressed some political history and the making of rum and coconut candy. Her eyes lit up when she mentioned the candy. It was her favorite. But he already knew that, didn't he? He knew everything about her, everything.

The two green iguanas hanging from a mango tree caused passengers to *ooh* and *ahh*, but meant nothing to him. He endured even more angst when the bus stopped at one of the roadside souvenir stands.

Patience. It will all be worth the wait.

The buses finally arrived at the Dominican National Rain Forest Park, releasing eager tourists on the trail that led to the rainforest and the Emerald Pool.

He exited and pretended to look for something

in his bag, waiting for Rebecca to move along the hard dirt path leading to the park's building complex. She took off, and he followed, knowing she had no responsibilities for a couple hours and was going to do what she always did.

The tour guide stopped at the last sun-beaten cabin, glanced both directions, then marched through the door reserved for employees only.

Jenkins stepped closer. His body buzzed like a swarm of bees. Even the purifying fragrance of rain coming from the rainforest intensified and seemed to magnify his senses a thousand fold. He felt everything.

He pulled the cloth from the sealed zip-lock bag concealed in his backpack.

The bamboo rods of the door sounded like hollow drums as he knocked. After a few seconds, the thick door swung open, and he was greeted with the sweet, pungent odor of marijuana swirling lazily from the room.

"Yes?"

"Hello, Ms. Tillerman. Allow me to introduce myself. I'm Eli Jenkins, and you're going to be the best yet."

CHAPTER-35

"Are you all right with this?" asked Manny, placing a hand on Sophie's shoulder. His partner hadn't spoken a word since they had left Gavin on the Lido Deck.

She looked up at him, and then over to the CSI, her expression focused, determined. "Yeah, we need to do this. We have to find out what happened, to make sure."

Both Manny and Alex nodded. But Manny knew what she was really driving at. She had to be absolutely positive Lynn didn't kill his wife. No one wanted to think they were that far off the mark judging the character of another. Furthermore, how do you rip sexual intimacy with a cold-hearted killer from your soul?

They stepped from the glass-paned elevator at the sixth floor. "We've got an hour to get this done, so no dinking around," said Manny.

The three Lansing cops hurried down the carpeted hall and stopped at the Casnovsky's room. No yellow crime-scene ribbon adorned the door. No ship security personnel stood guard either. Manny knew it would attract too much attention, and Carousel wanted no part of that. But to leave the room unattended was just sloppy.

He slid the card in the door, and led Sophie

and Alex in. He closed the door and stopped, taking in everything at once.

What the hell?

The ship's CSU hadn't processed the room at all. Nothing had been touched. The bathroom light was still shining and the bed and luggage was as Manny and Louise had last seen it. Even Lynn's wallet and cell remained unmoved. Liz's phone blinked steadily in response to the messages Manny had left.

"You gotta be kidding me. Is this a joke?"

He was suddenly angry. Like when you found out your best friend had betrayed your most private of secrets. Fury rose up in his chest like a volcano ready to ignite. This was unacceptable. It wasn't fair to Liz, and for all he knew, Lynn—it wasn't fair to anyone.

"What do they think is going to happen? Are they hoping answers are just going to jump up and bite them in the ass?"

"Easy there, big fella," soothed Sophie. "We need that slick brain of yours in full gear. You can't afford to be pissed, at least not right now. We have to find out what happened here."

She was right. Anger was a dead-end road that caused mistakes, and God knew there had been enough of those already. Besides, he had to keep together for Sophie too. Lynn was still out there, and they had to find out where.

He took a deep breath and ran his fingers through his hair. Sophie and Alex were waiting for him, for instructions on what was next. He got it in motion.

"Okay, this is how this goes. Don't touch anything and don't step on anything. I don't want to mess with evidence. Use your eyes, and let's see what we can see. They know that I was in here, so my prints won't be an issue. But I don't want to explain how either of yours got here."

"Not a problem," said Alex. He pulled three pairs of latex gloves from his back pocket and handed Sophie and Manny each a pair. They looked at each other, then back to Alex.

"Don't ask," Alex said, pushing past Manny and ducking into the tiny lavatory. "I'll take the bathroom."

"Oh no, you don't get off that easy," answered Sophie. "Why do you have these, especially on a cruise, kinky boy?"

"I said don't ask."

"I heard you. Are you doing weird stuff to Barb? I want to know what. Come on, give it up."

"I'm not talking, and it's none of your business, got it?" Alex barked. He closed the door of the bathroom.

Relentless, Sophie pounded on the door. "Okay. Okay. But I'll find out. Women talk. I'll get it out of her."

Manny stood staring at the bathroom door, then back to Sophie.

"I don't know," she whispered. "But I think he and latex are in love, in the biblical way."

"More things I don't need to know," said Manny.

She grinned, shrugged her shoulders, and began moving her way through the eight drawers of the vanity.

Manny started at the bed. Bending close to the comforter, he went over every inch, making mental notes of what he saw—or of what he thought he saw. Everything was important.

The threesome searched the stateroom for

fifteen minutes without any significant revelations. Except for a small spot of blood Alex found on the bathroom wall.

"There is no way to tell who's without DNA testing. It could have been from a cut while Lynn was shaving, or it could have even been from another cruise. Damn, it could have come from the killer," he moaned to Manny.

"Okay. Keep looking, and we'll check it out when the room gets processed."

Sophie had finished searching the drawers and closets, and she was now down on her knees getting an up-close-and-personal look at the floor in front of the closet.

"Do you need any help?" asked Manny.

"Nope."

"Okay. I'm going out to the balcony." He stepped out to the verandah, careful where he moved, hoping for something to jump up and bite him in the ass. It took a couple of minutes.

After seeing nothing obvious on the table and chairs, he leaned over the railing for another look at the lifeboat below the Casnovsky's cabin, taking in every inch of the orange covering. On the far border of the lifeboat's tarp, near the center's edge, a three-corner tear flapped ever so slightly in the breeze. Just enough to catch his attention before the sunlight hid it again. The tear didn't fit with the character of the immaculately maintained ship. It could be something, or nothing, but he'd have Alex check it out as soon as the meeting was over.

When he turned to leave the deck, something else caught his eyes, waving at the corner of his vision. Manny knelt down, twisting closer to a section of the narrow, white gutter running underneath the railing.

"Sophie, Alex. You better take a look at this."

Sophie arrived first, and then Alex squeezed onto the small terrace. He looked like dough popping out a cylinder of store-bought biscuits.

"What is it?" asked Sophie.

Manny pointed to the small area of the drain.

"I'll be slapped shitless," muttered Alex.

Resting against the side of the drain was a small green, oval shaped leaf. A dark-red semicircle dotted the left half of the leaf. The stain winked at them through the midmorning light.

"What kind of leaf is that?" asked Sophie.

"The killer's favorite kind. It belongs to a rose," whispered Manny.

CHAPTER-36

Manny was already seated at the large, round table in the captain's extravagant conference room when Sophie sat to his left and Gavin and Alex plopped down on his right.

There was little doubt that this meeting arena was designed for comfort and not necessarily for optimum function. The cherry-trimmed chairs were leather and thick-cushioned. The smell said they were new.

"Spare no expense" came to mind.

Leaving the Casnovsky's room the way he had found it, his impatience grew and questions multiplied. He was eager to get on with this meeting, to find Lynn, then to begin the real search for Liz's killer. Who knew, maybe one search ended the other.

Manny tapped his foot on the thick carpet. The captain had called the damned meeting, and he was late. Where was the man? They were wasting time, and that gnawed at his gut. Liz deserved better.

But there were other emotions too. Not the least was his irritation toward Richardson. The idiot had let the possible murder scene sit too long. Way too long. Late was the worst kind of police work, and everyone knew it. Clues could be lost and information distorted because the "Sentinel of Security" on the *Ocean Duchess* feared upsetting other guests.

Richardson sat opposite Manny, talking and joking with three of his security staff who seemed as clueless and oblivious as their poor excuse for a leader.

Why hadn't they processed the room? They can't be that incompetent. What do they think this is? Some training exercise for first-year cadets?

The answer was obvious as white on rice: The head of security still wasn't taking this seriously. Even after Liz's body had been discovered, Richardson thought her death was some kind of domestic.

Manny burned.

What about canvassing the area to see if any of the guests had noticed Liz or Lynn or maybe someone hanging around outside their door? Had he talked to staff to see if they heard or saw anything suspicious around the lifeboat? Richardson had to know the longer the wait, the less effective an eyewitness interview became.

It was probably this strain of slacker attention to detail that had caused Richardson to leave the big city force and accept a cushy assignment on this boat.

Manny's hand traveled through his hair, never taking his eyes from the security chief.

"Take a deep breath, cowboy. You're going to blaze a hole in that jerk's face if you don't knock it off," whispered Sophie.

It was too late. Richardson had finally honed in on Manny's pissy stare. How perceptive.

"Can I help you with something, Detective Williams?" Richardson smirked.

"I don't think there is anything you can do to help me. And I'm pretty sure there's nothing you can do to help solve the murder of Liz Casnovsky either."

A slow, creeping red began its tour up Richardson's neck.

"What's your problem, detective? You're a guest on this ship, not in charge of this investigation. First off, you have no jurisdiction. Secondly, this isn't Hicksville, Michigan. This is a real investigation. This isn't putt-putt golf. We're teeing off at Pebble Beach."

"Yeah well, doesn't it take balls to tee it up? So far, I haven't seen any in your sorry excuse for police work."

Richardson's eyes flashed. He stood up, and his chair shot back, hit the wall, and rattled to the floor. "You don't know what the hell you're talking about."

The security chief started around the table, his staff reaching to restrain the large man. Manny jumped up, scrambling over the pristine table to cut him off. He felt Sophie and Gavin grab him, but he was stronger than the two of them, especially now. He didn't slow down until Alex joined the melee, grabbing him around the waist. It looked like a scene from a redneck bar or an out-of-control brawl at a European soccer match.

"Why haven't you processed their room? What are you waiting for? The next damned cruise?" Manny yelled. "Explain that to me."

"I don't have to explain shit to you."

Just then, the door from the captain's office swung open, and Serafini led three others into the room.

Manny caught the surprise that registered on

all four faces. He guessed the last thing they had expected was a rumble scene from *West Side Story*.

"Richardson, stand down, now!" ordered the captain. "Detective Williams, that's enough. Return to your chair."

Despite the captain's orders, neither man moved. Tension hung in the air as Manny waited for Richardson's next move. Finally, the security chief shrugged off his staff, righted his chair, and sat down. Manny reluctantly followed suit, but only after he tossed a last *kiss-my-ass* look in the chief's direction.

"That's better," Captain Serafini said. "We have a serious problem here, very serious. We need to work together. That will happen, or I'll toss each and every one of you off my ship."

His dark eyes demanded full attention, as he glared around the table. He got it.

"Is there anything I haven't made perfectly clear?"

In Manny's view, no one in the room wanted to test the captain's peremptory question.

"Good."

After a few moments of tension-riddled silence, the three newcomers—two men and a woman—sat down with the captain.

First impressions were important, so Manny gathered his.

The medium-height Latino woman wore a large, golden crucifix in the hollow of her throat. Her hazel eyes reflected bright, searching intelligence that indicated she wasn't easily fooled. Probably a bit paranoid. Not a bad thing for a cop.

Her angular face was blemish-free and pleasant to look at, and she was in great physical condition, maybe a runner. Manny guessed she was the detective from San Juan.

The two men were dressed in dark suits and thin ties, and their demeanor was familiar. They were cops, but not just cops: Feds, probably FBI. The captain was right. They had a problem—a big one.

CHAPTER-37

"This is detective Christina Perez with the San Juan Police Department," said Captain Serafini.

The Puerto Rican detective flashed a warm, professional smile. But she was definitely a cop. Manny guessed she had seen a thing or two, but it hadn't hardened her. There was an air of persistence and toughness about her. He liked her immediately.

"This is agent Josh Corner and agent Max Tucker from the FBI. Agent Corner will be in charge of the investigation."

The men nodded greetings to the others seated around the table.

Corner stood six feet with a strong build, maybe thirty-five years behind him, and definitely ex-military. He was good-looking, and his hair sported the popular, almost-shaved style. His piercing, blue eyes were no-nonsense, and his demeanor left little doubt concerning who was in charge. Manny knew the type; agent Corner expected results, and fast. Exactly the kind of attitude that led to bigger and better things for his career.

Tucker looked a little younger and stood about five-ten with a much slighter build. His black hair was slicked back, every lock in place. His large nose sat between small, intelligent eyes, missing nothing. Manny guessed the African American agent was the forensics expert. If he was right, and he was sure he was, Tucker had to be very good at what he did. The FBI didn't hire from the bottom of the barrel.

A small spark of hope flickered somewhere deep within Manny. There was no substitute for bright minds and vast resources for information—in spite of the Feds' famous, or infamous, lack of a personal touch.

Tucker circled the room, passing out identical blue files with the official FBI seal stamped on the front, each containing a hundred pages or so.

These guys didn't miss a lick. And why should they? Lansing could only dream about having the resources at the Feds' disposal. Money talks.

"These are all of the crime scene pictures and forensic information from the murder of Ms. Henkle in San Juan. It also contains as much information as we could gather from the murder of Park Ranger Maxwell in St. John yesterday."

Tucker's statement ripped through the room like gunfire.

"There are two other murders?" Manny asked after regaining his poise. The scene at the hotel charged back like a runaway rhino.

Agent Corner nodded.

"I told you. You didn't know what the hell you were talking about," said Richardson.

"That's enough, Chief," warned the captain.

Manny ignored Richardson as Corner continued.

"Three in three days with almost identical MOs. Obviously, you can see the urgency. We have a serial killer running around the Caribbean, and we believe him to be on this ship."

Corner's gaze settled on the Lansing side of the table.

"We won't beat around the bush here. We have three murders to discuss, and the preliminary supposition is that they were committed by the same perp. I'm sorry for your loss. I actually worked with DA Casnovsky on a case a few years ago. She did a stellar job. The reason you're here, however, has nothing to do with your relationship with her. In fact, that almost kept you out of this meeting and off the case.

"But if what you suspect is true, that Robert Peppercorn could be involved with the Martin case, it stands to reason that he could somehow be involved in the others because of the killer's MO."

The agent reached for his bottled water and took a thoughtful drink. "There aren't many profiles jumping out at us that match the kind of savagery that Peppercorn committed. He seems to be a prime lead unless we have a newly evolved unsub. We don't think that's the case because of the specifics of the MO, primarily because of the rose. With that in mind, frankly, no one will have more insight than the Lansing officers.

"As thorough as our databases are, there's only so much information they can give us. Even the Behavioral Analysis Unit can only give us a possible profile. The investigative analysts are helpful, but I find the local enforcement officers invaluable."

Corner's eyes shifted directly to Manny. "Detective Williams, your chief has recommended that you be the contact person for the LPD. You need to understand that you have no jurisdiction here and that you are involved to assist us. Is that clear?"

Manny nodded. Clear, for now. Some things never change. The FBI's reputation for dictating procedures, processes, and who got to play and who didn't was world-renowned. But this would be a tough one for them to control. He suspected Corner knew it, and Manny had no intentions of waiting for orders. Not on this one.

"I need you all to think clearly, set aside any differences you may have, and lock up your emotions." He looked at Richardson and waited for confirmation. The ruddy-faced security chief gave a slight nod toward Corner.

Tucker stepped to the front of the table. "I want you all to take a few minutes to leaf through the file. Maybe you can see something right away that will help speed up this investigation."

He spoke with a slight wheeze, like a long-time allergy sufferer. The muggy Caribbean air likely would not improve that situation. But he got a sense that Tucker would tough it out. Persistence is a good trait in a CSI, and Tucker seemed to fit that mold.

The room grew silent as the rest of the members of the task force reviewed the information. At one point, Manny saw Richardson gawking at his file in disbelief. So much for the easy gig he'd hoped for.

Ten minutes later, Tucker broke the silence. "Let me brief you on what we have. And please feel free to ask any question you'd like, because anything could be helpful."

As Tucker presented his overview of the three cases, it became apparent to Manny that the agent was not just a CSI, but a forensics expert—a damn good one too. His spark of hope flickered into a small flame.

“All three murders were committed by manual strangulation. No artificial ligature marks were found. He used his hands. The bruising isn’t totally clear because of the mutilation, but you can make out vague finger lines. He has huge hands and is extremely strong. There were no apparent signs of forced entry in the first two murders. It doesn’t appear to be the circumstance in the Casnovsky case either. He seemed to know their routines, or he is a charmer, or they knew him.”

Manny rejected that Liz’s murder was a “case.” She was a friend. It sounded cold, uncaring to address her like just another statistic.

But how many times have I done the very same thing?

He focused on the agent’s last comment: “. . . they knew him.”

Lynn. Could he kill like this? Did his dark side travel that far into the terrible? He remembered Sophie’s emotional confession, how Lynn had hurt her and enjoyed it. Could he have tortured and killed not only his wife, but the other two women too?

Agent Tucker squirted germ sanitizer on his hands and continued.

“Again, the killer used his hands to kill, but the tearing and ripping on each body was done with his teeth. He has a strong, psychotic fixation with oral mutilation, and he takes great joy in the torture process. He needs to dominate.”

“There didn’t appear to be any ingestion of flesh. It was mostly there, just shredded. We believe that he tears the throat to symbolically quiet his victims. At least that's what our analysts think. I'm not sure about that. The evidence indicates that he just loses it.

"It's possible that he was maltreated by a woman who may have verbally abused him to an extremely vicious degree. Maybe even locked him up or restrained him in some way." Agent Tucker removed his jacket and hung it carefully over the back of his chair.

"We think the victims were unconscious for most of or, perhaps, the entire ordeal. There are chemical traces of chloroform in each of their respiratory systems. Chloroform also leaves small red blotches wherever it comes in contact with skin. All three victims have that type of blotching around the nose and mouth. The fact that they were drugged during the assault reinforces our opinion that the victims were unconscious, at least during part of the attacks. We haven't gotten much so far from the initial toxicology reports."

Tucker pulled an asthma inhaler from his pocket, took a shot, and continued.

"He's extremely bright. He wipes each victim's neck with bleach to destroy any saliva evidence. We are trying to find untainted samples from the first two victims, but nothing yet. There is evidence of sexual activity, postmortem, but he must have used a condom because there is no semen left at the scene. He also clips the victim's fingernails to remove any possible skin or hair samples that may have been left during the assault. Like I said, very smart. The rose he leaves behind has some personal meaning, but we're not sure what.

"We brought in our best people from Evidence Response Teams to St. John and San Juan. They are using every collection process available to find fibers, hairs, trace of footprints, and body fluids. But, as I said, this killer is very careful."

Sophie twisted in her chair, and Manny gave her a side glance. Each business-like word Tucker spoke must have brought more sardonic doubt to her. She had to be wondering the same things about Lynn that Manny was. She's a good cop. Good cops looked at the possibilities. He heard her breath tangle in her throat and knew what was coming next.

"What about Lynn Casnovsky? Should he be a suspect?" Sophie offered. Her voice was cool, calm, professional. He hoped no one else saw the emotion living just under her composure.

Agent Corner responded. "We all know the stats on domestic violence and spousal murders. But we don't think Mr. Casnovsky is a viable suspect, at least in all three murders. He has never had anything in his past that would predict this kind of behavior."

"How do you know?" growled Richardson.

Corner flashed a condescending yet polite grin.

"We are the Feds, Chief. We do have access to a few things that local authorities don't. Besides, on the night of Ms. Henkle's murder, there are several cash advances issued in the casino from his debit card, and two casino dealers recognized him from his picture. We believe he was gambling during the time of her death. We would still like to talk to him once he's located," he said, looking at Sophie.

For now, it didn't appear that Sophie's former lover was a homicidal maniac hurtling through the Caribbean engulfed in a binge of violence.

"Witnesses?" asked Gavin.

"Detective Perez?" deferred Agent Corner.

"A bartender at the Wyndham saw Ms. Henkle speaking with a tall, well-built man just before she left," Perez said. "It was too dark for the bartender to make out details of the man's face, so we really won't be able to have a sketch drawn up. He thinks that the man left a few minutes after her, but he was busy and couldn't say for sure. He said the guy was a little creepy and definitely American.

"We didn't find anyone who saw anything unusual at the hotel. We're not even sure he stayed there. With cruise ships in and out, it's hard to get a handle on the coming-and-going confusion. We checked with the people at the front desk, but no one remembers anyone who resembled the bartender's description.

"It's amazing what sunglasses, a hat, and baggy clothes can do to make someone just part of the crowd."

Manny's blood turned to ice. The man in the courtyard at the Wyndham. It was him.

"Wait a minute. I may have seen that guy," he said.

He explained what he thought he saw on the night of Mike and Lexy's wedding.

Gavin stared at Manny, his face turning as white as his shirt.

"Why didn't you say something to me? That's my kid," demanded Gavin.

"I thought I was seeing things. It was dark. It was late. I didn't want to overreact. I just thought I was having a hard time getting out of cop mode."

Gavin looked at him and sighed. "You're right. No reason to panic over that. It's a little scary, that's all."

Corner said, “It could be nothing, but why don’t you compare notes with the bride and groom, see what they remember?”

“I’ll talk to Mike and Lexy when we get out of here.”

“Good place to start,” agreed Corner.

Agent Tucker explained that no one saw anything at St. John either. Just the woman who had found Dot Maxwell.

“Dot Maxwell was a pretty unfortunate lady. She had been assaulted about six months ago in that same office. Her statement said that she had been sure she was going to die, but something had scared him off or he’d just left. She wasn’t sure. Not so lucky this time.”

“Did she have any idea who it may have been?” asked Alex.

“Not really. According to the file, she described her attacker as a big man. Tall and overweight. But that’s all she could remember. Her therapist said she blocked out most of what happened, and it might take years to uncover anything, if ever,” answered Tucker.

“This doesn’t make sense. If it is Peppercorn, where did he get the money to do a cruise? How would he get here? And if I remember right, he wasn’t going to win any Nobel prizes for intellect. He wouldn’t know anything about forensic evidence,” observed Sophie.

Manny mulled over the possibilities. There was a thousand ways Peppercorn could get what he needed to make an appearance in the Caribbean, even on cruises. Prison could be a source for almost anything a man wanted, once he was released and found a few bucks. And did it matter how he got here? Manny didn’t think so. At least not yet.

"Has anyone tried to talk to Peppercorn's prison shrink, Dr. Argyle? Maybe he can shed a little light on Peppercorn's behavior," said Manny.

"I have a staff person on that as we speak," answered Tucker.

The room fell into an anxious silence. Everyone recognized the importance of capturing this killer soon. The preternatural knowledge that he would kill again veiled the task force like a moonless night.

Agent Corner passed out assignments and scheduled another meeting for the afternoon. Manny was even more impressed at his organization than his demeanor. The man was more than good.

Alex was to go with Tucker and process the Casnovsky's room. Then they were to head to the morgue for a discovery session with Liz's body and Dr. Kristoff. Richardson and his staff were to search the rest of the ship, including the rest of the lifeboats. Because no working security cameras were located in the passenger hallways due to privacy issues, the staff, especially on that deck, needed to be questioned. Corner wanted to see if anyone saw the Casnovskys or anybody else enter their cabin—and if anyone saw something near where Liz's body was found. Manny was to review the file with a fine-tooth comb for anything that would step up the pace of the investigation. Sophie and Detective Perez were to go to security and order pictures of all the male guests. Corner wanted them also to walk the ship when the excursions returned, looking for anyone who might resemble Peppercorn or the suspect Manny saw in the courtyard. Corner asked Gavin to stay after the meeting for a few minutes because he had a special assignment for him.

Corner then fixed on Richardson. “I have a couple of questions of my own. Why wasn’t DA Casnovsky’s room processed?” He turned toward Manny. “And how did you know it hadn’t been?”

The chief explained that his staff was limited and that it had taken four hours to process the scene where Liz’s body was found. He lowered his eyes. The excuse must have sounded deplorably weak even to him.

Manny never blinked. “I had one of the cabin keycards, and we stopped by this morning to see if we could find anything that the ship’s CSU may have missed.”

“Did you?”

“Did we what?”

“Find anything.”

“Yes. But I’ll let Tucker and Alex tell you about that when they’re done with the room. There’s more to find.”

Richardson snorted. “Good job of tainting evidence at the scene.”

Before Manny could respond, Corner’s cell phone rang. The room became as silent as a church on Monday morning. “Damn it. Okay, thanks.”

Corner turned off the cell and panned the ceiling, his face grim and hard.

“A body just showed up in a fisherman’s net off the southern coast of Puerto Rico. He was identified by his inscribed wedding ring. We have located Mr. Lynn Casnovsky.”

CHAPTER-38

Christina Perez told Manny and Sophie that she needed to go to her room to unpack and freshen up. She agreed to meet Sophie in twenty minutes at the security checkpoint on Deck One to request copies of photos for all the males on board, even the crew. The Puerto Rican detective had a decisive, but pleasant demeanor. Manny figured she was just as good getting her kids to confess to misbehaving as she was eliciting confessions in the interview room. He knew she had two boys because of the pictured button attached to the strap of her leather purse.

"Handsome boys," he said.

"Thank you. Pedro and Ivan. Both named after famous major-league baseball players who were born in Puerto Rico."

She beamed with more than a hint of maternal delight. It was easy to see they were her life, her pride and joy.

Through the flow of life, and being a cop, Manny had learned that certain things were universal. Every cop needs a familiar port in the storm. A place or a person who keeps them grounded and brings into focus why they do what they do. It went hand-in-hand with the conundrum that entangled homicide work. Her boys were her grip on the positive things in life, like Louise and Jenny were his.

"It was their dad's idea. What the hell? Pick your battles, right? Besides, they're fine names."

Bright and practical, a good combination.

He and Sophie left Perez at the elevators and walked down the hall heading to Manny's cabin.

"So. Is she hotter than me? And don't lie."

"You'll always be the hottest detective I've ever seen."

"Really? You're not stroking me?"

"I told you that I'd never do that to you," he smiled.

"Okay. Just remember that I can tell when you're less than sincere. You suck at lying."

"Do I? I guess that's good."

They walked a few more steps. "Are you all right?"

Sophie gripped harder, refusing to release the strong, emotional hold on his left arm. Her quiet voice cracked as she wrestled for words that he wasn't sure would emerge.

"I guess I hoped there was a chance Lynn was okay, that somehow he wasn't dead. It hurts more than I thought. "She wiped at a wayward tear. "I just can't seem to get this man thing right."

He wrapped one arm around her shoulders and gave her a squeeze.

"Remember that old song that asks if it's better to be with the one you love or with the one who loves you? Maybe it's time to make that call."

His advice set a fresh batch of tears in motion.

"I have. But it still hurts," she choked.

They stopped at his door, and she turned to face Manny. She stood up straight, brushed off her blouse, and dried her eyes. "I want a piece of this asshole. We need to nail him to the wall. I'm going to go tell Randy what's up. See you in a couple hours or so." She reached up and gave him a kiss on the cheek. "And thanks."

He gave her his best *it-will-be-all-right* smile. She broke into the first real grin he had seen from her in a day.

"You're such a bullshitter—and I'm glad," Sophie sighed.

Manny watched her walk down the hall to her room, to the one who loved her. He thought it the best call she had made in months, maybe years.

He stopped at his door and gathered himself. Telling Louise what had happened to Lynn was tough, but telling her that he was working Liz's murder, as well as the other two, was going to be tougher. He eased into the room. "This is going to go over like a lead balloon," he mumbled.

Louise was sitting on the deck, door cracked, dressed in her white, two-piece suit, reading the newest J.A. Konrath novel. Jazz sounds poured from the stereo like a fine, velvety Cabernet. Her perfume hung in the air, and he loved it because she had been wearing that scent when they'd met. It was *her*. Experts say that the sense of smell is the strongest link between memories and events or people in your past. No denying that.

When he slid open the balcony door, the love of his life jumped like an awkward teenager caught making out in the corner of the gym.

"Easy there. It's just your favorite Lansing cop."

"You scared the heck out of me . . . and how do you know?"

"Know what?"

"That you're my favorite Lansing cop? I may

just take Gavin up on that nude deck thing."

"Are you going to take pictures? I think I can get them loaded on his Facebook page."

Louise raised her eyebrows. "That's a thought."

Manny reached for his wife's hand. They had been through a lot together. Getting married young isn't easy. Some couples grow apart when they mature, and some grow up together. Louise and Manny had hung in there and finally grown up. They had proven to the world—and more importantly, themselves—seventeen years later, it had been right.

There hadn't been a magic formula. Love, hard work, and acceptance of one another went a long way, a very long way. But he knew she had gotten the short end of the stick when it came to overlooking faults, by far, and it made him love her even more. It didn't seem fair she had to deal with this mammogram situation too. But no one ever said life was fair. Never any promises.

Louise watched his face and read him like an open book.

"It's all right, Manny. I want you to find out who killed Liz. She was my friend too. We can do this another time. This animal has to be caught, and they need you."

His hand tightened around hers. "A fishing boat near Puerto Rico found Lynn's body this morning, and there were two other women murdered in the last two days. It looks like the same guy may be responsible. Here's the kicker: It could be Peppercorn."

Louise shivered, and Manny felt it run from her hand to his. She was all too aware of the conviction of Robert Peppercorn.

"My Lord! Poor Lynn. That's just awful. Two

more women too?" Louise bit her lip. "Peppercorn? Are you sure?"

"No, not yet. But it looks like his MO."

Louise hugged him tight, tight enough to relay the message. An anxious alarm had just gone off, and he knew she was afraid for him. There was always an underlying uneasiness for spouses married to cops. And this was magnified many times over. Peppercorn was a nightmare morphed into reality.

"You need to get him." She moved past afraid, running toward angry. "Be careful. I want my husband to come home with me, but get him."

There was nothing Manny wanted to do more. And fast. This killer's party was just getting started.

CHAPTER-39

"Do I have reason to be concerned?" asked Agent Corner, glancing at Captain Serafini then back to Gavin.

Gavin gazed at the hot latte as steam rose into the air with an indolent dance. He lifted the mug and drank cautiously.

"This is the best latte I've ever had, the best."

"Gavin, I—"

Gavin interrupted Agent Corner. "Concerned? That's funny. Manny Williams is the most talented investigator I've ever worked with. He sees things that aren't noticed by other cops, good cops. Maybe more than that, he feels things. He has solved cases that, in my opinion, would never have been closed without his insight."

"I've read his personnel file, and I must admit his record for cases-assigned to cases-solved is amazing. But I'm not con—"

Gavin cut off the FBI agent a second time. "Do you know how he put the hammer on Peppercorn?"

Gavin could see that Corner wanted to reverse the table, to butt in. Like that was going to happen. He seemed like a nice enough guy, but he was still a Fed. He was going to give Corner a taste of his own medicine. The FBI didn't always get to win. Besides, it could help catch the killer.

"After the third attack, he came into my office to ask for the evidence bags from the first case. He said he had noticed something from one of the pictures that wasn't addressed by the CSU or the FBI's ERT lab. No one thought anything of a tiny, black hair caught underneath a button on the first victim's sleeve. Hell, we must have seen it a hundred times, but never really saw it, you know? I reminded him that the first girl had short, black hair, and it belonged to her. I told him we had pulled several like it from the victim's clothes, and all of them had been hers. He said it didn't look right. More than that, it didn't *feel* right.

"So we pulled the hair from the shirt and, damn, he was spot on. The hair belonged to a black Labrador retriever. Not just a black Lab, but an American black Lab. The hair is just a tiny bit smaller and less coarse than a regular, block-headed English black Lab.

"There were only two kennels in the Lansing area that sold this kind of dog. We went through their sales records and made a list of people we wanted to speak with.

"Williams was on the way to see Peppercorn because he showed up as one of the people who had bought a dog. He had gotten the pup for his mother as a birthday gift. Just as Manny pulled into his driveway, he heard a scream. Peppercorn had just dragged his intended fifth victim into the house. The son of a bitch was in jail an hour later."

Corner nodded. "I knew some of the story. Impressive. It's also the kind of effort we're going to need in this case. But you didn't answer my question."

Gavin lipped more of the choice coffee.

"Did I say this is damn good stuff?"

Captain Serafini smiled. "Only the best for our guests here at Carousel."

Gavin turned back to an almost-impatient Agent Corner.

"I have only seen him upset like that a couple times. He lost a partner about a year after he joined the force. He took the afternoon off to play golf and his partner went on a routine domestic alone. Manny used to be a hell of a golfer . . . two handicap. Anyway, it should have been a routine call. But the asshole slapping the daylights out of his wife also had an assault rifle. He shot Manny's partner nine times. Manny's always blamed himself." He stroked his mustache. "Seeing Liz like that got to him. It got to all of us, but Manny's taking it personally. He thinks Richardson should have moved faster, and it pisses him off. Your security man *should* have moved faster. *Much* faster."

Understanding mirrored in the eyes of the other two men.

"I've seen him shift to this gear before. He won't sleep until this is over. The only concern here should be on the part of the killer. If he can be caught, you'll need Williams to do it."

CHAPTER-40

Ethel Manis forced her damaged eyes to focus on the glowing face of the cheap dime-store watch wrapped around her wrist.

These damn eyes.

She was finally able to make out the green, digital shapes: 9:42. It was Tuesday morning, and the docking in Dominica had gone smoothly, as far as she could tell. She was just glad the relentless rocking was over. For two days, she'd felt like she had been riding the most vicious roller coaster ever built. On top of that, her back screamed because of the collision with that man on the Lido Deck.

A full tray of breakfast sat virtually untouched. The aroma of cooked bacon and fried potatoes almost caused her jumbled stomach to lurch up the two or three bites she had managed to keep down.

The seasickness was finally subsiding, thanks to Dramamine. She took three times the prescribed amount on the bottle, but she was a big woman, and sometimes it took a larger dose of medication to achieve the desired results. She didn't think doctors ever thought about that, but by God, she did.

She rose slowly from the bed and trudged to

the porthole, the room's only opportunity for a visit from the sun. She squinted and closed the drape. The sunlight hurt her eyes, especially in the morning.

Her cabin immediately retreated into gray shadows that felt familiar, comfortable. The remaining, solitary source of light, spreading from the bathroom, stopped just short of her bed. But it was enough, for now. Darkness had evolved into a cloak of solitude and understanding, and she embraced it. She was all right with not being able to see well as long as no one else could see her, the real her. She couldn't allow anyone else the opportunity to dig deep into her soul and expose her secrets. The dark helped her keep that promise.

A mother's secrets.

Ethel felt for the creased sheet of paper hiding in the breast pocket of her flannel shirt. He had sent her a letter, after all of this time; he had at long last sent a letter. Her son had decided to contact her—no one else, just her.

The letter explained how he had been living a simple, discreet life in another part of the country and how he needed, and wanted, a new start. He missed her very much, but it was just too risky to call her. The letter said that he hoped he could trust her and would see her soon. He'd put $2,000 cash money in the envelope. She was to use the money to book a cruise, this cruise, so she would be able to see him.

After a moment, Ethel squeezed the letter and cursed the fact that she hadn't brought her magnifying glass. Reading it again would reassure her, comfort her. Instead, she recalled that terrible trial and those awful accusations and damned, barefaced lies. He wasn't the terrible man they had accused him of being, and he simply couldn't have hurt those women. Not like that, not like they said. She hadn't raised a monster.

Licking parched lips, she became aware of the solemn doubt creeping in, memories she hated to visit. Her only son hadn't been like other children. There had been something within him. Something different. That thing, that persona, seemed to lie in wait until his brilliant emotions ran high. He would change. Not much at first. Then . . .

There were times she thought it her imagination or perhaps side effects from medication she had been taking. That's all. But deep down, she'd known better, hadn't she?

Ethel released the subconscious grip on the front of her shirt. When he'd gotten like that, she would have to lock him in that windowless basement until Bobby, the real Bobby, came back to her. Any mother would have done the same.

A mother's secrets.

NO!! Ethel Manis wouldn't allow that kind of misshapen image of her son, her Bobby. She couldn't allow it. No good mother would . . . and she had been a good mother. He had written her and paid for this cruise. Didn't that prove her virtues?

Her son.

To touch that face one more time, to smell his hair, and to feel his strong hands was all she wanted.

This would be her last chance. The doctors said four to six months was all she had left, maybe a little more, maybe a little less. It didn't seem right, but thinking about it only made things worse, and she had promised herself that she wouldn't dwell on her remaining time. But it was hard, so hard, and this life had been short. There were . . . regrets.

She snorted. People were just flat out lying when they said they had no regrets. Bullshit. No one's closet was empty. No one lived a life void of mistakes.

Waving her hands in rebellion, she chased away the last of her austere reflections.

The next day was all that mattered. Her boy would come. She smiled. God had answered her prayer. She was sure of it, and his visit was all she had.

That and a mother's secrets.

CHAPTER-41

The gruesome, crime-scene photos were disturbing, each one emitting an intonation of pure evil. Hell, even "evil" would have to skip up a notch to match this.

Manny wondered if Peppercorn could really do this. The man had a hard time getting from A to B, and murder was a giant step from rape.

The pictures escalated the pain he felt for the unfortunate victims and their stunned families. His heart broke for the dead, but equally as much for their broken loved ones. For a while, if not forever, their lives would cease meaning, rhyme, or reason. They would lay awake trying to control the senselessness of it all. Frustration would be their closest friend and "why" the only question that mattered. He knew; he'd been there.

His hand quivered ever so slightly as he studied the photos. No one deserved to die like this. But it did the investigation absolutely no favors if he approached his role without checking his emotion.

He had run into his fair share of psychotic horrors over the years, but this unrestrained creep show took the cake, won the grand prize.

After going through the pictures once, he flipped the file back to the beginning. The first time through was to see if he could collect a better feel for the perp's mind. Just maybe he could develop some ideas that could help catch him before he killed again—and he felt sure this lion would feed again.

Sophie and Detective Perez had left to work their assignment, including Manny's request for a list of people who had purchased excursion tickets to Trunk Bay. The detectives were also going to snoop around the security checkpoints near the boarding ramps and see if anyone could remember someone who matched Manny's description of the man he had seen approaching Mike and Lexy and again in the casino.

The killer's motive hadn't become totally clear, but it seemed logical to assume he wanted to be noticed, to start some cat-and-mouse game. That was evident by his display of Liz's body. Narcissism was a common thread for psychopaths. They wanted to be noticed, appreciated. It fit.

And if it was the same man Manny saw with Mike and Lexy, and if that man had really wanted to hurt them, why hadn't he?

Manny had another, less overt reason for his request of the two women detectives—he wanted more time alone with the files. No distractions. No questions. Just him and the evidence.

Sophie had become more than familiar with the game, and he knew he hadn't fooled her. In fact, he was beginning to realize just how hard it was to fool her. But she was willing to go along with him and see if any of the legwork led to a lead. If there was something, she would find it.

Louise and Barb left his cabin to swing by Gavin and Stella's suite. The three women were going to lay out on the Sun Deck and work on their tans. Translated, they were going to get out of their law enforcement husbands' collective ways. They all knew the drill. Except this time it was on a cruise ship deep in the beautiful Caribbean. At least the women had that going for them.

Manny stood and stretched, cracking his shoulder in the process. He grimaced. Old football injuries only got . . . older.

His nose suddenly honed in on what he had ignored for the last fifteen minutes. Room service had brought the two Rueben sandwiches Manny had ordered from the New York deli, and the inviting scent of corned beef, Thousand Island dressing, and sauerkraut harassed his groaning stomach. He had been concentrating on the file and had forgotten about the manna from heaven. He grabbed the sandwiches and walked out to the balcony.

The band was getting cranked up on the Lido Deck. He had almost forgotten how much he enjoyed steel drum music. "Hot, Hot, Hot" was one of the best island songs ever written.

Liz would've loved this. He could see her swaying to the bold sound of the band. Truth is she would never love anything again. Not on this earth, at least. There was something more than unfair about that. He suddenly wasn't hungry.

The air-conditioned cabin felt good as he came in from the heat and sat down. It was time for round two. He flipped open the FBI file and began to finger the appalling pictures and neatly typed reports a second time—much slower, studying each page with a renewed, deliberate purpose.

Every piece of evidence at each scene was

marked and numbered with a yellow tab so it could be cataloged sequentially. It was that way for the Henkle and Maxwell murders, but not for where Liz's body was found.

Alex and Agent Tucker would handle the Casnovsky's room with great expertise, but lifeboat sixteen had been so compromised it may never give them anything to work with. Richardson and his staff, so far, had been a bad joke. They had even screwed up printing the photos of Liz's body, and he would have to wait for Tucker's report to see them. The paperwork was fairly detailed, but that was it for Liz's file.

Part of Manny was relieved. Seeing her that way once was bad enough, and he could wait to revisit that lair. Besides, he didn't think there would be much variance between the three murders. This killer was just too organized.

He continued working his way through the set of crime-scene photos. Each woman was viciously strangled with bare hands, just as Agent Corner had observed. The size of the deep, violent bruises around each of the murdered women's necks confirmed it. Tucker had been right on that too. He scrutinized the blurred bruising. The intense bite marks made the purple, horizontal striations harder to see, but they were there. It looked like four marks on one side of the throat and one on the other. He grabbed similar photos from Dot and Juanita and put them side by side. Although the quality of all the pictures wasn't identical, the markings on each woman's throat were generally the same. A thought struck him like a stinging slap on a cold winter's morning.

These women were killed with one hand.

It would take a hell of a grip to kill an adult

female with one hand. If his suspicions were true, then what was the killer doing with his other hand? Masturbating? Something else?

The strangulations of the women were part of the ritual, his ritual. An element of the process? The killer put the women under, and then took his sweet time to finish what he started. He had undressed them and neatly stacked their clothes. What was significant about that? Neat freak? His notion of gentlemanly behavior? He couldn't have raped them right away. It would have taken a few minutes to undress them and fold the clothes. Did it take him awhile to awaken the one-eyed snake? Foreplay? He didn't know for sure, but he reasoned he was close.

The killer's biting of his victims was savage and wild. Anger? Frustration? Power? Hatred? What made this asshole tick? And why biting?

It was becoming more difficult to leave Peppercorn out of the equation.

Agent Tucker had said he thought the victims could have been unconscious when they were killed, at least for much of the attack. That maybe because this predator wanted peace and quiet. No resistance. But if that were true, why would he clip the fingernails of the victims? Did they wake up?

Manny continued to leaf through the files and reread the reports, taking note of the carefully placed position of the bodies. The tilt of each victim's head. It was as if each woman were staring into the eyes of their killer. As if he wanted them to look at him. Lover's eyes?

The truth struck him like those sudden revelations do. The killer *needed* them to *wake up.* He drugged them just enough so the sick son of a bitch could prepare for the final step.

My God!

When the victims had come to, he'd murdered them slowly with purpose. The killer had wanted to watch them die.

CHAPTER-42

The shade provided by the steel overhang running the circumference of the Sun Deck sheltered the killer like an iguana lounging under a palm. The glass of red rum punch felt cold in his hand as he crossed his long legs, watching the flurry of activity in the deck's pool area. Preteen children and drunken adults splashed around in the briny, pristine water with no conscious perception of who should be acting older—and not really caring.

They are all idiots. Pimples on society's ass. Pigs wallowing in the trough.

He hated them and despised their superficial pretense. They masqueraded at enjoying each other, but in the end, they really only cared about their own self-indulgent desires. At least he was honest. He knew what he was about and embraced it.

The *Ocean Duchess* was scheduled to leave Dominica in a few hours. That was good. The day's work had been completed. A satisfied smile ranged across his face.

Don't you just love it when a plan comes together?

The killer's mind blazed with thoughts of the next step. It was perfect. Just like him. Today's agenda was a critical cog, no doubt, but reaching Aruba would be the culmination of his hard work.

He wondered if this was how all of the great composers and painters felt when they had finished the one creation they knew would capture the world's imagination. He was the Rembrandt of death, the Monet of pain. He laughed out loud.

Damn, he loved being in control. This was the most exhilarating game he had ever played. Nothing had ever come close to this, not even at the prison. No one would see the purpose of his plan, with the possible exception of Detective Williams, who was smarter than he remembered. But then again, he needed the detective to be.

The band started again, and the music quivered with a life of its own. The killer tapped his foot to the performer's version of "Hot, Hot, Hot."

"Not great, but it works. I give it a seven."

Slowly, he began to scan the deck. Back and forth. His head moved like a great white shark, seeking its prey, injured and near.

She would make her long-awaited entrance soon. He knew her patterns already, and the next shining star of this production was like a dog salivating at the ring of a bell. He marveled at how people inadvertently trained themselves. Their subconscious responses to a particular set of circumstances never wavered. It happened every time. Freud may have been on to something, for an anal moron.

A blond bombshell in a red, thong bikini, large breasts swaying, gave him a double take, but he wasn't interested. Another time perhaps. He had only one goal, and she wasn't it.

Finally, he saw who he wanted to see.

Standing in the sunlight on the opposite side of the kiddy pool was the leading lady of his next big show. He knitted his brow. There was one small detail, a tiny distraction that needed to be attended to by dinner, before the headline show went on, but he would handle that. Distractions were to be expected. The unsuspecting young woman spoke to her friends with excited animation. She laughed without a care in world. She had no inkling of what was in store for her. No idea of how the last few hours of her life would play out, how things would change.

He watched her with the group, stored the picture of her appealing body in his mind. Intense heat began to spread to his groin. He could hear his heart thumping in his chest as his unchecked imagination climbed to new heights.

His mark's skimpy two-piece exposed her for the slut she was. Still, she was attractive, and tonight's task wouldn't be too daunting—for him. He would enjoy this phase of his homework. Just like he had enjoyed them all.

Draining his drink, he rose from the deck chair and strolled directly toward the unsuspecting source of his attention, each step bringing him closer to her and the evening's festivities.

The distinct fragrance of her coconut-butter sun lotion rose to his nostrils as he moved closer.

"Excuse me," he smoothed as he brushed against her. This was so intense.

The Lansing woman with the piercing eyes and wide, white smile responded. "Sorry. I guess I should get out of the aisle."

"No problem, no problem at all. We're all enjoying the time of our lives," he answered, then strolled away whistling "Hot, Hot, Hot."

CHAPTER-43

Sophie stood motionless in front of lifeboat sixteen. She wasn't sure what she had expected in coming here. Anything comforting, she supposed, would be welcome. Hell, maybe the boat would talk to her.

The afternoon sun beat on the back of her neck like a blast furnace, but she didn't care. The sullen numbness she felt couldn't be dispatched, not completely anyway. Nor could the heinous one-two punch of guilt and denial.

Why am I here?

Clues? A glimpse of the killer . . . because they always seemed to return to the scene . . . which she knew was almost never true. Something the CSU had missed? That was what she told Christina Perez. But that wasn't really the truth, was it?

First, her friend Liz, and now her freshly crowned ex-lover, were dead. Never mind he just happened to be Liz's husband. She shifted her feet and bowed her head as she blushed a convicting scarlet.

Liz had been her friend and even a confidant, the way women can be to others in their profession. The DA had helped her get through some rough times during her divorce, and Sophie had repaid this kindness by bopping Liz's husband.

Her head dropped even lower. "Some friend," she whispered.

Sophie had put herself in the middle of one of those ill-advised love triangles always written about in romance novels. She would never have thought that could have happened to her. But it had. She felt dirty. The kind of hell-born dirt that bad girls never remembered and good girls never forgot.

She looked intently at the place where Liz's bloodied arm had dangled the night before. The blood had been cleaned away, but the stain would never leave the deck of her guilt-ridden heart.

"Liz. I'm so sorry. I don't know what came over me. I can't tell you why I was sleeping with your husband. It just . . . happened," she confessed. "If you can hear me and can find it in your heart, I'm begging your forgiveness."

Just then, as if by some divine cue, a warm ocean breeze blew her long hair from her face. The wind danced and circled her moist eyes, as if to dry her repentant tears. The gentle wind was like a baby's breath, and her eyelids fluttered shut. She let herself become lost in the moment.

Sophie didn't believe in omens, but she had seen a prayer answered a time or two, and confession always seemed to be good for the soul.

In the interrogation rooms, she had witnessed hardened killers bawl with unadulterated relief after admitting their crimes, hoping against hope their confession could erase their treachery.

She wasn't sure if the breeze had been heaven sent, or if it had even been real, but she suddenly felt better.

Perhaps her solitary confession had been good for her spirit.

Was there really a God who forgives and brings about a peace that surpasses all understanding? At that moment, she believed there was.

"I'll do all I can to find your killer. I owe you that. And Liz, thanks," she breathed softly.

Turning to leave, she noticed a small piece of blue-and-white paper, resembling a torn movie pass, resting underneath the white crank handle that controlled the raising and lowering of the lifeboat. She glanced around the deck and was still alone. She was sure it hadn't been there a minute ago, but in her current state . . .

She squinted, stretching her arm to pick it up, halting in mid-motion.

It was a used excursion ticket for Trunk Bay, calling her like early-morning coffee. Her heart thudded in her ears as she gawked at the clean imprint in the middle of the pass.

There was nothing latent about the flirtatious fingerprint winking at her from the surface of the stub.

CHAPTER-44

Eli Jenkins glanced down the hallway of Deck Six's starboard side and watched the blue-haired couple squeeze through their cabin door, giggling like young lovers. The rest of the hallway was clear.

Damn, how I hate having to be cautious.

But soon all caution would be as unnecessary as a fur coat in Aruba. Every spinning molecule of his body brayed with enthusiastic prospect. This was what he was born for. He was here to set things in order. This was just another predestined step structured by destiny itself. He felt invincible.

A few seconds later, he raised a huge paw and rapped on the steel door with authority.

I wonder if she likes surprises.

The cabin door swung open and, dressed in a Carousel embroidered pink tank top and hiking shorts, her shining black hair tied in a neat ponytail, stood Detective Christina Perez.

Her eyes became slits when she scoped the tall man dressed in the room steward's uniform. After a few seconds, her right hand pulled reluctantly away from her back. Jenkins knew she was ready to pull the .38 Smith and Wesson revolver, her back-up weapon. The one she hadn't turned in when she boarded. He had counted on her having the gun, and she didn't disappoint.

All cops were the same. They lived lives as borderline criminals who didn't think rules applied to them. Perez was a bit jumpy. Good. That meant that she and paranoia were dining at the same table.

"Yes?"

"Here are the extra bath towels you requested. My supervisor said to bring you these right away," he spoke in his best Middle Eastern accent.

Perez looked at him and smiled. "No. I didn't request any more towels. But thank you anyway."

She was more of a looker than he thought. Nice legs too. Then again, he had only seen her from a distance, until now. They were about to get closer than she ever bargained for.

"This is room 6578, yes?"

"It is, but you must have the wrong room."

The detective began to shut the door just as he lost control of the stack of bath towels. They tumbled in slow motion to the floor just inside the cabin's entrance.

"My apologies, miss," pleaded Jenkins as he bent to recover the scattered mess.

Perez stepped back and waited for him to finish.

With suddenness and agility that was incredible for a man his size, Jenkins clutched her waist and pulled her to him, slamming the door with his foot. The detective never saw the drug-saturated cloth until it covered her face.

He felt her reach for her gun again, but she was far too late, and he was far too quick. His strong hand clasped around her arm and squeezed with the force of two men, causing her to yelp in pain, breaking her wrist in the process.

****

The drug was efficient. Perez's right arm wouldn't obey her brain's command to unholster the .38. It was as if someone had unplugged her nervous system. She wondered how she could have been so stupid.

Her world spun, uncontrolled. She thought of Pedro and Ivan and wished she could hold them one more time before black waves of unconsciousness washed over her. Her arms wilted to her sides as she descended to the waiting darkness.

CHAPTER-45

“This is fricking unbelievable,” moaned Alex, sitting on the edge of the bed, his thick legs pointing out at forty-five degree angles, right foot tapping to an orchestra only it could hear. “I thought we’d find more than this. Who is this maniac, a damned forensic expert?”

“I’ve seen stranger things,” answered Agent Tucker. He was finishing the complicated process of packing away the FBI’s portable argon laser.

Man, Alex loved these new toys. He saw how this one had located latent fingerprints so that they could be lifted in more detail than just the brush-and-lift method. The laser illuminated residual finger oils, and in many cases, picked up the hidden print. It was a modern wonder that cut down processing time. But not on this occasion. Because of the machinery’s propensity for detail, it had revealed at least thirty prints that needed to be lifted and cataloged, then run against the IAFIS database.

“We’ll run these prints and find out who belonged in here and who didn’t,” said Tucker.

“There have been hundreds of people in this cabin, and besides, how long will it take to get the results?”

Tucker pushed his glasses forward on his

nose, "About eighteen hours." His voice rattled with frustration. "I know. I know. We don't have that much time, but we'll have to wait."

The two men grew silent. They didn't have eighteen hours. That fact did little to boost Alex's mood.

"We did fine, Alex. We know this guy is using bleach to clean up the scene. He obviously has knowledge of how some of these procedures work. Like Corner said, very bright. We also knew there would be less information here. Hey, at least we've determined this is where she was killed."

"Yeah, that'll have to do for now," Alex said. "Somehow there's no consolation in that. Liz is gone."

"I'm sorry Alex. We can't fix it. We have to do all we can to stop this guy."

"You're right. But I'm not sure how much closer we got to that."

Alex looked at the labeled evidence bags stacked on the loveseat and felt his stomach drop. There were only half as many as there should be. No fabric or fibers that were out of the ordinary. No detectable shoe prints. They had found several hairs, but Alex would bet his next paycheck they belonged to Liz and Lynn or previous guests and staff. They had combed the bathroom for any sign of irregularity and it was clean, except for the blood spot on the bathroom wall, but he doubted it was anything important. In fact, *everything* was *too* spotless. It was obvious the room had been cleaned to hide something, or someone.

Tucker and he had worked meticulously through each closet, each dresser drawer, and each suitcase and found little. Nothing on the balcony was really out of the ordinary except the rose leaf—just busy work and exasperating dead ends.

The whole thing was maddening. Was this all there was, all he could do, to help find his friend's killer? He had hoped for something palpable. He hadn't found it. But that was the dichotomy of forensic science. It wasn't like Hollywood depicted it. Hardly. Occasionally the microscopic evolved to an open book, and he hoped it would in this instance. But the forensic gods could be cold and uncaring, and he hated praying to them.

He had just returned from the lifeboat with the torn cover that Manny had seen earlier. There were definite signs of blood, and he was also able to recover a minute swatch of human skin Alex was sure would match the DA's husband. Poor bastard. Lynn hadn't been everyone's favorite person, but to be murdered and then bounced off the ship like a piece of garbage was unthinkable. At least his body had been recovered. Dead is dead, but it would help to bring elusive closure to Lynn's family.

They had slightly better luck locating DNA samples with the help of a forensic scientist's best friend: luminal. The magic concoction caused body fluids like blood, saliva, semen, vaginal fluids, and even perspiration to glow when exposed to black light.

There were eighteen different areas from which they had swabbed samples. Alex winced when he thought about the "good time" couples had enjoyed in the room.

The gathered samples would be shipped, including the blood-stained rose leaf and the fingerprints, to one of the FBI's crime labs. The techs would run the DNA samples through

CODIS, the Feds' DNA profile database, hoping for a hit that would help.

"Do you think the blood on the leaf is Liz's?" ventured Alex.

Tucker shrugged. "Probably. Since the rose was lying across her chest. We'll know in a day or so. I guess the real question is how did it get there?" He snapped shut the black, padded case containing the laser. "Maybe we'll get lucky. Maybe the perp poked himself with a thorn and his DNA will be in the computer," said Tucker without much conviction.

Alex hoped that was true, and often that's all there was—hope. It was fragile, but hard to destroy.

Rubbing the back of his neck, Alex studied the room, noticing its cozy layout. The cabins were small, but enough. The ship's architect did a wonderful job of designing intimacy with efficiency, and the rooms weren't set up to spend a lot of time in. After all, this was a party boat.

His eyes followed the narrow aisle leading from the outside door, past the bathroom, and to the main part of the room just past the closet. Suddenly, he was inspired.

Jumping from the bed, he stepped to the door and placed his back flat against it. Alex called to Tucker. "Come here for a minute. I need to check this out."

"What for? We've been over—"Tucker's brain kicked in with understanding as he watched Alex.

"Lynn was a tall guy and in pretty good shape, right?" asked Tucker.

"You got it."

Alex tried to stand shoulder to shoulder with the agent, facing the inside of the room, their backs to the outside door. There wasn't enough room for the two men to occupy the narrow doorway unless one of them stood at a fifty-degree angle away from it. The walls were too close together.

"There is no way the killer would have been able to get into the room, at least without a struggle, if someone were standing right here. Liz may have answered the door, but the killer needed to take Lynn out to get to her, right? So it stands to reason Lynn answered the door, or came to help Liz, and the perp would have had to incapacitate him first," said Alex, stepping away.

"Since there's no room for two grown men to stand in the aisle leading from the door, one of two things happened," Tucker said with a tinge of excitement. "So if it was Lynn, when he answered the door, he was taken out like that." He snapped his fingers to drive home the point. "The other possibility is that he or Liz was expecting someone, maybe room service, and never bothered to check who was at the door before opening it."

Alex stroked his chin like Basil Rathbone playing Sherlock Holmes. "So either way, the killer would have had to do it quickly."

Tucker dropped to the floor in front of the cabin door, reaching into his blue, dress-shirt pocket, and unsheathed the magnifying glass from its fleece-lined case. "The fastest way to take someone out of the picture is a sucker punch to the jaw . . ."

". . . and you just might split open a knuckle hitting someone that hard," finished Alex.

"Thus, split skin could cause minor blood loss. Low-velocity impact bleeding could mean drops on the floor. But since we've already checked the carpet inside the room and found nothing. Maybe . . ."

Tucker opened the door and Alex held it, allowing the agent to get to his knees, bending his face to the colorful hall carpet. He ran the magnifying glass about two inches from the floor in grid-like fashion, and then stopped abruptly. A low, triumphant whistle escaped his lips. "You're the man, Alex!"

"What?"

Alex took the magnifying glass and scrambled to his knees near the spot where Tucker was pointing.

There, just below the hinge side of the door were two dark-red stains half the width of a pencil eraser. A triumphant grin spread across Alex's face.

"This psycho bitch bleeds," he said.

CHAPTER-46

Agent Corner tapped his silver Cross ballpoint on the table of the conference room as he waited for the second meeting of his makeshift task force to convene. It had been a long-ass day, and it was getting longer. The flight and lack of quality sleep were catching up to him, but it was more than just a little jet lag, much more.

As an agent on the rise within the FBI, he had been witness to some ruthless, perplexing, and bizarre forms of behavior. But it still shocked him to see these kinds of disturbing acts against God's prize creation; and this rampage was disturbing.

To add insult to injury, he was out of the comfortable environment he coveted, instead sailing on a cruise ship that was going to dock in sunny Aruba without his full resources. Every question had to be communicated via phone or fax without easy access to department heads or their expertise. He had to send whatever Tucker and Downs had found to the airport and then to the ERT lab in Miami. Then have the results faxed to the ship and the originals couriered to Aruba. He didn't like it. There were too many things that could go wrong.

Out-of-sight, out-of-mind was not some justifiable metaphor; it was the truth, even for an

FBI Wonder Boy. He squeezed the pen a little tighter.

There were far too many variables ricocheting out of his control, and if he hated anything, it was lack of control. It would be fourteen to eighteen hours before the results would be available. Time was a commodity he didn't think they had. In fact, he was sure of it. These demented psychos didn't stop playing the game; they just made up more rules.

They had nothing. Maybe a tall, muscular man who Detective Williams may have seen making threatening gestures to some newlyweds—who could be some biting rapist from eleven years ago.

Damn it.

Rubbing his tired eyes, he reached for more coffee. This unsub was way too far ahead of them. Keeping them off balance so they didn't have time to focus on what might be next. And the profilers were having a hard time pinning him down, too. It was almost as if he were toying with them. Josh hated being mocked, but hated even more that they were helpless to stop it.

But maybe they had an ace in the hole. Detective Williams. He couldn't stop the wry smile. A little too emotional for his taste, but a brilliant detective nonetheless. He had seen this type of personality on other occasions. They weren't all as intense as Williams, but it seemed to work for him, and there was no denying his talent.

Manny Williams probably didn't even realize his gift as a profiler. He thought he was just doing good police work and putting things together. He guessed that Williams had no idea how rare it was for one individual to solve cases at the rate he did without "the gift."

The FBI had a half dozen or so criminal investigative analysts who did the work of profilers (true profilers like Manny were rare), most were assigned to the Behavioral Analysis Unit, but none with more potential. Most held PhDs in psychology and criminal justice, but not much field experience. (Good thing because they had each other to talk to when some of the real sick stuff was over.) But Josh thought the best were cops that had seen a thing or two—if their insight didn't drive them towards some psychotic episode, or worse. But he didn't think Manny had to worry about that. He didn't drink, and his family life seemed stable and strong. Even if the Lansing detective did work too many hours, there were worse things.

Family. He thought of his young boys and his loving, patient wife, and the time he spent away from them. He wished he were home for a famous Corner family hug.

He shook his head like a punchy boxer trying to shake the effects of a big right hand. "Stay on the case, boy," he uttered.

None of the detectives-turned-profilers that worked for the FBI had the Lansing detective's closing rate on open murders. It was the real reason Corner wanted Williams involved. Even his own Chief had said that Manny *felt* things. He hoped like hell that Detective Williams was feeling something—anything—now.

The door opened softly, and Captain Serafini shuffled in throttling a piece of paper in his right hand. His demeanor told Corner that things had gotten worse.

"We have more problems," the captain said, barely loud enough to hear, handing Corner the paper.

"What's this?"

The letterhead belonged to the Dominican Police Force. That got his full attention.

Suddenly he felt suffocated, like he was standing in a room full of smoldering cigars. He studied it again, hoping it read differently the second time. The killer had struck again. This time, he had shredded a tour guide at the National Rain Forest.

"They want to speak with us and are threatening to delay our departure."

He followed the captain to the door. This time, Corner hated being right.

CHAPTER-47

The last vestige of a normal vacation was hopelessly obliterated, at least for Manny Williams. The faces of the killer's victims coursed through his thoughts like runaway trucks, and he would see them everywhere until this was over—and probably long after that.

He ran his hand through his hair. They had to stop him, now.

Everyone was seated in the conference room except Corner and the captain. An uneasy feeling tapped Manny on the shoulder. Detective Perez was late too, but Sophie said that the San Juan cop was going to bring her superiors up-to-date and that could take some time. Sophie guessed Perez would be here soon. But where were the other two?

This was off. He felt it, and lately, his feelings were far too accurate for comfort.

"I'm sure they'll be here shortly," announced Agent Tucker, like he had been reading Manny's mind. "I gave Corner the forensics material from the room and the ticket stub that Sophie found. He had to make sure they were going to be delivered appropriately."

The door swung open, and the captain and Agent Corner stepped into the tension-riddled meeting room. Manny took one look at the two men, and his angst shot to the stars. Corner's drawn expression circled the chamber while Serafini stared at the table top. It didn't take a genius to figure this one out.

"He's killed again, hasn't he?" asked Manny.

Without speaking, Corner sent a manila file sliding along the table to Manny's waiting hands. He opened it, and his heart rolled to his feet. The all-too-familiar scene in the God-awful photographs was as unnerving as a clown to a two-year-old.

"Damn it," he whispered.

"At 4:45 today, we received notice from the local authorities that this unsub had killed again. The victim was Rebecca Tillerman, a young tour guide whose body was found behind the employee's lounge at the National Rain Forest Park." Corner spoke in a tight, professional tone. There was a hint of a soft, southern drawl that Manny hadn't noticed before. Maybe Georgia or South Carolina. It seemed you really couldn't take the country out of the boy. He wondered if Corner had ever seen anything like this back home.

"We had to wrangle with the Dominican government to let the cruise continue. They wanted to hold us here until we gave them the killer. Luckily, we were able to convince them that the best chance of catching this creep was to keep things as close to normal as possible. To stay in port any longer, no matter what excuse we concocted, would have caused concern with the rest of the passengers, maybe even a shade of panic. It could even give the unsub a reason to suspect he was the reason for the delay."

"Not to mention the economic impact it would

have on the island if Carousel were to discontinue docking in Dominica, right?" queried Manny.

"It came up," stated the captain with a stoic, half-smile.

Corner rubbed his stubble and continued. "They are going to send us the rest of the crime scene file when they are done processing the murder site. There is really nothing more we can do until then, so let's talk about what we found out from our assignments this afternoon."

The team leaders brought the task force up to speed on what had transpired between meetings. No new info from the staff. Richardson said there were lots of tall men on the cruise, but no one who seemed out of the ordinary so far.

Agent Tucker and Alex had taken more pictures of Liz's body, but saw nothing obvious from their physical exam. The new pictures would be ready in a couple of hours. Then they processed the Casnovsky's room, and Tucker relayed how they had found blood at the Casnovsky's cabin that could belong to the attacker. Manny thought that might be a break.

When it was Sophie's turn, she explained how she had found the bloodied excursion ticket near the lifeboat. The killer had apparently made a mistake, and that was cause for optimism.

Manny wondered.

The ship's records showed that the ticket was one of two issued to the Casnovskys so the killer must have used it when he went to Trunk Bay. There was no way to trace it from there so that translated to another dead end. At least until they got the results from the print. Sophie said that Perez had info from the ship's photo database and would share when she arrived.

Agent Corner relayed that his staff in Miami had tried to contact Dr. Argyle about Peppercorn's profile, but he was out of town. His receptionist said she would contact him as soon as possible.

Corner looked at Manny. "Detective Williams?"

Manny let out a breath and began. "I think Peppercorn, if it is Peppercorn, is worse than we thought. He likes to wait until his victims are awake and then watches them die."

Silent revulsion rippled through the room.

"I don't know if it's a power game or some kind of God syndrome, but the killer watches the light go out. He may think he's catching some part of their essence, their soul or spirit."

"How do you know that?" demanded Richardson.

His acrimonious tone barely registered with Manny.

"If you look at the close-up head photos of the victims, each one has a pattern of faint bruises along the crown of the head. They were made with the killer's other hand. The pattern is consistent with someone holding their heads still."

"That bruising could have happened at a different time during the assault," countered Richardson.

"Maybe, but I don't think so. There would have been no reason to hold their head still if they were already out. Besides, the bruising is blurred, like it took him a minute to get control of each victim."

Richardson glared at Manny, but said nothing.

"His fingers and hands are like those you would associate with someone at least six-four. Like agent Tucker said, he is incredibly strong. It takes serious strength to kill the way he kills."

"His height would lend credence to your theory

that he may be the same man you saw," stated Agent Corner.

Manny nodded.

"Anything else?"

"Yeah, one more thing." Manny turned to Agent Tucker. "Did you find any spots on the bed that may have been makeup or looked like makeup?"

Tucker looked at Alex, then back to Manny and shrugged. "Yes. We assumed it was Liz's. But we swabbed it and sent it to the lab anyway. Why?"

"I think he may use disguises. It could be just enough makeup to alter his skin tone or maybe to change his whole look. I'm not sure. But I noticed a small, tan blotch near the foot of the bed and it seemed out of place."

Uneasy silence filled the room. If Manny were right, they not only had an intelligent homicidal lunatic on their hands, but one who could change his appearance. No one wanted to add chameleon to this killer's skill set.

Corner finally broke the silence. "We are going to change some things. I want to have six teams of two on watch at all times. When I say watch, I mean strolling around the decks, scoping out the casino, checking out the bars, and attending dinner in the main dining rooms. I want a team as near to every kind of passenger activity as possible.

"If they're tall, I want a picture of them. Anything or anyone that looks remotely unusual is to be documented and photographed."

Captain Serafini cleared his throat to speak, then didn't. Instead, he turned toward an arched armoire that matched the color of the oval conference table. He pulled out a key from his short, white uniform jacket and unlocked the large door. Reaching in, he pulled out eight holstered Glock 19, 9mmhandguns. Each weapon was a polished-smoke color and fitted with a fifteen-shot clip.

The captain's piercing eyes were alive as he addressed the mixed crew around the table. "I trust that each of you know how to use these and use them safely. I am taking a calculated risk in handing out these weapons." He tilted his head like Clint Eastwood in a *Dirty Harry* movie. "Desperate measures for a desperate time. I am pledged to protect my passengers and crew, and I will not allow this heathen to kill again. Agent Corner and I have consulted on this and believe it to be prudent."

He threw a quick side glance toward the FBI agent. Corner was looking at the guns and said nothing.

"I know that you all will do what is necessary if the situation presents itself."

The captain handed a firearm to each one of the seven cops plus an extra clip. The last one sat on the table like a lonely statue in a deserted park.

Manny leaped to his feet. "Damn. Where is Detective Perez?"

CHAPTER-48

Fearing the worst, Manny raced through the narrow hall of Deck Six, making a beeline toward Christine Perez's stateroom. His lungs were ablaze, but the only thing that mattered, that was important, was getting there. He prayed they hadn't been outplayed again.

A glance over his left shoulder confirmed that Sophie was only a few yards behind, with the others at her heels. Good partners were hard to find.

He picked up the pace, hoping Perez was all right and that he was simply overreacting.

But something had happened, hadn't it? Something horrible.

The premonition haunting Manny wouldn't leave, wouldn't pay the bill and check out.

Damn it. Why didn't they react sooner? There is no way she would be that late for the meeting.

He quickened his gait again and was now motoring at a full sprint. He passed 6546 and was just paces away from Perez's cabin.

After a few more strides, he pulled the Glock from its holster and flipped the safety to off, hoping he didn't need it, but feeling he would.

Manny slid to a stop and began hammering the door. "Detective Perez? Detective? "No answer.

"Christina. This is Manny Williams. Open the door."

Silence was the only sound, and his anguish spiraled higher. The others pulled up quick behind him, and Sophie immediately began pounding on the door as well, yelling Christina's name even louder. A few onlookers peeked from cabin doors to see what the ruckus was about, but Josh told them to get back inside. The guests quickly obeyed jumping back into their rooms.

"We need to get in there, now," Manny urged. "Sophie, find a room steward and . . ."

Richardson cut him off. "Relax, I have a key."

Manny whirled around in time to see the chief fingering a worn, black ring teeming with silver and gold keys. Attached to the very bottom of the oval menagerie was a white card equipped with a black magnetic strip. It was hard to miss Richardson's slight look of triumph.

"I am the head of security and have a master key or card for every door on the ship. Every door." Richardson eyed Manny and said, "You don't even know if anything is wrong. Maybe she lost track of time and is tanning on the deck."

"C'mon, Chief. That's bullshit, and you know it. She's not the type to forget or blow off a meeting, just open the damn door," Manny demanded.

"Now, Chief," ordered Corner.

Richardson rolled his eyes. "All right, all right. Just hold on to your weenies." He reached for the key slot, card in hand.

"I got your weenie," muttered Sophie.

Manny bumped her and motioned for her to move to the other side of the door.

"Okay. I get it. But when this is over, I'm going

to kick the living shit out of him," she whispered. "Twice."

Sophie and Corner drew newly acquired weapons and took positions at different angles pointing to Perez's cabin.

Richardson grasped the handle, slid the card in the slot, and pushed the door inward.

CHAPTER-49

The heavy door hung open, and Manny not only saw the darkness, but it whispered to him to come in, to take a chance. No guts no glory. He burst into the room, Corner and Sophie on his heels, and not surprisingly, Richardson bringing up the rear. Each had their 9mm pistols raised to a readied, ninety-degree angle, prepared for anything.

The room was as silent as a fog-shrouded graveyard after the witching hour. The thick curtains were drawn taut, forcing the room to embrace the dark. Manny nodded, and Sophie flipped both light switches. The brass overhead fixture flickered into life, simultaneously with the bathroom lamp. He waited motionlessly for his eyes to adjust. He could swear he heard each officer's stammering heartbeat.

Richardson emerged from the tiny bathroom shaking his head. Manny moved to the closed drapes and tore them open. There was no sign of the San Juan detective. He cautiously stepped through the deck door and peered over the railing, not sure what he was searching for, but covering every possibility. He saw only more sun, ship, and deep ocean.

Stepping back to the crowded cabin, he

noticed Perez's suitcase lay open, resting on the front edge of the bed. There were a few personal items laid out in an orderly fashion near the pillows. Running shoes, makeup bag, toothpaste and brush, red large-toothed comb, and the dark-leather Smith and Wesson shoulder holster for her service revolver formed a silent brigade of useless witnesses to the whereabouts of the woman who set them there. Her Sun and Fun card, just like in the Casnovsky's room, rested on the cabinet.

"I guess this throws your sunbathing on the deck theory down the toilet, eh Richardson?" said Sophie in a voice dripping with sweet sarcasm.

Richardson's look told her to get bent. She blew him a kiss.

Sophie had regained her composure completely, and her acid tongue to boot. Manny was grateful. He needed her. All of her.

"Maybe she locked herself out and had to find help getting into the room," said Agent Corner.

"I don't think so. Her shoes are here, and why was the curtain closed?"

At that instant, Agent Tucker and Alex arrived, both breathing like they would never catch their breath again.

"If she's not here, you four need to step out of there . . . maybe we can see something . . . that once resembled . . . a damn clue to . . . what may be going on here," wheezed Agent Tucker, motioning as he spoke with his best *"you just stepped all over the evidence, but I can't breathe"* hand signals.

"Just a minute. We want to make sure everythin—" Manny's response stuck in his throat. "hit," he huffed, focusing intently at the empty holster. "Did she bring a weapon aboard, and if she did, where is it?"

"I thought you couldn't bring a gun on board under any circumstances," said Sophie.

"You can't," whined Richardson. "Only the security staff has access to firearms."

"I didn't even know she had one. She didn't turn any in when she boarded, so I thought she didn't bring her piece. Even Tucker and I agreed to give up ours," said Corner.

"I bet it was her backup," said Manny.

Corner took charge. "I'll have her paged. Williams and Lee start down that side of the hall and knock on every damn door. Richardson and I will take the other side. I want to know if anyone even though they saw or heard something out of the ordinary."

"Are you sure that's a good idea? We don't want to panic any more guests," offered Richardson.

"We have a missing detective and five murders here, Chief. I don't give a shit about panicking guests, not anymore."

Manny couldn't help but see the venomous look spewing from Corner's blue eyes, staying any other thought Richardson wanted to express. The man was in charge, and a little emotion at the right time was a good thing.

Sophie nudged Manny as she headed out of the room. "I like him. He's hot and bossy . . . like you."

"Thanks, I think."

After one last look around, Manny had started to follow the others to the door when he heard it. Stopping stiff in his tracks, he cocked his head and listened. *There*! Coming from the closet, the sound begged again.

Indistinguishable, the echo was barely audible.

He turned toward the closet and raised his gun.

CHAPTER-50

An unsavory chill ran the length of Manny's spine while he backed away from the closet.

What the hell?

As he pointed the Glock and took another step back, his thoughts were scorched with burning possibilities, accompanied by all too familiar uneasiness.

"Partner, move your ass. We have doors to—" Sophie never finished.

He waved her toward him. The quizzical look on her face vanished when the light bulb switched on. She raised her gun, moved to the opposite side of the closet, paying attention to his lead, her demeanor alert and ready. By then, Corner and Richardson had come back to the room.

"Did anyone check this closet?" Manny said to Sophie.

She shook her head and shrugged. "Not me," she whispered.

The other two cops shook their heads.

Incredible! In the heat of the pressure-crammed moment when they had entered Detective Perez's cabin, everyone had assumed that someone else had secured the closet.

It was the kind of thing that could get a cop hurt—or worse.

Heart pounding in his ears, he motioned for Sophie to get into position. The door swung from left to right, and he wanted her to pull it open, while he readied his aim.

Agent Corner squeezed past Sophie and stood a couple of feet behind Manny, gun ready. Corner's forehead beaded with clear perspiration and not from the heat either. There was a trace of excitement in his youthful face.

Manny glanced over to his partner, and she nodded her head. He wasn't sure whose role in this mind-wrenching process was worse, hers or his, but knew she would do her part in flawless fashion. He prayed he would do his.

Sophie let out a slow, bleeding breath and clasped the polished, pewter handle, eyes wide.

Manny flexed his left hand and brought it slowly to his waiting right hand, his gun hand. He remembered his academy instructions—two hands were better than one. He had to be steady. They might only get one chance at this.

Sophie and he had routinely done this dozens of times before. But this time was different.

He tried to quiet the cacophony running amok in his head. It worked, a little. Catching Sophie's eyes with his, he nodded ever so slightly.

Sophie pulled open the door without a hint of hesitation.

"Freeze!!" yelled Manny.

The air came alive with the fetid odor of fresh blood. Instantly, he wanted the truth before him to be an illusion. But it wasn't an illusion.

Dropping his arms, he realized he wouldn't need the gun for this one, none of them would. His heart was already coming apart.

Agent Corner gasped an involuntary, shocked

breath.

"Oh my God," escaped Sophie's mouth.

Detective Perez hung from the crossbar of the closet, secured with a white, nylon rope that ran under her arms. Gray duct tape stretched across her swollen mouth. A black rose extended up from under the rope with the petals touching her bloody left cheek.

Crimson trails ran down her face and covered her naked chest. Bite marks jacketed her face and breasts; part of her right ear was missing.

Only that wasn't the worst, not this time.

Manny's gaze had settled on her face, hoping to see some flicker of light in her eyes.

But that wasn't going to happen. Christina Perez's beautiful, hazel eyes were no longer there.

CHAPTER-51

The US Coast Guard Medevac helicopter became a small, opaque speck as Manny watched it race north through the cloudless Caribbean sky. Forty or fifty rubbernecking passengers stood behind the restraining ropes, each one positive they knew the inside skinny behind the helicopter's appearance. The official word was a heart attack involving one of the elderly guests. He wished that had been it, with all of *his* heart.

Detective Perez was alive—barely. She had lost a lot of blood and was in critical condition. Luckily, she had blood type O-positive, the most common human blood type, and Dr. Kristoff was able to administer transfusions while Captain Serafini put in the call for the chopper. The doctor's fast work had probably saved her life, for now. He prayed she would make it, and prayer couldn't hurt. He was at least sure of that much.

Manny didn't recall seeing anyone—still breathing that is—as wrecked as Perez. Her skin, the non-mutilated part, matched the white terrycloth robe that he tore from the top of the opened closet to cover her disfigured body. And what could match the spectacle of her empty eye sockets?

Her chances were not good, but she was a

fighter, and fighters hung in there. He had seen it before. There was no way of measuring the human will to survive. Some seemed hell-bent and unusually determined to see their families or even to tend to something unfinished. Some didn't.

On top of that, it was fairly obvious that she had been the target for a terrible message, a dare. The killer was trying to say something, but so far, it escaped Manny.

Looking to the cloudless sky, he gritted his teeth. He wanted the memory of Detective Perez's closet to disappear, eternally erased. But he knew those stubborn images lived a life of their own. When they decided to stay, they caused many a cop to drink too much or swallow too many pills. But he'd never thought that way. He only thought of making the killer pay.

The investigator in Manny Williams shifted into full gear, and the questions rushed him like waves to the beach.

Why leave her alive? Why was the murdering piece of garbage changing the pattern? She was messed up, very messed up. But not to the extent of the other three women, except for the eyes. Was he interrupted? That didn't seem likely. He wouldn't have had time to put her in the closet the way he did. He purposely stopped the maiming short of killing her. To what end? Was he attempting to prove he could do whatever, whenever he wanted?

Dr. Kristoff was positive she hadn't been raped. There was no tearing of the vaginal tissue and no bruising around the thighs. He admitted that his examination was hurried and he had her life to worry about. The rape kit results would confirm or deny the doctor's suspicions.

These creeps often escalated their perverted rituals to the next level, and Peppercorn's "dating" habits had been way out there, but Manny wondered for the hundredth time if Peppercorn could be responsible for this kind of maiming.

He pulled down his sunglasses and walked toward the railing. The killer hadn't taken "souvenirs" before. At least, no keepsakes they were aware of. Maybe he was taking pictures of the murdered victims before, and now that wasn't enough.

The thought of the killer breaking his pattern was chewing at his twisted insides like a bad meal. Did he subconsciously want to be caught? What exactly was the reprobate bastard thinking? Figuring out this guy was like trying to set Picasso to music.

The perp was a killer of passion. He seemed to thrive on raw emotion and uncontrolled anger. Smart, but emotive.

Was this a part of his evolution or was he deliberate in this change-up? Cold, calculating, intentional didn't fit this MO. But serial killers never followed the rules. They reveled in their own reality, whatever they perceived that to be. They used whatever they deemed necessary to use. Like Christina Perez's Smith and Wesson .38.

The sending of a message?

Was the killer's arrogance starting to rise to the surface? Manny thought so.

He could almost hear the murderer laughing.

Manny took a deep breath and leaned over the veneer railing, taking in the glassy ocean. The cruise ship was carving through the water, and he smelled the salt as the persistent, summer breeze carried it.

He would have really gotten into this vacation. He wagged his head back and forth slowly—part in frustration, part in disappointment. One more payback to collect on.

Maybe Louise could salvage something out of this wreck, but that was going to get tricky. It was clear that things weren't safe, and they had to be more careful.

Manny zeroed back to the killer, to his apparent message of superior intellect. He thought himself uncatchable—and why not? They had squat. There were no real clues. No suspects. No mistakes. Only dead bodies littered around the Caribbean.

Just as Perez was being rolled out of the room on the ship's gurney, Richardson had come back from canvassing the rooms on Deck Six. He reported that no one had seen anything . . . except an older gentleman just stepping out from his room, who recalled a tall room steward knocking on Perez's door, or at least close to it. Richardson would check it out and let them know. Manny knew it would be a dead end. The killer must have somehow gotten his hands on a room steward outfit.

Real careful. Real smart.

Manny wasn't sure, but he wouldn't be surprised if the lab reports came back with little or no help. Lynn's recovered body, after a day in the ocean, wouldn't be much help either.

As Manny stared at the raised veins on the back of his hands, his mind assumed the mush position. He had examined each scenario a dozen times. Maybe more. Nothing clicked and he wasn't used to that.

He squinted in the direction of the horizon and

watched as a line of brown-winged pelicans gliding in perfect formation dove and dipped leisurely, yet with precision, into the blue Caribbean water, never warning their unsuspecting prey. Boom. It was over. The fish never knew what hit them. It brought new meaning to the term survival of the fittest.

Never warning their unsuspecting prey.

The truth hammered him like a jarring uppercut. Manny straightened up and blinked his eyes.

"That's it, my God. That's it!"

He ran along the hardwood deck toward the polished glass elevators.

He had to get to Perez's room.

Agent Tucker and Alex were giving it the forensic once over, and he needed to be there. There was no question in Manny's mind, not anymore. The killer had left them a message, and he was sure it wasn't an invite to dinner. The unsub was telling them, somehow, who was going to die next.

CHAPTER-52

Graceful despite their bulky size, the pelicans dove into the deep and seconds later emerged with their hard-earned prize, their catch of the day—much to the killer's delight. They abided by no laws, adhered to no rules, just simple survival of the fittest. It was a panacea that he eagerly embraced and understood on every level. Weakness would be disposed of and the strong would live as gods, *should* live as gods.

The weak existed only to submit to men like him. It was now a way of life etched forever in his way of thinking. His religion.

Nature had intended it, no doubt. It was how things worked, and men like him seemed to be the only segment of the human race to understand and accept the perfect harmonic that life sang.

Ironically, his kind was deemed less than human by those who embraced some kind of moral compass.

"Moral compass, my homesick ass," he snapped. These were the same men and women who were caught doing the nanny or the pool boy and stealing from their congregations.

He took another long drink from his new favorite drink. He was pleased with himself, very pleased. He had left them a map, a clue to figure out what was next. Hell, he even wanted them to find it. But alas, it just wasn't going to happen. The morons couldn't find their asses with both hands.

How could they figure it out? He was he . . . and they were they. But in the off chance that they, maybe Williams, did catch on, it would be too late. This story was going to be written on their watch. Their pathetic watch.

"How important am I now?" he raged.

The killer reached for the Smith and Wesson that had been in Detective Perez's holster not two hours before. The gun's wood-grain handle and steel surface felt cool against his fingers as he turned it over. He had never used a gun before, never needed to. He aimed the polished weapon at the smudgeless mirror, put his long finger on the trigger, and levered the safety switch to off. His hand was as steady as a surgeon's.

Slowly, patiently, the pressure from his strong finger tightened. Little by little. Sweat trickled down his temple. He was going to do it! He was going to fire the gun right through the mirror. Ecstasy ran amok through his tensed body.

How good is this going to be?

Then, at the last possible nanosecond, he eased the pressure, removing his finger from the trigger.

A picture was worth a thousand words, and the picture in the mirror had revealed a hideous, unexpected truth. The dreamlike image of him pointing a gun at himself had startled him. For a brief, dread-filled moment, his plan evaporated. His skin crawled, and his ever-present confidence stumbled. He realized that he could die. A fortunate guess, leading to a lucky shot by one of the law enforcement imbeciles, could undo everything he had worked for.

Eventually, he turned away from the mirror and slid the gun into the waistband of his shorts. The doubt had dissipated. Nothing could go wrong. Not for him. Not on this trip.

He *never* made mistakes. He wasn't about to start now.

CHAPTER-53

"We haven't found anything weird. Nothing that looks like a message, a clue. Not a damn thing."

Manny caught the not-so-subtle hint of exasperation in Agent Tucker's voice.

"It's been like freaking Grand Central Station in this room, and it makes the going slow, so just hang on to your asses." Tucker's eyes burned holes through the three impatient detectives.

"Okay, okay. But we don't have all night." Manny looked down at his watch—6:35.

Sophie, Agent Corner, and he were bunched in the hall just outside Perez's cabin.

Corner faced Manny. "Are you sure about this? It just doesn't make sense to start leaving obscure clues and covert messages now. It means he's changing MOs. It's rare; these people don't do that. It's not who they are."

The faint odor of the lemon carpet cleaner lingered in the hallway as Manny pulled in a long breath and looked intently at the FBI agent.

"I've been running this over and over in my mind."

"Great, we're in trouble now," said Sophie.

"Just listen."

"Sorry. I'm antsy and could use about nine

Long Island Iced Teas." Sophie looked at Josh. "I'm a lot of fun when I've had too many. Want to see?"

"She means with her husband," said Manny.

"No I didn't, but he could come too, I guess. Ever partied with a hot, Asian woman?"

"Uhh, well, I think we should try to catch the killer first, don't you?" asked the agent, his face turning red.

"All right then. It's a date, FBI man."

Manny cleared his throat. "Like I was saying, maybe he's evolving. Changing as his needs escalate. It happens. Some serial killers even stop killing because the thrill is gone. Granted, most stay at it until they're caught. But once in a while, their mind goes in a different direction. These assaults appear to have been attacks of passion, pure rage. He loses it. The biting, the close-up style of killing, the rapes, and even the control he craves with postmortem sex could all be part of it, of him." Manny furrowed his brow and dove deeper. "How about the way he holds the victim's heads facing him so he can watch them die? I think it might be some off-the-wall, bizarre expression leading to a way of closeness most of us don't understand. It's a connection with intimacy, *his* understanding of it, anyway. His actions are all produced from sadistic compulsions that he has to act out. But maybe it's not enough anymore."

That's it, isn't it? He looked back to Sophie and Corner. "Maybe new thrills are the order of the day. It's rare, but not without precedent."

Corner's eyes narrowed as he searched Manny's face.

"You really think this guy could be changing

his approach? And that he's now in it for the chase?"

"I don't know. There have been cases where the killer turns up the thrill with risky stuff. How about Son of Sam? Jack the Ripper sent letters to Scotland Yard for the sole purpose of mocking them. It had apparently evolved into a sick game for him. Some experts think that the Ripper's type of communication is a perverted cry for help. I don't. I think it's a way to turn up the heat, the danger. The thrill is another way for him to win, or maybe to lose. But mostly these guys have to win. It's part of their persona derived from abnormal perversion they saw or were a part of somewhere along the line. Like the molestation Peppercorn had experienced. They shut out all emotion. It makes them free. Sociopaths."

"Thank you, Dr. Manny Freud," ribbed Sophie. The three laughed, in spite of themselves and the situation.

"Maybe a little guilty of overanalyzing, but I believe everything I've said to be true about these guys. But there could be something else going on here. By breaking the pattern, he could be trying to confuse us, to get us to chase our tails. What if this guy wanted us to think these were crimes of passion? Choosing random acts of violence because it fits the known profile. What if he's always had a hidden agenda?"

Sophie wagged her head slowly. "Like what? I mean why go to all that trouble?"

"I don't know. Ego? Religion? Revenge?" said Manny.

"If he did have a different agenda, like you suggest, this would be a hell of a way to hide it," interjected Agent Corner. "You don't have any proof. Besides, let's face it. No one really knows why these psychos do what they do, right?"

"True. But if I'm right, he believes he can do anything he wants, and we can't do a damn thing about it. The man's condescension has grown to the point he believes he can send a message, and we won't find it. Even if we do, we'll be too late. He wants more out of this ride. It's like the rush of his compulsions are now secondary to something else. I mean look, he didn't rape Perez, and she's still alive."

"The adrenaline rush to keep us tied up is now driving this guy?" Sophie asked as her eyes filled with doubt. "I don't know, Manny. I kind of agree with Josh; it seems to be too much of a swing."

"I know it doesn't make much sense, but it could be true." Manny flipped his hands in the air. "To this point, the guy was at least somewhat predictable, but now its way out of whack. This sure as hell isn't textbook. At least none I've read."

"Man. You made my head hurt. I could really use those drinks about now," moaned Sophie.

The three detectives stared at the floor in tense silence, the air conditioner throbbing its peculiar cadence from the ceiling.

Doubt abruptly stole some of Manny's certainty. He had been so sure of himself when he left the Sun Deck. He could be wrong. Maybe there is no message. Maybe this murderer is exactly like he described; a total sociopath. If that were true, then what?

"It's almost like there were—" started Manny.

"Hey! You guys need to see this, NOW," yelled Alex from the bathroom. "Right now!"

CHAPTER-54

Sophie squeezed into the small bathroom, and Manny and Josh pressed as close to the entrance as the space would allow.

Alex was under the stainless steel sink, down on all fours, with his ample backside high in the air. Manny suppressed a grin at what could have been the first real reason to laugh all day. He filed the visual away as a point of reference for when this was over.

"You know, with one of those butt-burner machines, you'd have a pretty good ass. For an older man," said Sophie.

"Do you think so? And what the hell do you mean older?"

"You know, way over forty."

Alex waved his hand. "Just stick with the case, got it?"

"Damn, you're no fun. Okay. What is it? What did you find?" questioned Sophie.

"Something that shouldn't be here," he huffed.

The CSI was reaching into the farthest, shadow-covered corner, small chrome tweezers in his thick fingers. The miniature jaws of the pinchers were fastened securely around a small morsel of material. Alex backed out from underneath the sink, grunting like an old hog.

Sophie stepped back into the small shower stall to avoid Alex's four-limbed shuffle. It was about the only way two people could fit into the undersized room.

Alex stood up, breathing hard, and flexed repeatedly. There were two distinct bone-cracks as the CSI's vertebrae protested. "I need to lose some weight," he complained.

"And the light goes on," said Sophie.

Alex didn't respond. He was already rotating the small particle of detritus, which he had removed from the floor. Back and forth, in front of his spectacled eyes, with ninety-degree twists like it was pure gold.

The minute shaving was semi-clear and appeared to be made of a waxy material. The reflection from the bright bathroom light gave it a smooth, glossy sheen. To Manny, it could've been a thin fragment from a crayon, or maybe even a transparent bar of soap.

"Okay, what is it?" Manny asked.

"I'm pretty sure it's good old CnH2n+2."

"What are you talking about?" asked Sophie.

Tucker had joined the gathering near the cramped room. "It's paraffin wax. It's used for a ton of things, like sealing boxes, waterproofing corrugated material, pharmaceutical supplies, and even makeup. But it's used mostly for candle-making."

"It looks like a shaving from a clear candle or a block of wax. See how it's curled? Someone put a sharp, serrated blade to a block of wax, or more likely, a candle," explained Alex.

"But we aren't supposed to have candles on a cruise ship because of the fire hazard thing, right?" asked Sophie.

"That's right, so what's it doing here? Detective Perez had no candles in her baggage, and these rooms are cleaned thoroughly after each cruise," added Agent Corner.

Manny put his hand on Alex's shoulder. "Okay. Someone had an illegal candle in this room, or the shaving stuck to someone's clothes, or maybe the cleaning people missed it. Why show us this . . . what's the point?"

Alex was running his hand gently over the large, bordered mirror. He pulled his hand away and smiled a crooked grin. It reminded Manny of Sylvester the Cat after he'd popped Tweedy Bird in his mouth.

"I'll show you, smartass. Sophie, out of the shower. Chop. Chop."

"What?"

"Just do it, girl. Out. Now."

"Damn. Okay. Okay." Sophie saluted and did what he asked.

Manny watched the CSI reach in and turn the faucet toward "H." Hot water cascaded from the chrome spout.

Alex shooed Sophie out of the room, and he stepped through the door right behind her. He pulled the door shut.

"Let's give it a few minutes. The steam will stick to everything except the wax I felt on the mirror. If I'm right, the killer . . ."

Manny finished the sentence, ". . . left a message just for us."

CHAPTER-55

MISERY, MISERY, MISERY
WHAT SHALL YOU DO?
DEATH RIDES THIS SHIP
NOT FOR STILLS, NASH AND YOUNG
BUT FOR WHOM?

Jarred, Manny read the poem again. The crude rhyme screaming from the steamy mirror was as chilling as any January night. The warning carried a sense of prophecy that felt as real as the ship under foot. His body swayed without really moving, like he was about to have an out-of-body experience.

And he read the terrifying message again.

"What in God's name?" asked Agent Corner, incredulous.

Manny regained his composure. "This whole thing isn't about random rapes and murders. He wants *us*. Anyone who's from Lansing law enforcement is a target. He's telling us that Gavin Crosby or his family is next." Manny's eyes closed in frustration. "This thing has been a set up since San Juan . . .maybe since those murders back home in April and May."

"But why?" Sophie asked with more than a

trace of anxiety. "How would he know we would be here?"

"Probably from the wedding announcement—or he knows us. But we can figure that out later. Right now we need to call both Crosby cabins and make sure they're all right."

"I'll call Mike and Lex." Sophie was already dialing the wall phone, and Manny switched it to speaker mode. He watched the phone as the first ring to the young Crosby's cabin pulsated through the handset. No one breathed. It was so quiet in the cabin that everyone could hear the dull drone of each precisely spaced chime. As the third ring began, Manny started for the door.

"Yes?" filtered through the speaker when Mike Crosby answered. The released collective breaths sounded like a gust of wind.

"Mike, this is Sophie. Listen, don't ask why, just make sure your door is locked and chained. I need to call your dad, and then I'll stop by to explain. Okay?"

The hesitation in Mike's voice was obvious. "Ummm . . . okay. You . . . ahh . . . don't need to come down to explain. You can tell us at dinner."

"No problem. I can come to your room in a few."

"Lex and I are kind of busy, you know?"

"Well, okay then. You call Manny or me when you're ready to talk, got it?"

"I will." Mike hung up the phone.

Sophie covered her mouth and snickered. "Sorry, Manny. Mike said to visit later or he'd call. They were . . . busy."

"Yeah, I got that. Speaker phone, you know. Call Gavin and Stella."

She wasted no time dialing Gavin's room. After

the fourth ring, Manny didn't wait and headed out the door, running to the stairwell that led to the seventh floor, fighting every uprising fear sent his way.

This was a nightmare coming to fruition right before his eyes. It felt like some concocted story from a vivid, hard-crime novel. Except in real life, killers don't expose part of their hand, but this one had—at least that's how it looked.

Was he that sure of himself? That confident?

The murders weren't some kind of random, homicidal rampage by a deranged sociopath. The assaults had been driven by vengeance, the worst kind of motive.

As he hopped the stairs two at a time, Manny tried to sort through years of arrests and investigations. He mentally reviewed specific threats from punks and pros alike, but it was hard to concentrate on that just now. He boss, his friend, could be in grave danger.

Manny reached the top of the stairs and rushed toward Gavin and Stella's stateroom. As he approached their room, he couldn't stop the dread that was beginning to draw a sickening portrait of its own. He hoped that they had figured this one out in time.

CHAPTER-56

The barrel of the .38 Smith and Wesson formed a small, circuitous imprint in the back of Mike Crosby's head, and the man-mountain knew it hurt like hell. He pressed harder. Mike groaned.

The new groom's hand shook as he fought for sufficient composure to hang up the phone on the waiting cradle, trying not to let it tumble to the floor. The killer smiled as Mike was able, somehow, to complete his mission. There was no way that the Crosby's kid had ever before experienced the fear now running through his body.

No daddy around to take away the bad man?

Mike's trepidation excited the killer. "Some hero cop you turned out to be," he taunted, slapping the back of Mike's head.

This had been a bold undertaking, even for him, perhaps marginally risky, but he reveled in it. The pathetic task force was now on full alert. Obviously, they had found his special memo. That's why that little oriental bitch had called. He wondered if Williams had been the one to figure it out. He would ask him when the time came.

All part of the quest, if they were able to keep up, and frankly, he was surprised they had gotten this far. Although it did make things more vivid, more deadly.

I'm right under your dismal noses, and still you run around like chickens with your heads cut off.

"You did well. Very well. If you would have said one wrong word to that oriental bitch detective . . . well, I would have hated, but certainly not hesitated, to splatter your slutty new wife's brains all over this room."

He allowed Mike to glance into the large mirror and see the center of the bed. Lexy was bound around her ankles and wrists with gray duct tape and her body bent in a slight reverse "C." A smaller piece of tape covered her tremulous mouth. She was dressed only in a white, sheer-lace bra and panties, looking like the low-class whore she was. Tears shone in her large eyes.

Mike spoke to his captor. "Why are you doing this? What do you want?"

The killer didn't answer. Instead, he pulled his gun-wielding hand back and smashed the revolver against Mike's head with the force of a jackhammer. The sound was sickening, like dispatching a jack-o-lantern with a bat. Young Crosby slammed against the protruding closet and crumpled to the floor, blood streaming from the long, deep gash gouged into his left temple. His lean body shuddered spasmodically and then grew still. The big man watched with fascination and then laughed out loud, turning toward Lexy. "I don't think he'll be playing with us anymore today. What do you think?"

Lexy tried to scream through the sticky gag, but nothing except muffled spasms of fear leaked from her mouth. He watched her eyes widen even more as she saw that her wimp-ass husband stayed down. Her bronzed body quaked with anguish and panic.

He stood near the queen bed and ordered her to stop making noises. She did.

Sitting on the edge of the bed, he began to slowly run his hand along her shapely leg. Beginning north of her silver ankle bracelet, he slowly maneuvered up her calf, past her smooth knee, and eventually massaged soft, fleshy thigh. The hand's journey had purpose, meaning. His action exhibited an intimacy that was far past his preference in the normal world. But this was his normal world, wasn't it? No sense in splitting hairs, not now.

His awakening was clear, and Lexy's body stiffened as she made extraordinary efforts to move away from his advances. "Careful, you might hurt my feelings, and you wouldn't want to do that, would you?" She shook her head, reminding him of the Martin woman. Ahh, good times.

He explored her rigid face like a lighthouse searching for a troubled ship. Steady. Relentless.

After his right hand reached the top of her thigh, he stopped short of where body and leg became one, just short. The young bride glowed, and he could smell her unique odor mingled with the scent of melon body lotion. He closed his eyes in appreciation. There was nothing that matched the sweet smell of pure fear. Especially fear he called his own.

Labored breaths escaped Lexy's nostrils as her chest began a rapid rise and fall, too rapid. He knew what was happening and wanted to see it play out. He had to see her asthma attack run its course.

Her eyes grew even wider while she struggled to capture precious air. Lexy thrashed around on the bed still harder, but he steadied her, his eyes never leaving her face. He was transfixed. Eventually, she stopped moving. Her pretty features had taken on an ominous, blue tint. Lexy's eyes took on a glassy sheen, like reflections off a clear mountain lake, and then fluttered shut.

Rage exploded from within him, and he tore the tape from her mouth. Her lips were deep blue. *Damn it. The little bitch can't die. Not yet.*

Bending his head to her chest, he ripped the bra from her full bosom and listened. Lexy caught a breath from somewhere and—yes! There it was: a faint, but steady heartbeat hollow to his ear. It had almost gone too far. Almost.

He nuzzled Lexy, touched her breasts. The pleasure would still be his. The opportunity remained perfect, and there was no reason to lose the moment.

Stepping from the bed, he lifted Mike Crosby from the floor and propped him on the loveseat facing the bed. Mike would be his silent but appreciative audience, his own special observer.

No reason to lose the moment at all.

CHAPTER-57

The icy-cold beer winked at Gavin from the small patio table, and he didn't ignore the provocative invite. "This beats the hell out of murder scenes and dead bodies," he pointed out to Stella while they sat quietly on the small terrace just off their stateroom.

"I believe you're right on that one," she said as they both marveled at the purple and orange beginnings of a Southern Caribbean sunset.

He had just returned from walking Louise and Barbara to their rooms, and made them promise to keep the doors locked at all times, telling them to make sure they fastened the safety chains. He didn't have to tell them twice.

Michigan rarely displayed these kinds of sunsets, and he couldn't help enjoying it just a little. That demented, murdering bastard wasn't going to ruin everything. The killer had made shambles out of what should have been one of the most joyous weeks of his and Stella's life. But Gavin could, and would, steal back some of the hijacked happiness. The sunset was a great beginning. So was his wife.

Still, he'd never be able to imagine this week without thinking of Liz's and Lynn's horrible deaths. Somber convictions of guilt traveled through him like pulses of physical pain except there was no pill to help dull the throbbing reminder of friends lost. Maybe Lynn and Liz would still be alive if he hadn't invited them on this damned cruise. Maybe it was his fault they were dead. He struggled against ill-willed postures that wanted a pound of flesh.

His flesh.

They pressed in, but Gavin dismissed them almost as soon as they appeared. That unconscionable sociopath had killed Liz and Lynn, not him.

He understood crimes of passion, at least some; they were as old as Cain and Abel. People sometimes snapped. But planned homicides that made Genghis Khan look like Gandhi were another story. Those killers held no regard for human life, and he didn't get that part. They just took what they wanted. Maybe what they needed.

Getting older had some perks, but the idea that aging was golden was fantasy. Maybe he was just getting too old for this crap. The stress was more intense, and God knew he couldn't take the physical part anymore.

The old days were better. Not nearly as many sickos, gangs, and not as much senseless stuff. Maybe it was those damn video games, like some people thought.

At least there was comfort in the fact that his three folks were working these murders, especially Manny. He hated that the boy never learned to relax much, that he was a bona fide, card-carrying workaholic, at times. Gavin was glad this was one of those times.

Stella reached for his hand. "Penny for your thoughts?"

"Only a penny?" He smiled at his wife of thirty-four years. She had a couple more wrinkles and maybe five more pounds than the day they were married, and her hair was more white than blond these days, but she still looked damn good.

She had put up with an inordinate amount of junk being the wife of a cop, then police chief. Life as a cop's wife was tough enough, but throw in the politics and, well . . . there had to be a special place in heaven for her.

"I was just thinking how things have changed over the years. How many more psychos are running around than before. How violent our society has become. There just isn't any respect for human life anymore."

"And how glad you are to be married to me, right?"

"That too," he laughed.

Stella's gaze was steady, and he knew she was reading the rest of the story on his face like a newspaper headline.

"Don't worry, honey," she said. "I know that this isn't what we bargained for with Mike's wedding week, but it is what it is. It's not your fault."

Nodding, he felt the gratitude that can only come from a marriage like theirs. She always seemed to know what he was really thinking. Sometimes that was a pain in the ass, but not today.

The beauty of their surroundings brought about another observation: the dichotomy between God's natural beauty and the hideous ugliness epitomized by these murders. Amazing that both could exist in the same world. He'd been a cop for thirty-five years and still wasn't sure how to get his mind around that concept.

The knock on the door interrupted his thoughts. He would never have heard it if they hadn't propped open the balcony door.

Never giving fate a thought, he got up from the chair, beer in hand, walked to the cabin door, and pulled it open.

Fate could be, and often was, a two-edged sword. Sometimes it labored for you, and you won the lotto or captured the heart of the only lover you ever pined for. Other times, it took your soul and ripped it into so many miserable pieces. Fate had no allies or enemies, it just was.

Gavin Crosby stared into the intense eyes of fate and instantly wished it had been an ally.

CHAPTER-58

Manny recorded the despondency on Gavin's jowly face. For one fleeting instant, he could have been Methuselah's older brother. He'd never seen that look from his boss before. He was pretty sure he didn't want to see it again. Manny felt Gavin's heart sink.

"What is it? What's wrong Manny?" Dread vibrated through his gruff voice. "Has he done it again, the killer I mean?"

Manny shook his head. "No, at least not yet." He looked his boss square in the face. "But we have a warning that he's going to kill again. He left a poem on the mirror of Detective Perez's bathroom. Alex found a sliver of wax on the floor and figured out the rest from there. All we had to do was steam up the bathroom mirror. The message was, ahh . . ." Manny's eyes dropped to the floor as he studied his sandals.

"This guy's no Robert Frost, so spit it out. What did it say, the poem?"

Hesitating, he slowly reached into the front pocket of his khaki shorts and pulled out a piece of paper with the Carousel crest stamped in the corner.

The note still smelled of the black felt pen.

Gavin read the big, block letters, and his face

drained of color. "Did you talk to Mike?"

"Mike and Lexy are fine. Sophie called to check on them, and she spoke to Mike. I tried to call you and Stella, but you didn't answer."

"The phone stopped ringing before I got to it."

"All due respect, Chief, you scared the hell out of me. I thought, well, that you and Stella might be in trouble," his voice trailed off.

"I'm sorry. I didn't mean to worry you." He looked at Manny, and his faced softened. "Thanks for worrying."

The chief motioned Manny through the door, and he followed him to the vanity near the TV. Gavin put the ship-issued 9mm in his waistband. "If this jerk off wants to dance, he picked the wrong band."

Manny clapped his boss on the shoulder.

CHAPTER-59

Agent Corner stood in the hall with the three Lansing cops outside Gavin's closed cabin door. He wished he could see or sense what they were thinking. Too many options and not enough time to second-guess a wrong choice. Not exactly what the doctor ordered.

They looked tired, maybe more than tired, and especially Manny.

He had gotten a sense of how hard Williams would throw himself into this case, but the Lansing detective had run a much harder race than Corner had expected. Talent and hard work rarely existed in combination these days.

Manny looked back at the agent. "What?"

"You look like hell."

"Well, thank you. That's what I get for going on a damn vacation."

"Actually, he looks like this most of the time," grinned Sophie.

"Thanks for your kind words."

"Any time. That's why I'm here."

The four slowly settled into an uncomfortable silence. Corner had been in more than a few of these gatherings, and his experience told him that no one wanted to contemplate—or worse, take responsibility for—the next decision. Disregarding this conversation, however, wasn't an option. It was like a persistent bill collector; at some point, you had to answer the phone.

Gavin started. "Now what? Do we put everyone in the same suite until this is over?"

"I don't like that idea," stated Manny. "If everyone is in the same place, one attack is all he would need to make us go bye-bye."

"Yeah, but what about that divide and conquer thing?" asked Sophie.

"That could be what he wants," said Corner.

"I don't know. He likes to kill up close and personal, but if he does have a plan we don't understand, we could play right into his hands by putting everyone together," said Manny.

Sophie bit her lip and frowned. "But if we don't gather a little strength in numbers, are we being set up to be picked off, one-by-one?"

"He might try, but this just might be one of those best-guess things. All I know is that we need to make sure everyone is as safe as possible, especially the Crosbys," said Corner.

Gavin spoke. "Okay. Let's, at least, double up and put four to a room. We can get security to stand watch and make sure there is at least one gun in each room. It's not what the captain or Carousel wants, but it's too dangerous not to take the next step."

"Awesome. Josh can bunk with Randy and me. I'll make Randy sleep on the floor."

"Thanks for the offer, but I . . . ahh . . . well, Max will need a place."

"That's a thought. Never been with three men in the same room, all night at least."

"Sophie!" barked Gavin.

"Sorry, boss. Just trying to help."

"Okay. I'll check with the captain and see if we can rustle up a few suites instead of these one-bedroom deals. You're right; he won't like it, but he'll do it," said Josh.

Gavin looked at Agent Corner and shook his head. "I hate this." Gavin wiped his hand across his chin and shrugged. "But, as my wife says, it is what it is." He reached for the door handle. "I'm going to tell Stella and then call Mike and Lexy to have them come to our cabin until we get something different."

"One more thing," Corner said. "I want you all to get some rest." His eyes fixed on Manny. "Some of Richardson's people are patrolling the ship and the rest of his staff is on high alert. I won't get the forensic results back for a while, and you and Sophie haven't really slept in the last twenty-four hours. You won't do this investigation or the rest of us any good if you are out on your feet. Go get some shuteye, and I'll call you when I have new accommodations—that's an order."

"You don't have to tell me twice," said Sophie. "Josh, you coming?"

Manny started to protest, but Corner's gaze discouraged the Lansing detective from any further objection. "Okay, okay. What about you, Josh?"

"I'm going to do the same, right after I talk to the captain, and don't worry about me." He gave Manny a big brother look. "You need to do this because you have to be one-hundred percent ready when we get the break we need. We all do. Got it?"

Manny pressed his lips together. "All right. I'll go take a nap. Happy?"

"No, but it will have to do," responded Corner.

CHAPTER-60

Knocking at the door of his cabin, Manny waited for Louise to open it. Each second the door went unanswered, his anxiety escalated. Apprehension was taunting him like an older sister, and he was seconds from breaking down the door when the safety chain rattled and the door swung open. He let go of the breath he was unconsciously holding as Louise grabbed and hugged him in the same motion. He could feel her heart thundering through her vice-like grip while she burrowed her head under his chin. The natural scent of her hair engulfed his senses, and he closed his eyes in appreciation.

"I hate it when you don't let me know you're okay. You should have stopped by."

Manny held her close. "I'm sorry, honey, but that freak threatened the Crosbys and we had to make sure everyone was safe. There was just no time. I'm sorry, really."

She mumbled something about being an asshole, and he smiled.

"Don't do that again. I didn't know what was going on and that scared me." She released her grip on her husband, and they locked eyes. Manny could see remnants of an emotion she would never be comfortable feeling.

"I won't. I promise."

Louise searched his face with the intense stare of a CIA interrogator. She kissed him on the mouth, and they stepped back into the room.

"By the way, Agent Corner called and told me to remind you that you're to take some time off, and he'll call you in a few hours. He said you promised."

"I'm going to try, honey. I'm tired, but I need the mind to cooperate." He slipped out of his sandals. "We think it will be safer if we all bunk up with another couple and then have the ship's security provide guards."

Louise nodded. "Okay. That makes me a little nervous, but you guys are the experts." She frowned and shifted her weight. "Could he be whacked out enough to try something?"

"I really don't think so. He thrives on the one-on-one ritual to get his kicks, so an attack on a group would be totally out of his MO." Manny didn't mention that the killer's methods had already evolved, or maybe devolved.

Louise shrugged. "What do we do now?"

"Corner will call back when he gets the room arrangements so there isn't much to do until then."

She hugged him again. "Tell you what. I'll call the restaurant and order a couple of steaks with all of the fixings, and you can get into the shower. We'll just have a nice, quiet dinner in here so you can get some rest."

"Better make it three, if you're going to eat," he winked. "And that shower thing is the best idea I've heard today."

****

Gavin brought his wife up-to-date and told her he was going to have Mike and Lexy come to their cabin and wait until Corner called with new rooms.

"Maybe you should go get them. You have a gun, and they don't," said Stella with more than a little concern in her voice.

"Good idea. Go ahead and call them and tell them I'll be there to get them as soon as they're ready."

Stella reached for the phone as Gavin walked out to the balcony to retrieve his sandals and, in the process, catch one more glimpse of the glowing sunset. But there was another reason he left the room. Some of his courage had slipped out the back, and he needed to find it.

For one of the first times he could remember, he was afraid. Not for himself so much, but for Stella, Mike, and Lexy. He had never really had his family threatened, definitely not like this, in all of his years as a cop. This madman was different, and he wondered if the killer even knew what was coming next. He felt for the 9mm and hoped this move was the right one.

The balcony door slammed open and Stella hurried through, barely able to speak. "Gavin, there's no answer at Mike's room."

"Lock the door, Stella." He pushed past his wife and bolted through the cabin door, gun in hand, hoping, praying everything was fine, that the killer was simply playing mind games. Maybe Lexy and Mike were out on the verandah. But his hope was swallowed by the petrifying panic running through his gut.

CHAPTER-61

John Eberle was stretched halfway through the door of his cabin, looking both ways for any signs of commotion. He didn't see any and was thankful.

No telling what all that running and shouting had been about a few hours ago, and frankly, he didn't give a rat's ass. It was lobster night, and he had no intentions of missing his favorite cruise meal. God willing, he might even have three of them.

After a few steps down the hall, he swore. He had forgotten to take his pill. The magic one. Dinner would be a painful excursion without his acid-reflux medication. Heartburn had been an uncomfortable way of life for him until ten years ago when he discovered acid inhibitors. If his seventy-six-year-old body couldn't handle the surgery to correct his hiatal hernia, then the medicine was the next best thing.

"First the weenie, then the joints, then the guts, then the mind," he groaned.

He retreated inside and shuffled to the bathroom. His thin, arthritic hands struggled with the foil package until he finally released the pink, pain-saving tablet from its sealed prison.

"Safety packs, my ass," he complained, while

downing the pill with a shaking glass of water.

As he turned away to leave the room, he caught the reflection of an old man in the mirror and wondered when the change had happened. He hated sneaky and getting old was just that. He didn't feel like the wrinkled, age-spotted portrait flashing back at him.

Occasionally, his hands didn't work so well, and at other times, he had to hit the head ten times a day. Maybe he felt it a little then. And sometimes, when he lay awake at night for hours on end, and couldn't do a damn thing about it. Maybe then too.

He gingerly stepped out of the bathroom and looked around to make sure he hadn't forgotten anything else. His weary eyes settled on the navy-blue suitcase still resting on the vanity. Martha, his wife, had bought it about five years ago, when they had decided to start traveling.

Beautiful Martha.

There are lots of things you don't experience living on the farm in Bristol, Tennessee, and they had been ready to broaden their horizons. The farm life had been a good one, but not the fast lane for sure. They'd wanted to see some of the world they read about or saw on the travel shows. Martha had always wanted to go on a cruise, so they'd gone.

The Western Caribbean voyage had been a wonderful time. In fact, it had been so good, they planned another one six months down the road. This time they would travel in style and see the Southern Caribbean.

But Martha would never see the rich teal waters and white sandy beaches of St. Thomas or the Divi Divi trees of Aruba.

A single, lonely tear ambled down his wrinkled cheek as he remembered how that damned cancer hadn't taken no for an answer. It had grown so fast. Like hungry garden weeds after a warm summer rain. The doctors called it one of the most aggressive forms of breast cancer they had ever seen. They just couldn't stop it. The greedy son of a bitch wouldn't give her one more trip, and one more is all she really wanted.

His wife of fifty-one years had been laid to rest the day they were supposed to embark on that next cruise. He'd promised himself, after she passed, that he would take a couple trips a year and tell her all about them. It was the least he could do.

"This has been a good one, honey. A little excitement with two folks dyin' from heart attacks, but it's been a good trip, aside from that," he whispered, hoping she heard.

He pulled the handle of the heavy door, wincing until it swung open. He stopped dead in his wobbling tracks and blinked, but the sight before him was still there. Bigger than life.

A tall, muscular man was emerging from the young couple's room across the hall. Not that unusual, except crimson streaks of blood ran down his left bicep and on the sleeve of his yellow island shirt. The big man looked at John with contempt he'd never seen. His dark gaze burned a hole directly into Eberle's head.

This giant means to kill me.

Then, as if he were reading the old man's mind, the big man relaxed his stare and smiled. "Have a good one, old timer." He turned aft and headed down the hall, whistling.

Eberle stood still for a moment as his pulse

gained some semblance of normalcy.

He had spent time in Vietnam. He had seen things, but had never been as afraid of dying like he had been thirty seconds before.

Putting his hand on his heart, he risked a look at the front of his shorts. As he sighed in relief, Eberle was struck with a terrible, overpowering thought.

Where did the blood come from and what did he do to those nice honeymooners?

CHAPTER-62

Running his hand over his freshly shaven face, Manny realized he did feel a little better, but he was still beat. Even after the hot shower. The only real cure for what ailed him now was a few hours of hard sleep, and this murdering bastard in the brig. Or better yet, in the morgue.

And what of Louise? The last few weeks hadn't been a picnic for her. This week was supposed to be a no-brainer, a super vacation that would overshadow the delayed mammogram results.

Dinner at the swank Supper Club would have helped them both get their minds off that one, but not tonight. Maybe the only thing worse than not getting some R & R, aside from being keelhauled, was disappointing her.

No rest for the weary.

He ran fingers absently through his soaked hair and his thoughts swarmed to the message the killer had written on Christina Perez's mirror. Gavin and Stella were okay, so far. He wondered if Sophie had checked on Mike and Lexy again. He would call them too when he got dressed, just to make sure.

But the message could have been just a con, a brain screw. For all they really knew, the poem could have been some dark, derisive misdirection .

. . part of the killer's perverse, deadly game.

Manny threw on a pair of gym shorts and a tank top and stepped out of the tiny bathroom just in time to hear the knock on the door. He reached for the 9mm and glanced at Louise, who had risen from the bed.

"Must be dinner," she declared.

He nodded and looked through the door's peephole to confirm. He dropped his gun behind his leg, unlocked and opened the door quickly. The startled look on the server's face almost caused Manny to laugh out loud.

"Sorry. Just wanted to make sure it was you."

"Yes sir." The server rolled the cart into the room. "Will there be anything else?"

"No, not now, thank you," he answered, glancing both ways down the hall.

"Wait." Louise reached past Manny and handed the server a five-dollar bill.

Manny began to close the door, when he noticed Alex and two of the ship's security staff coming down the hall in his direction. Manny waited, reading their body language and not liking what he saw.

Alex stopped, looked at Manny, and then cleared his throat.

Manny's senses didn't have to work overtime on this one. Alex wasn't here for a cup of coffee.

"Tell me I'm wrong, that he didn't kill again."

"We thought they were safe. It happened about twenty minutes—"

"Thought who was safe?" Manny interrupted.

"These two men will stay here, but you need to come to room 6214 and see for yourself. We may have a witness."

The pit of Manny's stomach turned to ice. For

a moment, he couldn't feel anything, like a 400-pound wrestler was standing on his chest.

But reality screamed and put him in motion. He turned to Louise. "Lock the door and don't open it for anyone, not even these two guards." Then he pressed past Alex, hurrying down the hall to Mike and Lexy's cabin.

CHAPTER-63

The energetic knock on Ethel Manis's door startled her. She had just finished her room service meal of double-cheese pizza and diet pop. Thank God her prolonged bout with seasickness was over. She didn't think food could taste this good.

Could it be him?

She didn't know another soul on the ship. The room steward had already come to roll down her bed and leave one of those tasty little chocolate mints on her fluffed pillow. He knew she was in for the night. There could be only one explanation and that enlightenment raised her hopeful heart.

Her son.

She pulled her stocky frame from the edge of the bed and waddled to the door, glancing at the mirror as she went by. She couldn't see much. Mostly lighted shadows, but she knew she didn't look pretty. She didn't care, not really. She wasn't here for a damned beauty contest.

Her stubby fingers dragged the chain away from the safety lock, and she yanked open the door. Standing in front of her was a tall man with massive arms and chest. It looked like him. She tried to focus on his face, but the combination of her poor eyesight and long shadows hanging in the narrow hallway diluted any clear look she might have otherwise had.

"Is that you son? Is that you? Speak to your old ma. Bobby?"

The silence seemed to have a mind of its own as Ethel waited for the man who stood quietly in her doorway to answer.

"Yes, Mother. It's me. Aren't you going to invite me in? It's been a long time."

The old woman couldn't believe her ears. It had been an eternity since she heard her son's voice. She knew everything about it. Everything. The high, the low, and even the subtle lisp. Ethel closed her eyes. She had rehearsed this blissful moment for what seemed like a lifetime. But now she was heartsick. The deep, intelligent voice belonging to the man at her door wasn't her son.

A mother knows.

"I don't know who you are, but you ain't no son of mine; you ain't Bobby Peppercorn." Bitter disappointment ripped at her very soul. "This is a cruel joke on a sick, old woman, and I hope you rot in hell."

She started to close the door, but it was too late. A strong right hand stopped it from swinging shut, and the big man stepped into the room, shoving her hard toward the bed.

Her body throbbed with pain. But the pain seemed to sharpen her senses. Her mind grew bright with the realization that the cancer robbing her body of life wasn't going to be her demise. It would never have the chance.

Ethel's bad eyes focused enough to watch him reach for the empty, plastic soda bottle. He pulled the Smith and Wesson from his waistband.

She wasn't going to see her son after all. Her

heart broke again.

"Oh, you're my mother, all right. You have helped me to develop into the man I am today," her visitor stated. "Don't you remember me? We used to talk so much." He threw back his head and laughed.

Ethel shook. She did remember.

A mother's secrets.

She heard him place the barrel of the gun into the plastic bottle and felt it rest against her temple. Ethel clutched the letter in her shirt pocket.

He pulled the trigger.

The makeshift suppressor did its job. A muffled *mmmfffffttt* sounded as the right side of Ethel's face detached from her shattered skull.

****

He gazed at the dead woman's disfigured face as he wiped the blood and gray matter from his hand and gun. "Yes, dear Ethel. More of a mother to me than you will ever know."

CHAPTER-64

Manny saw that Agent Corner stood talking to Richardson and Captain Serafini in front of room 6214. The three were involved in a lively discussion. The FBI agent was extremely animated and appeared to be far more than agitated as he addressed Richardson and the captain. Whatever the conversation entailed, the FBI agent was getting his way.

When Corner noticed him, the agent's look turned from angry to grave. Manny could tell that he had wanted to hide his initial reaction, but it was too late. Manny saw everything in a blink of an eye. The agent's face told him all he needed, or for that matter, wanted to know. Manny's shoulders slumped.

"What happened? Where are Mike and Lexy?" he said softly.

Corner glanced at the other two men and then back to him, hesitated, and spoke.

"Mike is in the infirmary with a nasty concussion and multiple skull fractures. Dr. Kristoff says he got lucky. It could've been much worse. He'll have some side effects for a few months, but will be fine in the long run. At least physically. Tough kid."

The other two men remained silent as Agent

Corner rubbed the back of his neck. "Lexy wasn't so fortunate. She was . . . raped and bitten like the others."

Corner swallowed hard, causing a deep chill to run through Manny's spine. He hated what the agent was going to say next.

"I'm sorry Manny. She . . . she didn't make it."

Instinct caused Manny to reach for the door. He had to see for himself.

His hand hesitated on the silver handle while he sought some kind of purchase for the twisting realities spinning a tale he didn't want to accept.

It had only been days ago that Lexy and Mike had stood in front of the preacher and recited their vows. She was beautiful and so full of life, so happy. She wanted to be a mom, a wife. Do the PTA thing.

Tears are not uncommon in a marriage ceremony, but Lexy's had been the real thing, the kind that showered the wedding guests with genuine joy.

Till death do us part.

First Liz and now Lexy? He was going to wake up any second. He had to . . . because he wasn't sure he could take anymore.

The knob began to groan and turn in his hand. "Damn it," he sighed softly. "I should have known. We should have checked on them after Sophie called."

"You can't blame yourself, Detective. We all should have done something. Mike answered the phone and said he was fine. He's a cop, for God's sake. We all thought they were okay. How could you have known? You can't be there every time. It doesn't work that way, never has."

Corner gently placed his hand on Manny's

arm, "Manny, Max is inside going over the room. You'll just be in his way. Besides, what good would it do?"

The reality of what Corner said began to sink into another level. A sorrowful welling grew from the depths of Manny's gut, and he blinked away tears.

She had been just twenty-five years old, and now it was over. Not only over, but she had been treated like some meaningless piece of trash. And what about Mike? What could ever heal the scars that Lexy's murder had caused?

"Do Gavin and Stella know?" he whispered.

"Yeah, they do. Gavin is the one who thought there might be something wrong. When they didn't answer the phone or the door, he came to my room."

"Where are they?"

"Sophie's with them in the infirmary. They're doing as well as can be expected. The Doc gave them a sedative and they're resting, but they won't leave Mike's side."

Alex spoke through the silence. "I know you want to see them, but let them rest awhile and talk to them later. Besides, we need you on this."

Standing by the door, head bowed, he sought desperately to push the "on" button for detective mode and to leave personal feelings fighting for another time.

It was so hard. These murders were personal. The killer had seen to that. He clenched his teeth, removed his hand from the handle, and wiped his eyes. "How did this happen? We called them and they were fine."

"We think he may have been in the room with them when Sophie called," said Corner.

"Why would you think that?"

"A witness saw a man leaving their room no more than thirty minutes after we called. To have time to do what he did, he was probably there. I assume he was holding them at gunpoint. There was a small circular bruise on Mike's head, consistent with a gun barrel, indicating that the killer was pressing the weapon hard against his head."

The notion struck Manny that they all, himself included, seemed to be rats in a complex maze trying to find their way to some gratifying conclusion. Maybe that's what the killer was trying to promote: more confusion and no clear path to the end, just oblique teasing that led to nowhere and everywhere.

The shadows that separated "special detective" from "heartbroken friend" further dissipated as Manny's anger and sorrow began to recede. For now, he needed to focus on catching this lunatic asshole. He was ready.

"Where is this witness?"

Agent Corner turned toward the stateroom only a few steps across the hall.

"It's time you met Mr. John Eberle."

CHAPTER-65

Shaking the elderly man's boney hand, Manny sized up the one who said he saw Mike's attacker, Lexy's killer. Eberle returned the scrutiny with an even gaze of his own, and Manny thought that was good. He might be advanced in years, but Manny suspected Eberle had all of his marbles, and for that, he was grateful. Sound mind equaled solid description.

"I want you to tell Detective Williams what you told us," said Agent Corner. He turned toward the captain and Richardson. "But first, the good Captain and Chief Richardson have agreed that it is time to go room-to-room and see what we can see. Right?"

The doubtful look sprouting on the two cruise-ship employees confirmed to Manny what the discussion had been about just before he had arrived.

They didn't want to panic or inconvenience the rest of their guests, but Agent Corner was no longer concerned with that line of thinking. Manny could tell from the inflection in his voice that he flat out didn't care. They had a killer, a monster to catch.

Manny, Corner, and Eberle stood outside the old man's cabin as the others disappeared down the hall to mobilize the search. The witness glanced nervously toward one end of the hallway and then back. He reminded Manny of a grade-school kid checking to make sure no cars were coming before he crossed the street.

Eberle shifted his weight nervously. His knee joint cracked and sounded like a small-caliber gunshot.

Manny said. "That was a good one."

Eberle bowed his head and snorted a small laugh. "Almost as loud as those farts I get after eatin' a couple of those hotdogs with the extra sauerkraut."

"That'll do it," smiled Manny. Eberle was a good man. He felt a little better.

The three settled into a comfortable silence before Manny broke it.

"John, what did you see?"

Eberle hesitated. Whatever he had seen had frightened him. Manny noticed the military tattoo on the old man's forearm. Eberle was a veteran, and Manny bet he had served in Viet Nam. Vets from that war didn't scare easily. Most of them had seen far too many inhuman acts to be alarmed by anything on a cruise ship.

"I'll tell you again, if it'll help. Those are good kids. They always said hey and had a smile for this old man, a real one."

Then Eberle launched into his story for the second time. He paused when he spoke of the blood on the big man's arm and shirt. He was obviously affected by it, but more by its source. He finished his account of his meeting with the killer and took in a shaky breath.

"I could see his wheels turnin'. I thought he was going to punch my ticket. It scared the hell out of me."

Manny nodded and said nothing.

"Ya know. It was almost like he wanted me to tell you what I saw. I think that's the only reason I'm talkin' to you now."

"You could be right."

Manny asked a couple of clarifying questions about the killer's height and build, then a couple more about his attire. Eberle answered without hesitation. That was good.

His pulse quickened as a small ember of hope began to glow in his otherwise pensive thoughts. Most cases are broken wide open because someone saw something and was brave enough to come forward. Manny thought this could be the break they needed. Desperately needed. "Are you willing to look at photos of men on the ship when they're ready?"

Eberle nodded.

The two cops shook the gentleman's hand, and Manny thanked him for his bravado. John Eberle, with fading brown eyes, gazed at the two men. Their witness had something else to say.

"You know, Detectives, I started cruisin' after my wife passed with the thought of tellin' her about them when I got home. I know she's dead and it sounds goofy, but it's true. She loved the only one she got to go on, and it does my heart good to think, just maybe, she can hear my old chatterin' about the latest cruise and get somethin' out of it, you know?" His voice trailed to a soughing murmur as he searched Corner's face and then Manny's. "Does that make me crazy?"

"John, that's about the sanest thing I've heard on this cruise." Manny answered, putting his hand on the old man's shoulder.

Eberle gave him a grateful smile. "I just wanted you to know that even though I talk to my dead wife, I saw what I saw."

The old man looked down at the floor and then back to Manny. "I hope you get this devil. Anyone that would hurt a smart young couple like that needs to find his place in hell real fast."

"He will, trust me." Manny saw the trepidation and sadness in the old man's eyes, and it mated with his own grief. *Sorrow has no generation or gender gap*, Manny thought. *It exists completely without prejudice.*

CHAPTER-66

Josh Corner sat on the edge of his loveseat, dressed only in red boxers, and greedily gulped the last morsel of New York strip swimming in a generous pool of steak sauce. He had forgotten to eat all day and now, at 9 p.m., he had finally gotten to enjoy a cruise ship meal.

He wasn't sure if it was because he was so hungry or that the food was really that good, but it tasted like the best meal he had ever eaten. Maybe it was.

Staring at the empty platter, he thought—just for a second—against licking it, then did it anyway. Next, he lifted the two pieces of raspberry cheesecake from the tray and dug in. Moments later, the desserts were a memory and so was Josh Corner's hunger.

A shower and a good meal were just what he needed. He stretched back on the bed and closed his eyes to absorb the last couple of hours.

Captain Serafini had called and said there were no suites available for the rest of Lansing's finest. The cruise was unusually full. He apologized and offered more security guards for each room.

Corner thanked him and hung up the phone believing the extra security wouldn't be necessary because the killer had already made good on his promise. The Crosbys had indeed heard the bell toll. Their lives would never be the same. But more guards couldn't hurt.

Richardson had stopped by his cabin to tell him that they had no luck going door-to-door. There were just too many cabins with no one home, reminding Corner that this was a cruise ship and people had things to do, bars to frequent, shows to attend, and sun to worship.

A couple of folks had mentioned to Richardson that they had seen a man like he described, but didn't know where his cabin was. One woman, who traveled the excursion in Dominica where the tour guide was killed, said she had spoken with a tall, well-built man on the pier. She said his eyes bored right through her and made her feel uncomfortable. That he was creepy, but didn't know where his room was.

He reached for the second pillow and stuffed it under his head. The next thing to explore was the forensics reports, and they wouldn't be back from the ERT lab for a few hours. So until then, he was going to get some sleep. At least try.

He stretched out on the bed and his mind drifted back to Lexy's face. He was helpless to stop it. She had been bitten almost beyond recognition and strangled so intently that her eyes were virtually blood-soaked. He had never seen petechial hemorrhaging like that before and didn't want to see it again. He locked his hands behind his head and tried to concentrate on something else, anything else. Sometimes he hated this job. It did things to a man.

Rolling over, he found himself hoping the others were having better luck trying to get some rest. A tiny smile forged its way to life at the thought of Manny Williams trying to shut down for a few hours. That was totally against his nature, but he knew the Lansing cop needed some time off, and he hoped Manny could get the Crosbys off his mind long enough to make it work. Now was the time, because the bases were covered until the next batter stepped to the plate.

His eyes began to droop, and then he went out.

****

Two hours after Agent Corner had fallen into a deep, exhausted sleep, the loud ringing woke him with a jerk. He instinctively reached for his gun, blinking himself awake.

It took a few seconds to remember where he was and what the ringing meant. He stumbled from his bed and answered the phone on the fourth ring.

"Hello," he muttered. "This better be damned good."

At first, no one spoke. Quiet, distant breathing passed through the phone like a summer breeze.

His pulse quickened, "Who is this? I hope this isn't some asinine prank. I can trace this—"

"Agent Corner?" The deep voice carried a heavy Latin accent, and he had heard it before. His antennas were on hardcore alert.

"Yes. This is Agent Corner," he responded calmly. "Who is this?"

"I'm sorry to disturb you, but this is First Officer Pena, and we have received some faxed information for you. It is from your office in Miami and is marked urgent. Should I have it delivered right away?"

He stared at the phone in frustration. His imagination had just taken a trip on the Good Ship Lollipop, and he had to bring her quickly back to the pier. He kicked himself for his lack of professional control.

"Agent Corner?"

"Yes, First Officer Pena, please have it brought to me at once. Thank you."

He hung up the phone and sat back on the bed. This was going to be another long night. He dialed room service and ordered a pot of vanilla bean espresso and four bowls of chocolate melting cake.

He reached for the phone again and dialed Manny's room.

A long night indeed.

CHAPTER-67

The CD player blasted out a classic rock tune that seemed appropriate ambiance for the killer's mood. Steppenwolf hammered a driving beat as the lyrics coursed through the cabin.

A true nature's child . . . Born to be wild, Born to be wild.

The partially eaten BLT and large dill pickle offered an interesting mingle with the rest of the aromas spattered across the room. Shoe polish, menthol shaving cream, and spicy aftershave contributed to the hodge-podge of odors.

But the imposing figure that was Eli Jenkins hardly noticed as his thoughts ran deep. He was gripped with a single purpose.

Dressed in a black tank top, his stout legs were covered in full-length army fatigues. His high-top boots gleamed like buffed obsidian. The laces were in perfect tension, and the length of each lace between the eyelets was precise.

Small, dark patches of shoe polish gathered below each eye. Jenkins's freshly shaved head and face glowed as steady streams of light reflected against congregating perspiration. No demon born from hell ever looked more frightening.

But there was no arrogant smile pursing his lips. No expression inhabited his black, unforgiving eyes. He was all business. It was as it should be. The time had finally arrived. And he was ready. Everyone was born to a purpose, and what came next was the very reason he had come into existence.

It's not often one is allowed the opportunity to do what I am going to do next.

He would no longer have to shroud his intent with disguise and deceit. He had remained hidden for all of these months, and now it was near the appointed time to inform the world what Eli Jenkins was about.

They would discover that God wasn't found in an ancient, 5,000-year-old book, but in raw, unrestrained power. His kind of power.

The license to give and take life made gods, not notions of love, sacrifice, and kindness. He had seen the effect of his actions in the faces of his victims when they left this world. That was real power.

The black diving watch on his wrist said it was 10:59. Right on schedule.

Pulling the backpack over to his side, he checked and rechecked its contents. Once satisfied, he zipped it and placed it on the floor next to the bed.

The opened balcony door allowed the night's humidity to enter. The smell of the ocean was strong as he listened to the breaking waves keep steady time against the cruise ship's hull.

This is all for me, this stage, this audience. I won't disappoint.

After ten minutes, he pulled the door shut, turned down the music, plugged in special earphones, and flipped off the room's lights.

Jenkins stood staring out the window, as still

as a rock. Just a few hours to go and the prize would be his. No one could stop him or what was predestined.

He felt like a child on his birthday.

As he closed his eyes and relaxed his body, he heard it. At some indefinable time between the world of the unconscious and the conscious, the voice spoke.

For one brief, uneasy—maybe even sickening—moment, he heard Robert Peppercorn's plea for freedom, for deliverance.

With a sharp flex of Jenkins's will, Peppercorn disappeared like a wisp of smoke.

Jenkins had worked too hard to allow that wormy, feeble-willed punk back in control. Hell would freeze over first. He smiled again. He knew a little about hell.

CHAPTER-68

After hanging up the phone, Manny pulled on shorts and a red tee shirt. He shuffled to the room's loveseat and tried to stuff his wide feet into his sandals. They wouldn't go. Trying again, he bent the toenail on his big toe back far enough to get his attention. He scowled and looked down, finally realizing that Louise's pink-flowered flip-flops weren't going to stretch nearly enough for his EEEE wide, size ten-and-one-half feet. A tired grin broadened his unshaven face. They wouldn't go very well with the rest of his outfit anyway.

He continued to rub the sleep out of his eyes while he located his watch and wallet. Corner had let him know that more information had come in from Miami, and his presence was requested to go over the fine print. He also had said they would be staying in their original rooms, but with more security. Manny was grateful, but wasn't sure it was a problem anymore. Josh had agreed, but had taken the liberty of doubling up the security in the infirmary. No more trouble for Gavin's family. They'd been scorched enough.

The Crosbys. He was trying to be a good cop, to get the personal out of the way and focus on the investigation. But how could he really? He knew that the unspeakable pain of the past few hours could never leave.

But exhaustion has no allegiance or emotion. Proving an ally this time, Manny had actually slept some. A couple hours were better than none.

A few moments later, *his* sandals firmly in place, he stepped through the cabin door, making sure it locked, nodded at the two security guards, and headed to Corner's room. Grogginess was now a memory, and the thought of possible new leads hastened his step.

Corner was waiting for him, espresso in hand. Manny gratefully accepted the coffee and sat down on the loveseat. A thick file of faxed documents sat on the round table and glared ominously at him. He returned the glare. It wasn't the first time that the evidence displayed reluctance, even disdain, at the prospect of speaking to him. In the end, though, the words and photos would converse with him. They always did.

"Well, at least you look awake. No super model, but awake."

"Almost, and bite me," Manny said, returning the agent's grin.

"Those your kids?"

Corner glanced at the faded picture of two grinning toddlers pressed in the middle of his tee and smiled an unguarded, affectionate grin.

"Charlie and Jake. Four and three. Best time in the whole world." Corner's smile was replaced with a shake of his head. "I don't see them enough. You know how this career thing is."

"That's the truth. And I know the feeling."

It was good that Corner was a family man. Loved ones put the checkmate on all of the other pieces that could steal your sanity, your soul.

Manny poured more coffee and saw there were

only two cups to go with the small pot of espresso. "When are the rest coming? It's going to be a little tight in here. Maybe we should go to the conference room."

Corner rubbed the back of his neck. "No one else is coming; at least for now. I want you to look at this stuff and see what you see."

Doubt billowed in Manny's eyes. "I'm not the forensic expert here. I think we need Tucker and Alex to help us analyze this information. Not to mention, Richardson will blow a gasket if he's not involved in this."

It was Corner's turn to fill his cup. He studied the black liquid and tested the Vanilla Delight. "I'll handle the others. I want to get your impressions. Your thoughts. I want to see how you interpret fresh info without anyone else's input. Just like yesterday when I gave you the incomplete files. You saw things. I want you to look closer. I bet you do your best work when you're alone, away from others and their opinions."

Manny paused and then slowly nodded his head. That was no surprise, at least to him. Things just seemed clearer when he was running solo. He *did* do his best work alone. The voices of the dead were easier to hear when it was quiet. They spoke, and he made sense of their petitions, their pleas. He didn't know where Corner was going with this, but he was right. "If that's what you want. I'll do it. How much time do I have?"

"I'm going to call a meeting at 6:30 a.m. sharp. You have until then. How much time you spend looking at the lab reports and pictures is up to you."

He rolled his eyes and ran his hand through his hair. "You're a jerk. You know I won't get any more sleep tonight."

Corner flashed his bright teeth and shoved a piece of cake in front of Manny, tossing him a fork.

"We won't have the blood DNA and fingerprint results until late morning after we get into Aruba. That information is being sent via courier from my office. But you have all of the pictures and updated reports from Liz's file, including new photos, and the murders in San Juan, St. Johns, and Dominica. Plus, you have the semi-completed files involving Lynn Casnovsky and the attack on Detective Perez. It was as good as the San Juan Police could do on such short notice."

Corner hesitated and picked up another, much thinner folder carrying the FBI seal. Manny watched him turn it around in his hands nervously.

"What?"

"Max put together the preliminary pictures and report from Mike and Lexy's room. They're in this one. Like I said before, it's not pretty."

The two cops locked eyes, and Corner asked him the most simple of questions. But it chilled him to the core.

"Are you ready for it?"

The same anguishing, gut-clenching feeling from the early evening came snarling back. Barbed wire seemed to have wrapped itself around Manny's insides.

Hell no, I'm not ready for it.

How could anyone be ready for the horrible images that lay hidden in that unholy file? But what choice did he have?

Damned if you do and damned if you don't. He hated the phrase, but it applied here. He took the file from Corner's hand.

"By the way, we still haven't heard back from Dr. Argyle about Peppercorn. His secretary is supposed to get back with us in the morning. He must have his cell phone turned off because we have been trying to call him too."

Manny nodded, stood up, and tucked the thick files under his arm.

"Aren't you going to eat your cake?" asked Corner.

"Knock yourself out. I'll see you at six."

He left the agent's room and headed back to his.

He greeted the guards and stepped into his cabin. He didn't know what was going on in Corner's mind, but decided he didn't care. He liked getting the files first. It was going to be a long night, but it was the least he could do.

Bending low, he kissed his still sleeping wife, then sat down to catch a killer.

This kind of work made him more . . . alive.

Cautious enthusiasm bordered his thoughts. They were getting close. Things were ready to pop. He could feel it. They had a witness and this information, plus they were in a closed environment on the ship. The noose had to be tightening for the madman.

He would reflect later on just how accurate his intuition had been. In just a few, short hours all hell was going to break loose aboard the *Ocean Duchess*.

CHAPTER-69

Louise's slow, metrical breathing was the only sound drifting through the cabin while Manny turned each page of the thick files with methodical purpose. He tried to coax the cryptic stories, hidden in each case, to a measured, resolute rhythm. Like a conductor reaching the part of the concerto where tempo was everything. The inflection identified what the composer wanted to unveil. But the music's effect on the audience was almost always a mystery. Even to the skilled leader of the band. The same was true with an evidence file. It would sing, but could he hear the melody? Could anyone?

For Manny, the challenge was to put an emotion and a cadence with each picture, each report. He wanted to feel how the killer felt, how the perp thought of himself: Mozart or Led Zeppelin. Did he hate or did he, in his own perverted way, love? Did he see himself as an angel of God? One of Evil's dominions? One thing was sure—the madman enjoyed the fear element of his ritual. He wondered what made this killer tremble. What caused him to shudder, to piss his pants in fear? Maybe nothing, maybe everything. But if he had to bet, he suspected no fear cruised this man's core and compassion was only a word in the dictionary.

There really wasn't anything new in the information provided for the first four victims. Everything looked virtually the same. Orderly. Precise. Each body found with the black rose in place. Each throat wrecked and upper bodies torn to shreds. It all meant something. But what? He wanted them to speak, to reveal their stories of living, of dying. He needed to hear clearly when the concert began.

While turning the pages, he thought how hard it was at times to equate the pictures and reports, wrapped in official government file folders, with a once living, feeling person. No problem with that tonight, however. Liz, Lex, and the others would always be more than the contents of these miserable files. Much more.

Manny pressed his finger against his lips and wondered what was inside that he hadn't seen the day before. There had to be a screw-up, no matter how trivial. No one is that good. That perfect. Every one of these bastards, somewhere along the line, makes a mistake.

After the third time through, he slammed the files on the table in disgust and frustration. He wasn't seeing it. There was something else here. He knew it. Could feel it. But what? Then again, what did he expect at 4:30 in the morning? Miracles? Walking on water wasn't in his repertoire.

He ran his hand through his hair again and tasted from the white mug. It didn't smell or taste as good as the vanilla espresso that Corner had, but it did the trick.

Lynn Casnovsky's file was next. He leaned in to get a better look at each graphic photo. Lynn had bruising on the left side of his face that showed definite signs of knuckle imprints. His jaw had been broken in four places, antimortem. He must have been in serious pain, and Manny felt the empathetic tug at his heart.

There was some bruising on the other side of his face, indicating that it had been squeezed or grabbed with tremendous pressure. That fit with the fact that his neck had been snapped like a twig in a storm. There were other postmortem injuries. A few broken bones earned from being thrown over the balcony and bounced off the lifeboat. There were also several places where the body had been stripped of tissue by sea scavengers. Not pretty.

A rookie detective could recognize what had happened here. The killer had hit Lynn in the jaw, maybe putting him out, then stole his life with a violent twist from behind.

That took raw strength or knowledge. But he didn't believe this guy had any military training. His best guess fortified what Tucker and Alex both thought; he killed with pure strength. Not someone to go toe-to-toe with.

The ocean had washed away anything else that Lynn could tell them. No fibers. No blood traces. No hair or epithelium to process. Just a clean, ocean-soaked body.

Manny tilted away from the table and thought about Sophie's affair with the dead man. He knew neither one of them would have guessed an ending like this.

Well no shit, Sherlock.

People wanted to manipulate the whens, the hows, and the whats—it gave them a sense of control of their destiny. If he had figured one thing out in life, it was that no one had command of anything. Control was some cruel illusion that fate hung overhead like just-out-of-reach fruit. Dauntingly close, but impossible to touch. Maybe it was a good thing that God ultimately controlled eternity. At least there would be justice.

He closed Lynn's file and gazed at the dark file that hid the secret to Lexy's last minutes alive. It whispered his name, and he heard it, all too clearly. Like Sirens beckoning the sailors of a lost ship.

He locked his hands behind his head and gazed intently at the curtain-covered terrace door. Small rays of early morning sun eluded the flat edges of the drape.

Am I ready for it?

If not him, not now, then who would Lexy speak to?

After a few moments, he began to open the file and then pulled his hand away. *Déjà vu* put up a roadblock that he wasn't sure he could get through. Opening Lexy's file reminded him of when he'd had to gather enough courage to review his late partner's homicide file. He'd put it off for two weeks, and when he'd finally opened the cover to Kyle Chavez's file, he hadn't eaten for two days afterward.

Memories of his ex-partner's death had faded mostly. But like old scars, the wounds heal, but things never look quite the same.

Kyle still represented recollections of a past that Manny was helpless to change, but maybe that's how it was supposed to be. Maybe men like him weren't supposed to forget. It's what drove them.

The Guardian of the Universe took a deep

breath and opened Lexy's folder.

CHAPTER-70

Sophie sat on the edge of the firm bed and laced her blue-and-white Reebok cross-trainers. She was dressed in jogger's shorts, a white tank top, and a fanny pack, decorated with the LPD insignia.

A Carousel cruise line baseball cap held her long hair in place. Randy had gotten the hat for her at one of the lavish shops in the ship's mall. He could be so sweet.

She ran slim fingers around the edge to make sure it was on straight, and was struck with an odd thought. *She* hadn't gone shopping on the ship. Not one iota. Usually she and shopping were as close as sun and light. That's what she got for being Manny's partner. He owed her for that one, big time. A new, expensive pair of shoes would work.

A wide yawn came to visit while she stood and stretched her legs and arms. She was tired, and the last couple days had taken something out of her. But she always got up before 5:30 and ran three miles. Always. She thought of the old milk commercial.

It does a body good.

She glanced over to her husband. Small snoring sounds filtered through the thick pillow that partially covered his face. At least one of them was getting some sleep.

The 9mm felt heavy as she patted her fanny pack, but she couldn't leave it behind.

You never know when you might get to shoot the balls off a serial killer.

She adjusted the barrel and snuck out of the stateroom.

One of the security guards asked her if she wanted company. She shook her head and flashed the weapon. "This little darling is all I need, but thanks."

With that, she headed for the jogging track on the Sun Deck. She knew it was going to be about the only time, at least until they docked later in Aruba, that she would have to herself. After what had happened last night, the investigation was going to intensify, if that were possible. Especially if Manny and she had anything to do with it.

Poor Lexy. Poor Mike. Poor Gavin and Stella. She lowered her head. Someone needed to remind her again why she wanted to be a cop.

The information from the FBI labs would be in Oranjestad this morning, and she was sure that the good-looking Agent Corner (and he *was* good-looking) wouldn't hesitate calling them together.

He *couldn't* waste any time. Who knew when the killing machine would strike next? She had never seen anything like this guy and never wanted to again.

Sophie stepped from the elevator and stretched her calves and thighs, watching the red sun peek over the horizon. She felt its immediate impact on the already warm, humid air and took a deep, sweet breath. It just plain felt good. Maybe there is something to that old saying that things would always be better in the morning.

So far, this daybreak was the complete antithesis to the previous evening. It had to be—because *nothing* felt good about last night.

The collective torture of the Crosby family danced vividly in her mind. No one should have to cope with the death of a child. It wasn't natural, not the way things were designed. And in a real sense, Lexy had been Gavin and Stella's child.

Lexy. Sophie had always thought herself tough as nails and able to handle most things. She had seen plenty in the back streets of Chinatown in San Francisco. But seeing Lexy like that, like some kind of slaughterhouse mistake, had gotten to her, really gotten to her. The truth of the atrocity was driven home even deeper as she sat with Gavin and Stella. They wore identical, vague, glassy-eyed expressions. These kinds of things didn't happen to them, their family.

The quick sob came out of nowhere and surprised her. Lexy had been such a good kid. She had been a perfect match for Mike. But that train had hit the tracks.

Hot anger flared as she began her thirty-lap trek around the tan oval that circled beneath the weather towers and wind indicators.

With each lap around the deserted track, Sophie picked up speed, trying to exorcise the images from the previous night. Maybe even some of the ones that Lynn and she had hidden together. She steered away from thoughts of Lynn. There was enough to deal with today.

Her skin glistened in the early morning air as she pushed herself near the limit.

Who said sweating was bad for women?

She was so lost in her own world that she

didn't notice the big man pull up beside her until she caught movement out of the corner of her eye.

He was outfitted in a black tank top and army fatigues. His long, powerful legs loped stride for stride with her.

"It's a beautiful morning, don't you think, Detective Lee?"

Her head jerked to the right. "How do you kno—?" Sophie stopped breathing. He had changed. He was in astonishing shape, but it was him. Robert Peppercorn was no longer missing.

She slammed on the brakes and reached for her zipped-up Glock, but she never really had a chance. He sprayed the chloroform directly into her face.

****

Jenkins lifted the small woman over his shoulder like a rag doll and headed for the food court. His body language revealed just how pleased he was with himself.

"Hey! What are you doing?"

He turned to see First Officer Pena, dressed in jogging gear, running toward him from some twenty feet away. He raised his left hand and pulled the trigger of the Smith and Wesson. Pena's white shirt turned to crimson as he hit the deck, dead from a shot to the heart. A toothy grin spread across Jenkins's damp face.

Oh, what the passengers on the Ocean Duchess *will write in their cruise journals after this day is over.*

CHAPTER-71

The darkened room squeezed him. Not because the walls were closing in, but because the entities surrounding him, touching him, embracing him, were growing. Manny sensed them changing, evolving, and he was afraid.

The absence of light in the room ordered him to feel lost, forsaken, and caused his fear to escalate. The blackness enveloped all reason and logic and kept them isolated from him like a prisoner in solitary confinement.

As the objects pressed closer, he realized he couldn't move. He could smell the aroma of rank death as hot, putrid breath scampered across his face. He tried to scream, but nothing came out. Fright whirled closer.

What the hell is this? Why am I here?

As if to answer his questions, out of nowhere and everywhere came a deep, deafening voice booming directly into his brain. "It's all your fault. The reason that everyone around you is dead is because you let them die. If you had been any kind of cop, they would ALL still be breathing. Some Guardian of the Universe."

Then the voice changed gender, and it was Liz's turn.

"Thanks loads, Williams. I wanted to do this

cruise thing, but you screwed that up and now I'm dead. But you'll pay. Starting with Louise, she's the next to die."

A small movie screen sprang to life directly in front of him. The picture was as clear as life. He watched in horror as Lexy Crosby pointed a Glock 19 at Louise's temple. Lexy turned toward Manny, showing off her mutilated face as a vivid reminder of her fate. He screamed to warn his wife. But the loud report blocked out everything.

His body jerked as his senses spiraled back to him. The next loud knock brought Manny up from his chair like a jack-in-the-box—a terrified jack-in-the-box. He looked at his watch: 6:15.

He wiped at the moisture on his face and felt his pulse start to calm. He shot a quick glance at Louise, saw the faint rising of her chest, and knew the nightmare had lied. But it was still fiercely alive. He tried again, but couldn't quite shake the helpless binding that some nightmares bring with Jacob Marley-like chains. He took another deep breath and relaxed his shoulders. Better.

Wow. He had fallen asleep after he closed Lexy's file. He wanted the rest, but that kind of sleep he didn't need. No one did.

The knocking intensified. Manny grabbed his gun and went to the door. A fast look through the security peephole was all he needed to become fully awake. Adrenaline pushed through his just-settled body, and the pounding in his chest returned.

Richardson and Corner stood outside his door wearing looks of worry fit for a mother. "Damn!" He said as he opened the door and waited for Corner to speak.

Alex and Tucker joined them. The expression

on their faces only made things worse.

He noticed his partner wasn't in the hall. "Where's Sophie?"

Corner searched the floor and then went back to Manny.

"He took her. He's killed First Officer Pena and kidnapped Sophie. He's holding her hostage behind the food court. And damn it, now he's got Perez's .38 *and* Sophie's 9mm."

Corner shifted his weight. "He says his name is Jenkins, but it's Peppercorn. He's either playing with us or you hit the dual personality thing on the head. Regardless, he wants us, especially you."

Surreal dread grabbed at Manny and refused to let go. Not Sophie. Not another partner.

Pointing at the security guards, he said, "Don't let anyone get into this cabin." Then he turned to go.

Richardson grabbed his arm. "That's not all. He claims that he has pipe bombs and will use them unless he gets what he wants."

Manny stopped in his tracks. "I thought you said he wants me. What else does he want?"

Richardson threw up his hands. "I don't have a damned clue, but he said you would know."

"How would I know?"

Searching the others, he hoped to see the answer written in big, bold letters across their foreheads. No luck.

He ransacked every corner of his mind, looking for something he already had, a gift that Peppercorn had given him. His eyes burned holes in the floor, and then it hit him. He did know what the killer wanted.

It all made sense now. It was masked in the

madman's agenda for revenge, the real reason he did what he did, was who he was. The killer didn't even realize it himself.

"What do we all want?" He rushed to the Lido Deck with the others trailing close behind.

CHAPTER-72

By the time Manny reached the Lido Deck, Jenkins had moved to the very back of the ship, taking Sophie with him and using her body as a human shield, just in case anyone got trigger happy.

Manny pulled the card out of his pocket and eyed the copy of the ship's picture ID that Corner had handed him earlier. It appeared to be Robert Peppercorn. He had changed his hair, and his face was chiseled. His skin had been transformed by hours in the sun or tanning booths. The name under the picture read Eli Jenkins.

Was this name change an attempt at hiding, going underground? Or did his mind pathetically blow a psychological gasket and evolve into what Manny thought he saw in him those years ago?

How did this fit with the knowledge that Jenkins wanted to talk to him?

Manny had interrogated him several times, with different questions meaning the same thing, and on each occasion, Peppercorn had maintained his innocence. He'd been convincing too. But the evidence called Peppercorn a liar.

Is it possible to really do something that hideous and not know it?

How could anyone really know what hid in the

mind of a psychopath? Lucky him. He was sure he was about to get a glimpse of that unchartered territory. Maybe even a full-blown show.

"Hey, you with us?" asked Corner.

Eyes snapping away from the picture, he put it in his back pocket. "Yeah, just trying to put things together."

He looked around the lounge area surrounding the five eateries and noticed that Richardson's people had the doors guarded and had sealed off every exit leading to the very back of the deck. Peppercorn was trapped. He frowned. It didn't fit. Guys like Peppercorn didn't leave themselves in this kind of position. Unless . . .

What if he wanted it like this?

Manny didn't like how this was going down, but there weren't many options. Jenkins or Peppercorn, or whatever he called himself, had Sophie and that had to change.

"Are you ready to do this?" asked Corner.

"I'm fine. Let's go."

Manny piloted the others past both deck pools and the small winding waterslide that led to the end of the larger one. He sidestepped broken and tipped sun chairs scattered over the wooden deck. It looked like a bomb had gone off.

Sharp tension took hold of his hand, and he could see that the stress was affecting the others too. And why not? Peppercorn had been a step ahead the whole way, and they could be walking right into a trap—a death trap.

They neared the last sliding door that opened to the very back of the *Ocean Duchess,* to where Jenkins held Sophie hostage. They'd better get this right or Manny would bury another partner, or Louise would be a widow, maybe both.

Without warning, the door parted and a tangle of flesh tumbled through it.

Reflexes took control, and he leveled his gun at the snarl of arms and legs moving his way.

"No shoot! No shoot!"

A terrified Japanese couple toppled breathlessly to the deck like sacks of potatoes, covering their heads with unsteady hands and screaming in their very best English.

He quickly raised his gun to the cloudless sky and swore.

Corner motioned for the couple to go to the forward part of the ship.

"I'm getting too old for this shit," swore Richardson, lowering his gun.

Alex agreed. "I thought I was going to need new underwear there for a second."

"That makes two of us," Manny exhaled.

"Three," added Tucker.

Once the couple was out of range, he motioned to the others. The next step wasn't exactly proper protocol and probably wouldn't work, but Manny saw no other way.

"Let's split here. Josh and I will stay on this side of the ship, and you three come up the other side. With teams on each flank, we might be able to distract him. And for God's sake, let's not do anything rash."

He turned to Richardson, who nodded.

"If he wants to talk to me—at least I hope talking's on his mind—we're going to give him the opportunity. If we can divide his attention enough, maybe we can get a clear shot. I hate this, but we're just going to have to play it by ear. He's holding all the cards."

Corner turned to Manny. "You think you know

what he wants?"

"Yeah, I think I do. I guess we'll find out shortly."

"You better know, or it's gonna get ugly," snapped Richardson.

Manny looked at the burly ex-cop. The pissy attitude was getting real old. But he also knew the chief was right. "Just hold up your end."

Richardson grunted and led Alex and Tucker through the sliding door. Two minutes later, Corner put his hand over his ear phone. "They're ready."

Manny and Corner crawled to a group of steel dining chairs piled on hand carts—just to the left of where Peppercorn lay in wait—and hunkered behind them. Manny raised his head to get a look at Peppercorn and, hopefully, Sophie.

The scene in front of him caused the wind to leave his sails. It wasn't what he had expected, but the killer had been clever all through this ride, and now was no exception.

Jenkins was holed up in the rear left area of the deck with stacks of flat sun chairs on each side of him, protruding at forty-five-degree angles. Two rectangular food tables had been stood upright, just on the outside of the chairs. A tall, blue table umbrella covered the space so that no one could see in from the radio or weather towers. He had made sure no sniper could get a bead on him. The only way in was straight through his line of sight.

Sophie sat duct taped to a cafeteria chair just to the inside of the makeshift stronghold. Her head lolled on her slow-heaving chest. She was out, but alive.

There was something else. Something out of

whack. This scene looked too contrived. Too staged. There was no way out for Jenkins. Even if he tried to jump off the back of the ship, he would hit at least two protruding deck covers. No one could avoid them except maybe Superman.

No matter what happened to Sophie or with any alleged bombs, Peppercorn couldn't get out alive unless he surrendered. Manny thought that possibility had a snowball's chance in St. Thomas of happening. This was set up for a bad ending for Peppercorn. He frowned. These men didn't work that way. Life was about them and what they needed, and suicide just wasn't in their vocabulary.

What was he up to?

"What do you think?" whispered Corner. "Should we get his attention?"

"I don't know. There's something wrong with this set up."

"I think so too. But maybe he truly screwed up."

"Maybe, but not likely." He grabbed Corner's wrist. "But we can't wait for more help; Sophie's running out of time."

Corner nodded. "Let's see what's on his mind."

The agent turned in the killer's direction, the ship's bullhorn to his mouth.

"Robert Peppercorn, this is Agent Corner with the FBI. Put down your weapons and come out with your hands behind your head."

Immediately a shot echoed over the deck. The bullet ricocheted off one of the chairs to Corner's left.

"You stupid shit," screamed Jenkins. "Peppercorn is gone. Long gone. My name is Eli Jenkins, and I sure as hell don't want to talk to a damned Fed. I want to talk to Detective Williams, now."

Jenkins's voice had gone from lunatic screaming back to full control in one eerie second.

"I want him to come to me. Unarmed. You hear me, detective? If you don't get your pretty-boy ass out here, I'm going to kill your partner. I'd like to take the time to do it my way, but a bullet in the head will work. Don't you think?"

"Put down the weapons and come out—" Another bullet exploded near the stack of chairs, slamming into the deck. Shards of wood covered the surface.

"Are you deaf? You have two minutes before this skank's head goes inside out," yelled Jenkins.

Manny started to stand up, and Corner pulled him back. "What the hell are you doing? I can't allow this. He'll kill you before you get within fifteen feet."

"I don't think so. At least not until he gets what he wants. I'm not totally sure what this Jenkins is about, but I think I know how to get his attention. You boys better be ready."

Shaking off the agent's hand, he started toward Jenkins.

CHAPTER-73

Runnels of sweat streamed from every pore on his body, soaking his shirt, as Manny walked. Every cop knew that the real threat of dying went hand-in-hand with living. It came with the territory. But he had never really ventured into the realm of dying, at least not like this. It was crazy and against everything he'd ever learned. Not only that, he was going boldly into what came next.

Who's the crazy one here?

He hoped God did protect drunks and fools because he was a card-carrying member of the latter. But he had to try. He couldn't let Sophie die. If he didn't face him, he knew Jenkins would kill her. These men didn't utter idle promises. They weren't politicians.

Bright reggae hopped from the ship's sound system. The music hardly fit the mood, but it sounded better than the funeral march. He also noticed that the foamy trail left in the ship's wake had ceased. Captain Serafini was guaranteeing this scenario wouldn't be smuggled into the busy port of Oranjestad. This would be Jenkins's last stand, one way or the other. It might be his own too.

Eli Jenkins. What of this new persona that embodied Peppercorn? What did he mean when he said Peppercorn was long gone? Was this an alter-ego thing about the Dissociative Identity Disorder that the shrinks working Peppercorn's case had mentioned, or was Peppercorn really dead and this monster, somehow, had taken his place?

"That's far enough."

The sunlight was blinding. He squinted through it, trying to get a good look at the towering figure. Jenkins took a small step forward.

Surprise tapped him on the shoulder. He had seen this man around the ship. In the glass elevators. At Trunk Bay in St. John. In the dining room. But Manny had never recognized him for who he was. He had changed. Lost sixty or seventy pounds and had gone the route to extreme fitness. But the man who now called himself Eli Jenkins was Robert Peppercorn.

The two men exchanged looks, and Manny's sense of dread went up ten levels. The cold, uninviting black pools that were windows to the killer's soul almost caused him to flinch. Hatred, anger, and pain were the only things Jenkins was about. Manny got the unmistakable impression that any shred of goodness or compassion this man had ever held had been snuffed like a finished candle. He had never sensed this kind of wickedness. The man before him was more monster than human.

"How can I help you, Mr. Jenkins?" he asked softly.

"*YOU* help *ME*? Come, come detective. I think you have the roles reversed. You are in no position to help me. But I, on the other hand, can help you."

"Okay then, how can you help me?" he said evenly.

The killer's face twisted and his rage detonated. "Don't patronize me, flatfoot," he yelled, pointing the 9mm at Sophie's head.

"If you try that shit on me again, I'll kill her and then stuff one of these between your eyes before you can freaking twitch, got it?"

"I get the picture. No reason we can't work something out here." He bent his eyes to the deck. "How can you help me, Mr. Jenkins?"

"That's better. It's not often we get a chance at redemption, detective, but I'm going to offer that opportunity to you. I'm going to give you a chance to save your soul."

Manny brought his eyes up from the floor and noticed that Sophie was coming to. He never missed a beat as his gaze continued upward to Jenkins.

This man was so articulate, intelligent. Something that Peppercorn could never have been guilty of. What had happened?

"What is it that you want me to do?"

"Why, Detective Williams, I thought you would never ask. I merely want you and all of the rest of Lansing law enforcement to suffer. You see, I have discovered that suffering is worse than dying. Ask the Crosbys. I suspect that even Detective Perez could give you some insight. If she could talk, that is." Jenkins face grew amazingly calm. "You must choose, Detective Williams, another partner's death or your own."

Manny tried to ignore the lead ball that had instantly formed in his stomach. He'd been right. Jenkins wanted revenge. He fought the good fight to answer. "How does that save a soul?"

"You dumb-ass cop! Do I have to spell it out?" Jenkins shifted the gun to his other hand and continued. "Let me put it in terms you might understand. We all feel better when we pay our debts. Right? There's a sense of relief. I want you to experience that sense when you write this check."

He watched Jenkins's muscles tense. They were getting near the end. He needed to find a solution to this standoff—now—except none of the scenarios in his mind excluded death, especially his.

"What debt do I owe?"

The hateful reaction on the killer's face was chilling.

"You haven't figured it out yet? You are the very essence of ignorance. By killing this bitch, I get to watch you suffer. By you dying, your loved ones suffer. Either way, I win. I spent ten years in that shithole. This is the payment I require for sending me there. It's time to pay up. Your turn to choose. Her or you. Now."

Jenkins pulled the hammer back and pressed the gun against Sophie's head.

It was time to play his card. Now or never.

"Wait. Just wait." Manny let his breath out slowly. This was it. Lord, he hoped he was right. "What will your mother say when she sees you like this? She's on the ship. I saw her three nights ago."

Jenkins hesitated. For a brief moment, Manny saw Peppercorn's face emerge from the confusion, from whatever dark place he had been imprisoned.

"What? My mother?"

The gamble had paid off, momentarily at least.

Everyone wanted their mother to love them, to care for them, to tell them that they will forever be insulated from the pain this world invented.

Almost everyone's mother loved him or her, unconditionally. The man that was once Robert Peppercorn was no exception. He still cared what his mother thought.

This was the break he had hoped for. It would be a mismatch, but so were David and Goliath. Manny crouched to attack, never anticipating what happened next. The old saying about the best laid plans of mice and men was right on.

"You dick! You leave my wife alone," screamed Randy Mason, seemingly ignorant to the danger around him as he crashed through overturned deck chairs.

Randy rushed Jenkins with Richardson hot on his heels, screaming for Randy to get down. At the last second, just before Jenkins recovered from the mind-bending truth Manny had administered, the security chief tackled Sophie's husband. The thud was resounding as almost six hundred pounds of flesh collided with the deck.

Maybe it was Randy's screaming or just how Jenkins planned it, but Sophie was now almost fully awake and took her cue by rolling violently to her left. She went down hard with the chair still firmly attached, but out of Jenkins's line of fire, for the moment.

Manny closed the distance between them and staggered Jenkins with a hard right hand to the jaw. Most men would have been down for the count. But Jenkins wasn't most men.

Jenkins righted himself and grinned. "Is that all you got, detective? I bet your gook partner could do more damage than that." He stepped forward and swung his gun at Manny's head. Manny dove to his right, reaching for the 9mm in his waistband at the same time. He landed awkwardly on his extended shoulder and was greeted with crippling pain that jolted his senses. It felt like someone had stabbed him with a jagged knife. The gun slid from his hand like a skate on ice. Always the lucky one.

"You bastard! Let her go!" shrieked Randy, even as Richardson struggled to keep him on the deck.

Now fully recovered from his momentary shock, Jenkins turned away from Manny and pumped four loud shots toward Richardson and Sophie's husband. Manny heard an agonizing scream come from Randy. Jenkins swore and he sent two more bullets their way.

"I'll kill every one of you Lansing pricks!"

Manny knew that Jenkins meant it. Desperately digging for the gun, he twisted his body to get a better look, catching his shoulder along the wood. The pain caused motes of colorful stars to dance in front of his eyes.

His body told him what his mind wouldn't believe; he couldn't have picked up the gun even if he had found it. He was frozen in place, unable to get off the deck, and soon Jenkins would know it.

The killer fired a shot in Sophie's direction, and another. He then whirled and headed straight to where Manny lay, scattering chairs and tables Manny had dove behind. Jenkins was like a raging rhino honing in on his one true target.

"You're a dead man, Williams. Are you ready?"

He wasn't. He tried to get up again. His shoulder said no. He then grew surprisingly calm. His thoughts turned to his wife and daughter. He found himself hoping Louise and Jennifer would forgive him. He knew Louise understood that he'd had to do something. Letting Sophie die wasn't an option.

Jenkins leveled the gun at Manny's head.

He could smell the killer's pungent body odor as it mingled with the acrid, smoky smell of spent gunpowder.

Jenkins pulled the clip from the 9mm, checked it for ammo, then slammed it back and racked the slide.

Manny closed his eyes.

Loud shots rang out, and wood exploded next to his ear. The sound was tremendous as splinters stuck to his cheek and neck. But he was alive. Somehow, Jenkins had missed.

He opened his eyes, blinking into more bright sunlight, trying to locate his would-be executioner. He watched as Jenkins staggered to one knee, two round holes braying from the middle of his tank top. The next shot caused a large, red-rimmed third eye to appear between the killer's other two. The big man fell backward to the deck, his large limbs fidgeting in a gathering crimson pool. He grew still with the gun still clutched in his hand.

Manny let loose the breath he'd been hoarding.

He twisted to his left side and forced himself to sit up. He looked over his shoulder to the source of the shots. Agent Corner lowered his still-smoking weapon and winked.

"What kept you?"

"I had a date."

"Nice shooting."

"You didn't think I was gonna miss, did you?"

He was glad the FBI Wonder Boy hadn't. Real glad.

CHAPTER-74

Eli Jenkins or Robert Peppercorn—whoever he really was—was dead and wouldn't hurt anyone again. That made Manny happy. As much as he could be anyway. He unconsciously rubbed his bruised shoulder and watched Aruba become a small dot on the brilliant, blue horizon.

Yesterday had been a hell of a day. One he wouldn't forget, not soon anyway. The only consolation was that it was over. But an unsavory, maybe indefinable price had been paid. Innocent people had died because they had simply been in the wrong place at the wrong time, trapped in a madman's nefarious concept of how the world should turn.

What price, justice.

Manny sat in the middle of his phalanx of friends, eating breakfast and watching cruisers mill around the sun-drenched deck, just doing what cruisers do.

Most were unaware of the intense standoff twenty-four hours earlier. It took a major effort from Carousel's public relations department to downplay, and eventually smooth over, the disaster that had taken place. But cruise lines were good at it, maybe better than any other industry in the world.

This morning it looked as if murdering chaos had never occurred on the *Ocean Duchess*.

Louise sat close to his left and Sophie to his right, next to her husband.

Randy wore a fresh, white, gauze bandage on the right side of his neck, compliments of the grazing bullet fired from Jenkins's gun. He had been fortunate. Another inch and it would have hit his carotid artery. Richardson had reached him just in time. Manny still didn't care for the abrasive security chief, but he had acted like a good cop, and that meant something.

Alex and Barb Downs sat directly across from him, and they were flanked by Agents Corner and Tucker. Gavin, Stella, and Mike had decided to fly from Oranjestad to take Lexy's body home with them, compliments of Carousel, of course. Mike had made a fast recovery and the ship's doctor didn't see any reason why he couldn't fly in a few days.

There had been desperate sadness clouding his old partner's eyes as he gave Manny a gentle hug and headed to the taxi that took the Gavin and his family to the hotel. Mike still refused to speak about the incident.

No amount of time would ever really heal the deep, vacant pit that had taken up residence in the Crosby's collective hearts. But each passing day would lessen the pain; he knew that to be true.

Jenkins's wild voice still rang in his ears, that he had wanted them all to suffer. His vengeful mission had been carried out. Most of the Lansing law enforcement family had been, and would be forever, affected by Jenkins's terrible quest.

Manny shaded his eyes as a line came to him

from an old gospel hymn.

Forever changed, I'm forever changed.

Nothing could be truer. Manny had seen the dark side of human disposition for years. But nothing resembling Peppercorn. He wondered where the limits of human justification ended, or if there was one. He didn't know. Maybe no one did.

He was glad this one was over, but he couldn't rid himself of the questions nagging him. It was hard to understand why Jenkins had set himself up to die. Did he really think he was going to be able to escape from the deck? Force his way off?

Manny ran his hand through his hair. Did it matter? Jenkins was dead. End of story.

They had taken a tour of the killer's room and found nothing to shed light on any questions that remained. They did find a worn newspaper clipping from the Lansing Post, written by a young reporter named Eric Hayes, accounting the trial and eventual conviction of Peppercorn. Several of Lansing's finest were given credit, including Manny, for bringing him to justice. It didn't take a genius to figure out why Peppercorn had kept it.

If he wanted to kill us all, why make the mistake that would most certainly lead to his death?

And what of Jenkins's mother? They had found her dead in her cabin, shot like a sick dog. But the astonishment on Jenkins's face when he mentioned the killer's mother had been obvious. He had been surprised to find out she was on board—even though she had been killed with Detective Perez's Smith and Wesson, which Jenkins had possessed. Just another psychotic episode?

Chief Richardson came from the elevator and

approached the table. Sophie saw him first and jumped up, leaning toward Manny. "This has been a long time cooking, watch my coffee."

She walked quickly to the chief and stopped a few feet short. "You've got this coming." His partner took one step and leaped on Richardson, draping her arms around his thick neck. Richardson started to pry her off and then stood still, slowly wrapping his arms around her. Her quiet sobs shook her small body as she finally slid away from the big man.

"I want to thank you for saving my husband. You might be a prick, but a brave prick, and you can play on my team anytime," she quivered.

Richardson stood with a surprised look on his face. Then he smiled. "Ahh . . . thank you, detective . . . I think." He moved to the table. "I'm not good at this stuff, so let me say I'm sorry for your loss. And if I can ever help you with anything, let me know."

Sophie's eyes narrowed. "Did the Captain put you up to this?"

The chief leaned back and grinned. "He said you'd say that, but no. Let's just say you taught an old dog a new trick." He turned and walked away.

"Do you think we just got smoked?" frowned Sophie. "But maybe he's for real. Randy's still here, and that's good enough for me."

Just then, Agent Corner's cell phone started playing Jimmy Buffet's Margaretville. He rolled his eyes. "No rest for the weary. Corner here."

He left the table and put his hand over his other, sun-kissed ear. "Say again, I didn't get all of that." The FBI agent's head and shoulders slouched while he continued to hold the phone tight to his head. There was no denying the body language; Manny tensed and waited. Now what?

Corner dragged the phone from his ear and stood staring over the railing. His head was shaking slowly. Like he hadn't believed what he'd just heard.

"What is it Josh?" asked Manny.

Corner heaved a sigh. "Detective Perez died about an hour ago."

Stunned didn't cover it. He'd known her death was a possibility, but people expected the best and things usually worked out. Not this time.

"Damn," rolled softly from Tucker's mouth.

Jenkins had struck again, this time from beyond the grave.

CHAPTER-75

Manny's spirit ached for Christiana Perez's two boys and her husband. They had lost more than he could imagine. She was a good cop and loved her family more than herself.

Life seemed so unfair at times. It left wounds. But it does continue, like it or not. After deciding to make peace with that, Manny determined there was nothing more he could do, and that maybe he owed a little more to his wife than his job.

He made a concerted effort to enjoy the morning's post-breakfast activities that Louise had planned. They were going to go to the casino and then find a couple of empty deck chairs to work on their tans. But first, he wanted to finish reading the Western he had started in San Juan.

He hoped it would end with the same verve and swagger that it had begun. He pulled out the book, opened it, and began where he had left off.

. . . Sage began to fire, shooting from the hip, then from the shoulder. Each round intended for an outlaw that needed dyin' . . .

Marking the paragraph with his index finger, Manny turned to the next illustration in the book. The fascinating artist had created a masterful image—it seemed to come from the author's very own mind's eye.

Sage Noble, a farmer turned gunslinger, stood in the center of the illustration and was as large as life. Sage's face was craggy and lined with age, and he appeared to be tired from his journey. Yet, his pilot-blue eyes were alive and filled with a stirring purpose. His black hair was slightly out of place; hanging low on his forehead. His Western-style, blue tunic matched the gunslinger's eyes perfectly.

Manny raised his face to the hot sun and then stole a glance at Louise, who was lying on her back in the deck chair beside him. She was relaxed and wore a look of contentment on her face. It was good that she was finally enjoying herself.

It is good for me too.

Her tanned skin glistened with mango-scented sunscreen and painted a pleasant contrast with her bright yellow two-piece, a very pleasant contrast. He made a mental note to check things out a little closer when they went back to the room.

A tall, well-built man and his wife strolled across Manny's line of sight holding hands, prompting his mind to wander, wondering for about the millionth time how Jenkins had gotten himself cornered like that. It hadn't made sense then, and it didn't now.

He pulled the Ray-Ban sunglasses back over his eyes and looked at the picture of Sage again. It was hard to imagine him as a farmer. The man looked like a gunslinger. The huge, ivory-handled revolver was melted to his large left hand and spewed yellow and orange fire as Sage took deadly aim at the outlaws.

Large left hand! Manny sat straight up in his

chair. His pulse quickened as his stare seared a hole through the artist's work.

My God, that's it!

How could he have been so blind? It was so simple. It had been right in front of him. Pictures don't lie and neither does evidence. There had been something, but it had been hidden from him like an egg at an Easter hunt. Until now.

It took maximum effort to harness his poise and hide his suspicion as he tapped Louise on the shoulder. He told her he was going to the cabin to change and then to the casino. She mumbled acknowledgement, reminded him about dinner at the Supper Club, and turned her face toward the rising sun. He jumped out of the chair and walked quickly to the elevators.

Corner's cabin wasn't far, and he prayed he was there. He had to be.

His mind was churning with a truth that was now obvious, at least to him. He hoped the agent didn't think he was nuts, but he was sure he could prove it. He knocked on the Special Agent's door.

Evidence never lies.

It wasn't what everyone wanted to hear, not what anyone wanted to think about. But he was sure he was right. There was another killer on the *Ocean Duchess*. More deadly and clever than Jenkins had ever hoped to be.

CHAPTER-76

"What in God's name do you want to look at the forensic information for? This case is over. Jenkins is lying in the morgue. Right where we want him. This one is in the books," snapped Corner.

He stared at Manny as if he were some crazy panhandler in downtown Lansing. In spite of Corner's adamant declaration, Manny detected an uneasiness that the agent wished not to acknowledge.

"I've learned to trust your instincts, and you were dead-on about Peppercorn's profile, but I think this is over the top," Corner complained as he rubbed his stubbled face with both hands.

He looked at Manny again with the kind of expression you give your kid when they say they were late because they had a flat tire. He wanted to see the tire.

"Josh, sit down. Let me show you this." Manny didn't wait for the FBI man to sit. He spread out seven crime scene pictures, in a very specific order, on the table. They were close-ups of the six women who had been killed since they had left San Juan, plus one shot of Lynn Casnovsky's face.

"I never get used to this," said Corner.

"Me either. Shoot me if I do." said Manny. "But

these people need us."

Corner motioned for Manny to continue.

"I want you to look at the bruising patterns on the necks of the first four pictures. You can see four distinctive bruises on the right side and one on the left. The left mark is bigger, and because of the darker purple color, it could signify that there may have been more pressure exerted at those points, indicating it was his thumb on that side of each of these four women's throats."

"Okay, so he strangled them with his left hand. We know that Peppercorn was left-handed so that makes sense."

"You're right, it does. The other bruising, here on the head and temple, is consistent with pressure from his right hand. So that checks out. The rest of his MO is patterned virtually identical as well. Obviously the same perp—except when it came to Detective Perez because he didn't immediately rape or kill her. Everything else was almost the same, but not quite. Based on the markings on her neck, I still think it was Jenkins, but his MO changed. The trophy eyes, the hiding of the body in the closet. It didn't fit. It's like someone told him what to do."

"But we all know these guys can wander all over the board. They evolve for whatever reason. He may simply have had a change of heart. We've both seen it."

"Agreed. It could be true. But I don't think so. I believe, in this case, he would have changed his routine gradually. The act of removing her eyes *and* putting her in the closet didn't make sense. Too much change for one event. I think he had instructions."

Corner carried a look of disbelief. "Tandem

killers? Come on, Manny."

"It's not unheard of. Look at that sniper case in DC a few of years ago. Two killers—one dominant, the other submissive. They behaved like a surrogate father and an adopted son."

"Okay. So far you have shown me nothing but theory and a pattern change."

Manny's intensity grew as he tapped the other pictures with his finger.

"Look at the pictures of Liz and Lexy. Look closely."

Corner studied the pictures, and Manny saw the light go on, like sunrise banishing shadows. The marks on Lexy and Liz were mirror images of the other four. The thumb mark was on the *right* side of their throats and the finger bruising was on the *left*.

"Shit. The killer used his right hand to strangle these two ladies," whispered Corner.

To drive his point home further, Manny pointed to the photo of Lynn Casnovsky's face. "Lynn's face is bruised on the left, indicating that he was hit with someone's right hand and not their left. The only way that Jenkins punched Lynn that hard is if he was ambidextrous, which he wasn't. So the logical assumption is that Lynn was hit by someone who is right-handed."

Agent Corner looked at Manny with anxious, indelible amazement. "But Peppercorn was so messed up, he could have changed hands."

"I don't believe it. Right- and left-handedness operate much more from instinct and reaction when in a highly emotional situation. Murder is still just that."

The agent rubbed the back of his neck. "You really think there is another killer?"

"There's only one way to find out. Let's look at the results of the stuff that Max and Alex gathered and see if anything is out of place."

Corner hesitated and then stood up and headed for his room.

"Okay, okay." he said in an almost pleading tone. "I hope to God you're wrong."

Manny fell in line behind his agent friend. "I don't think hoping to God is going to change anything at this point."

They stepped into Corner's cabin. The smooth jazz saxophone of Bony James filtered quietly from the small speakers while Corner walked over and unlocked the room's safe.

He pulled out two sealed envelopes. Both were marked with the familiar "CONFIDENTIAL FBI FILE." One read IAFIS RESULTS the other CODIS RESULTS. They had been sent to Corner's attention.

"I didn't see any reason to open them until I filed my report when I got back." Corner held out his hand. "Your idea, you get to open it."

Manny smiled and took the file with the CODIS results.

The two cops sat on the edge of the bed as Manny unsealed the file and flipped to the name summary for the DNA results. Each case was referenced and catalogued with a date and a file number. He scanned down the list. He read it again. Then a third time.

No one is that good. There has to be something.

Doubt clouded his eyes. There was nothing at any of the crime scenes that shouldn't have been there. Nothing. In fact, two of the victim's names, Juanita Henkle and Rebecca Tillerman, hadn't shown up. They had no DNA record on file, so references to them came back "unidentified."

"Damn it! That wasn't much help." Manny cleared his throat and ran his hand through his hair.

"Hey, you know we don't get hits on all of them. That's why half of the murders in America go unsolved. Unfortunate, but true."

Corner reached for the file. "Let's see if we get any fingerprint surprises. It will probably be less helpful than the DNA profiles. Sorry Manny, but your theory isn't looking too good."

"You're right, so far."

Manny pulled open the folder and leafed through to Liz's and Lexy's reports. There were several identified prints. Most of them were staff, and the other list of unknowns had to be previous guests. They would check it out, but his face fell like a stack of dominos. No Peppercorn or any other name that was a likely link to the case.

Frustration smoldered like an out-of-control forest fire.

He flipped to the last, partial page and saw something that changed his mood. "Look at this."

Corner looked to where Manny was pointing, bent closer, and followed Manny's finger.

There on the last page of the report, after Lynn's case summary, was a small tag to the file. It was like an afterthought. It appeared as if the tech processing the prints had decided at the last minute that the information could be important.

The partial print on the stub Sophie found under lifeboat sixteen had been the last one processed and didn't belong to a past or current guest. It belonged to someone else, someone Manny knew.

The name that IAFIS had uncovered stared

back at the two cops like a cobra ready to strike—then it did. Dr. Fredrick Argyle, Peppercorn's shrink, had been on lifeboat sixteen.

CHAPTER-77

"There's no Argyle listed on the ship's manifest," observed Corner as he tossed the booklet on the bed. Then he rolled his eyes and raised his eyebrows the way someone does when the obvious slaps them across the face. "Well, duh. Of course there isn't." He stroked his chin. "I guess this explains why he hasn't called us back."

"He has another ID, and chances are he's changed his appearance. But he's here, or at least he was. I can feel it," Manny said.

"Your 'feelings' are starting to bother me. What are you, some kind of psychic wannabe?"

"Just call me Silvia Brown."

"Maybe I will," the agent grinned, then turned serious. "What do you want to do?"

"I don't want to panic anyone, including the captain and Richardson. There's no reason to get their panties in a bunch just yet. Let's keep this between us for now."

The guest picture book that had been printed digitally from the ship's database still rested on Corner's loveseat.

"Let's take out all of the single, male pictures in this thing and pay a visit to our only witness. Since we put Jenkins down, there hadn't been any reason to go over the pictures with Mr. Eberle."

"You mean since I saved your ass and put Jenkins down," Corner retorted.

"Yeah, but I didn't see you walking through the Valley of Crazy Bastard to confront him," answered Manny.

"Touché. But it did feel good to see him hit the deck."

"Even better from my vantage point," said Manny.

"Don't forget me at Christmas. I love presents."

"Okay. Let's go see John Eberle."

"Let's go."

Five minutes later, they were knocking at Eberle's cabin. After the second knock, the old man stuck his head out the semi-opened door.

"Mr. Eberle. Do you have a minute?" asked Manny.

"Call me John. Sure, detectives. I was just fixin' to go up on the deck and check out the lovely scenery around the pool, if you catch my drift." Eberle looked at both the smiling detectives. "I ain't dead yet, men, at least not all of the way."

"No sir, you're not," answered Manny, who remembered a saying he'd heard once: *Don't die until you're dead.* The old man was still living. Good for him.

"We need you to look at some pictures. It may take a few minutes, but we would really appreciate it."

Eberle's face came alive. "Glad to help. Come on in, I got me a little time."

The two detectives followed Eberle back inside his room and were hit with the pleasant aroma of mocha drifting through the cabin.

"Want a cup of double mocha latte? I'm not supposed to have it but, well whatever, we're all gonna die from somethin', right?"

While Eberle retrieved cups, Manny placed the stack of pictures on the table, purposely putting Jenkins on top.

The old man put on his wire-rimmed reading glasses and slid into the chair adjacent the table. His wrinkled hand shook slightly as he pulled the stack of photos close.

He hesitated at the first photo. "This guy is close, but a little different."

Manny and Corner exchanged glances and watched Eberle go over each photo with methodical purpose. The process was excruciating. Each second seemed locked in time, captured in a time warp. But neither he nor Corner said a word. This had to be all Eberle.

After twenty minutes and hundreds of pictures, Eberle stopped. Manny held his breath. The elderly man was staring at a rugged, square-jawed man, who looked remarkably like Robert Peppercorn. Eberle studied the photo without blinking.

"This is the son of a bitch, right here. You have to take away the goatee, but I'll never forget those eyes. He even has the same, cocky-ass grin."

"You're sure, John?" Manny asked, trying to stay calm.

"Yes sir, I am. This is the guy."

Manny scrutinized the photo and didn't see it at first. He traced his finger over the left cheek of the man in the photo. The make-up job was a good one, but not good enough.

The small crescent scar was barely visible, but it was there. A souvenir from one of Argyle's patients at the prison. An angry inmate, pissed because Argyle helped deny the con's parole, had attacked him with a filed-down toothbrush and had sliced his cheek wide open. Anyone who had ever met Argyle knew about the scar. It was like his red badge of courage. He even bragged, to anyone who cared to listen, about how he had gotten it. Manny knew of it because he had worked with him a few times, especially with the Peppercorn case. And of course, there was the incident between Argyle and Gavin Crosby.

He bit his lip. It all made sense now. "Shit."

"What?" asked Corner.

"There was a thing between Gavin and Argyle a few years ago. I'll tell you more when we get to his room."

The room number 6217 was stamped below the frame of the photo along with his name, Dave Prisby. It was just a few doors down from Mike's and Lexy's cabin.

"Thank you, John, you've been a great help," said Manny.

He gathered up the pictures. They had their man and his room number. Sometimes being lucky *and* good worked together. Like when a witness was sure of what they had seen. Like John Eberle.

"Detectives?"

The two men stopped. "Yes?" answered Manny.

"I have just one question. Do you think this lunatic would come after me? You know, for putting the finger on him?"

"No sir. I think he *wanted* you to drop the dime on him," said Manny.

CHAPTER-78

Richardson and his staff had shut down the elevators leading to the sixth deck and had sealed off the entrances in that section of the hall. They were doing a fairly good job of keeping this latest drama under wraps, but it wasn't easy. People wanted to go to their cabins when they wanted to, not when it was convenient for the ship's personnel. They didn't like to hear about "minor problems that would be cleared up shortly."

Standing outside of Argyle's stateroom, Sophie raised her 9mm as she stood to Manny's left, with Richardson and Corner to the right. Four additional security guards waited on each side.

"I want the first shot. Boom, right in the wong," muttered Sophie.

"No shooting, yet, but if it starts, feel free," whispered Manny.

They had been situated outside his cabin for five minutes and hadn't heard a sound. It was starting to look as if he wasn't in the room, which Manny thought made sense. He seemed adept at saving his own skin and wouldn't follow Jenkins's lead.

But to storm in could be dangerous. Argyle may have even set some kind of trap.

Argyle had thrived on making law enforcement

look bad. He wanted them to be like the blind leading the blind and to fall into the ditch. The arrogant bastard didn't think they would, or could, ever catch him and somehow he had set up Jenkins to be the fall guy. Manny's curiosity throbbed with how that had happened. How had Argyle controlled him? A thousand questions and no answers.

It was time to get this show on the road. He slid the key card into the slot and pushed slowly, stopping when the door cracked about an inch. He examined the gap for any sign of a trip wire and saw none. He pushed a little harder and felt no resistance. The muscles on his upper lip twitched, and his hands grew moist, but he couldn't risk wiping them.

Then like some distant drum, he heard a faint sound resonating from somewhere inside Argyle's room. *Thud.* The noise was muffled, but it was *something.* He held his breath, waiting for anything.

For the next minute, he stood like a statue. But he heard nothing else. Only silence. The deafening kind.

Manny had waited long enough. His instinct and lack of patience took over. It was time to get real, as they say. One glance toward the others was all it took for them to know what was coming. He shoved as hard as he could and dove into the room, flying low. Sophie dropped to one knee and held her gun with both hands. Corner stood above her, aiming high.

Bracing himself on the floor, he scanned the room. No one and no thing moved. No gunshots or fiery explosion. No raging Dr. Argyle running toward him with a two-foot dagger in hand.

The faint thumping he had heard from the hallway caught his attention again. It was louder, clearer, like a collision of plastic on glass. Poised like a gunslinger himself, he directed his weapon at the balcony door.

He approached the curtain and pulled it open with a quick wave of his hand. There, dangling from the top of the balcony, banging the door whenever the breeze was strong enough, was a small, covered plastic jar. It contained two objects rolling around in clear liquid.

Manny's stomach lurched.

Ogling back at him, through the crystal clear jar, were Detective Perez's bloodshot eyes.

Behind him, Sophie, Richardson, and Corner had rushed into the cabin. Sophie came from the bathroom as Corner slammed the closet shut, and they hurried to Manny's side.

"Good God!" moaned Sophie. "Doesn't this guy ever stop?"

She turned away, covering her eyes, as Manny opened the door and pulled the bottle down, quickly hiding it in the pocket of his shorts.

"Where is the piece of shit?" begged Manny.

Sophie flipped on the overhead light, but instead of radiance spreading through the room, the TV sprang to life. A small click filtered through the room as the DVD player switched on.

The voice coming from the player was almost immediate. "Good afternoon, Detective Williams. What kept you?" Argyle filled the screen with a conceited smirk. "I have eagerly anticipated this meeting."

CHAPTER-79

The doctor had changed. He'd always been tall, but not ripped. His neck was thicker, his face stronger. It was obvious he had spent countless hours in the gym. He might even have partaken in the crazy steroid world.

Argyle had dyed his close-cropped hair shining black and shaved his salt-and-pepper Fu Manchu, but there was no mistaking the prison psychologist. Except for the scar on his cheek, his appearance was uncannily similar to Jenkins.

It pissed Manny off that the narcissistic doctor was bigger than life on the screen. And only on the screen. He hadn't bothered to attend this tenuous gathering himself. Instead, he'd sent his mechanical lackey to handle it. Argyle was smart, but part of him wondered if the doctor was gutless too. In a perfect world, the homicidal lunatic should be standing in front of Manny instead of hiding behind some taunting video. But Argyle had their attention, in control—right where he liked to be.

"No doubt you are not singing my praises, but you know what they say: a prophet is without honor in his own home. Maybe you can appreciate some of my genius now." Argyle flaunted a triumphant, but charming smile. "Maybe you,

Detective, the rest of Lansing law enforcement, and certainly the FBI will think twice before disregarding research like mine as—how did Chief Crosby put it?—'ridiculous ranting.' He even suggested that I was the one who needed my head shrunk." His eyes blazed with hatred.

Corner reached over and paused the whirring player. "What the hell is he talking about?"

Manny looked at Sophie and back to Corner. "Is that what this whole thing's about?" he whispered.

"What?" demanded Corner.

Manny said a one-syllable expletive not used in church. "I said I'd tell you, so here goes. About five years ago, Argyle set up a meeting with prison leaders, two other shrinks—Drs. Martin and Orcutt—and invited police chiefs from most of Michigan's largest police departments to discuss a new therapy he was sure would work. He said it would fly in the face of traditional dogma, but he was convinced it would break new trails in treating prisoners with certain disorders."

"Specifically, DID, or Dissociative Identity Disorder," chimed in Sophie. "He thought if you could treat and eventually control each distinctive personality or behavioral pattern, you could 'cure' the subject." She shook her head. "I just said that and it sounded nuts."

Frowning, Manny continued. "He said that convention taught if you addressed the subject's problems and traumatic experiences, got them out in the open, the rest of the other behaviors and personalities, so to speak, would disappear or at least be significantly diminished, and the subject wouldn't need to 'hide' in other parts of their psyche. Argyle disagreed, citing the lack of success of those traditional therapies.

"Martin and Orcutt agreed with each other that treating this 'other' personality would give credence to its existence and consequently make it stronger. In short, the treatment would in effect be creating a monster. With Argyle pursuing this line of thinking, his colleagues thought he was flat crazy."

Corner's face twisted with irritation. "So let me guess, he thought someone like Peppercorn, who didn't recall any violent acts or behaviors because he hid in the 'other' personality, could be cured by this new approach."

Manny nodded. "He wanted permission to work his theory on Peppercorn: to locate or to draw out and treat the other personality. He said that Peppercorn had a particular type of DID, something about people who suddenly find themselves in another place or time and can't remember how they got there. He called it dissociative fugue . . . or something like that."

"I'm no psychologist, but that sounds dangerous. Messing with someone's reality, I mean," responded Corner.

"The other two professional shrinks at the meeting believed Argyle was way out there, whacked, and that his proposed treatment would only mess up Peppercorn more. The big wigs from the prison and a certain police chief thought so too, and they flat out denied Argyle's request. That police chief was our very own, grouchy-assed Gavin Crosby," said Sophie.

"Gavin wasn't real tactful," admitted Manny. "He completely went off on Argyle. He called him a ranting lunatic and suggested he had gotten his degrees from some witch doctor school in Dipshit,

Africa. He told Argyle they have enough troubles with psychos on the street without him creating one."

"So what happened?" asked Corner.

"Argyle picked up his files and started to leave. Then he dropped everything and ran toward Gavin, taking a swing at him in the process. He missed, but the riot was on. I grabbed Argyle and a couple of others got a grip on Gavin. Things settled down, and Argyle called Gavin an imbecile, then left," explained Manny.

"The doc got two weeks off without pay and was given a warning that if anything like that happened again, he would lose his job and his license to practice in Michigan," said Sophie. "If I remember right, the company that had agreed to publish his first research manuscript found out about his little meltdown and cancelled the deal."

"So, if we put two and two together, he went on this killing spree and somehow recruited Peppercorn to help, because he thought you all played a part in ruining his career, right?" said Corner.

"Could be," agreed Manny. "There's something else, Eight weeks ago, Dr. Martin's wife was brutally murdered in her bedroom, while Martin was away at a conference in Detroit. We thought she was a random victim. But it looks like Argyle got a piece of that one, too."

Corner reached for the PLAY button. "Let's see if confession is good for the soul."

The screen sprang back to life. "Well, I hope you and Detective Lee have clued the FBI in on my past. Everything you have deduced is probably true. Bravo!"

Argyle's face remained controlled and stoic.

"But you were all wrong. Dead wrong. I treated Peppercorn the way I wanted, and it led to my first meeting with Eli Jenkins. Fascinating man.

"Each time Peppercorn came in, I would hypnotize him and converse with the complex and very intelligent Mr. Jenkins. I was impressed with his freedom from guilt and remorse, his sense of power. He cared for nothing but what he wanted. While it flew against everything I had ever believed, I started to see the simple, magnificent truth in it. Only the strong should survive. Everyone else should serve the exceptional among us. Don't you think?"

"Sick bitch," muttered Manny.

"Come, come, come. You didn't think I would give up trying to prove my theory, did you? Genius is so overlooked." He cackled, raising the hair on Manny's neck. Argyle was crazy.

"After a year, I realized that Jenkins was the sane one. He had opened my eyes. His philosophy was brilliant and simple. I found myself wanting to be like him. No, more than like him, I wanted to be *superior* to him. With my training and greater intellect, I knew it would be just a matter of time before he'd do whatever I wanted. Anything at all. We had hundreds of sessions and progress was slow, but eventually I was able to control his actions, while I continued to grow in my new convictions."

Argyle's dark eyes peered past the TV and seemed to drive straight through Manny's soul. "It was unfortunate that Jenkins had to die, but it was all part of the plan. He accepted and even embraced it. He knew that his death was required to accomplish a higher purpose—my purpose. Jenkins thought of me as a father, and sons will do anything to please good old dad."

His laugh turned wild, almost out of control. It was unsettling how he reeled it back in.

"So there you have it. I won't bore you with any more details. I don't want to spoil all of our fun. But not to worry, Detective Williams, I'll leave calling cards from time to time, just to let you know I'm still out here. We must meet again because, quite simply, all scores are not yet even."

The doctor was in love with the platform he had created. Manny suspected what was coming next, and he was right.

"Oh, by the way, how is Dr. Martin doing after the unfortunate and untimely demise of his older, but lovely wife? I'd bet he's not doing that well. The sniveling wimp will probably just shrivel up and die. Poor baby. The incompetent moron couldn't even wipe his ass without her telling him how. Send my regards."

Argyle's face turned calm. "There is one more thing: I have left another little present for you. A clue, if you will. Can you find it? No, not the good Detective's eyes. That would be far too easy. By the way, do you think her children would want them back?"

The screen went blank. Dr. Fredrick Argyle was over and out.

Manny rolled his eyes to the ceiling and then promptly smashed the player with a driving punch.

"Easy there, big boy, we might need that disc for evidence," said Corner.

"Sorry." He hit it again and the tray popped open, displaying the disc. "How's that?"

"Show off," said Sophie.

CHAPTER-80

The tall man with the hands of a professional basketball player gave his passport to the security agent at the main terminal of Queen Beatrice airport in Oranjestad, Aruba, and waited.

The small, dark-complexioned guard studied his face, then the photo. He repeated the process two more times, then handed the passport back.

"Did you have a good time on our humble island, Mr. Ellis?"

"I had a splendid time. They don't call it 'One Happy Island' for nothing," he responded.

The guard moved his head up and down with such energy that Ellis thought he looked like one of those idiot bobblehead dolls.

"Have a good flight to New York, and come back soon."

Ellis moved leisurely through the final gate to the waiting area. He touched his short, strawberry blond hair and tugged at his cleanly trimmed beard.

He wondered how long it would be before they found the real Mason Ellis. Ellis had thought he was meeting his new lover for a forbidden rendezvous—that the free trip to Aruba and his hotel stay were appreciation gifts. In a way, they were.

What a pathetic fag. In the end, he had cried like a baby. The real Ellis had possessed the same look all of Argyle's conquests had—the one asking how they could be so stupid.

It had taken him just a few days to find Ellis a few months ago. He had needed to find a queer who looked enough like himself to make it work. It was easier than he thought it would be. He even had a few to choose from. The Internet is a wonderful thing.

Argyle had put Ellis' body in one of the hidden caves on the northeast part of the island. He wondered what the cave explorers would think of *that* discovery.

Shifting his carryon bag to his left hand, he continued his stroll down the center of the terminal like a peacock in heat. No reason to hide. All was handled.

He sat down on the airport bench and loosened a lazy yawn. It had been too easy. He had proved his theory that most cops couldn't catch a damned cold.

Jenkins had been right from the beginning. People like him were superior beings. They didn't have to adhere to the rules like the rest. Still, he had to be careful . . . because people like Detective Williams disagreed with his newfound philosophy.

His smile diminished as he dwelled on Detective Manfred Robert Williams.

The man was fairly intelligent and could prove to be a worthy adversary, especially with a little help from the clowns at the FBI. If there was such a thing as a worthy adversary for Dr. Fredrick Argyle, that is. Time would tell.

The flight would have him in the US a full six hours before the dolts found his disc. It gave him plenty of time to be at his next appointment. A lifetime really.

He had a surprise for Dr. J.T. Orcutt, late of Lansing, Michigan, and currently of Rochester, New York. He was pretty sure that Orcutt's horoscope had no idea what his real future held.

CHAPTER-81

The rest of the cruise proved to be calm and uneventful. Richardson's crew searched every room and any nook or cranny, but Argyle was off the ship. Sophie suggested that he had left them in Aruba and had somehow gotten a flight out. Manny and Josh agreed and alerted Aruba's police force. They wouldn't find him, but they had to make sure. At any rate, Richardson's people discovered what Manny already knew: Argyle was gone.

The FBI contacted Dr. Orcutt in New York and warned him of Argyle and his newfound religion. Corner sent agents out from the field office to offer protection to Orcutt and his family and hoped it would be enough.

Louise called her brother in Lansing, and he took their daughter Jennifer to his place until they returned. The LPD would make sure there was a round-the-clock vigil on Louise's brother's house. No need to take unnecessary risks now. Argyle had said it himself—the score wasn't settled.

At about four a.m., on the last night before the *Ocean Duchess* docked in San Juan, Manny walked the ship alone.

Before he had left the room, he watched Louise in silent adoration, remembering the Supper Club dinner they had experienced just hours before. He recalled how the scarlet-stained, glass dome at the ship's very highest point kept the Caribbean weather at bay. How it had cast a searching red glow across the white, Egyptian cotton tablecloth. The effect was enchanting, and the colors blended perfectly with Louise's gown.

The stuffed flounder and T-bone meals had been extraordinary. The service, impeccable. Not to mention the *crème brûlée.*

He touched Louise's face, his thoughts sweeping to how the band had begun with Jazz Master Paul Hardcastle's *Lost in Space.* He had whisked her to the small, intimate dance floor, despite her minor objections. The dance was as magical as any they'd ever dared.

But that hadn't been the most emotional part of the night, not by any stretch of the imagination. When they had returned to the room, after they had made love, Louise had gotten up, went directly to the dresser, and pulled out a white envelope and handed it to him. It had the name of her doctor stamped in the corner and remained sealed. He knew exactly what the woman of his life wanted, what to do. He asked her if she was sure. She nodded as her eyes moistened, and he never hesitated, tearing the envelope open.

He read the letter, and then read it again.

Louise's eyes scanned his face, hoping to get a sense of what Manny had seen. He looked down at the print again then turned the letter toward Louise, pointing to the last line.

". . . imaging error, no unusual readings. No carcinoma detected."

Her reaction was overwhelming. Almost as intense as his.

They had climbed on the bed and danced. Then they'd simply jumped up and down until his calves hurt, and her squealing had evolved to a squeak.

He had pulled her close, and they'd stood in the middle of the bed holding each other. Quietly, thankfully.

Was there anything like being rescued from the dragon?

Louise being cancer-free was the best news he had ever received, and he prayed no more of those trials were on the horizon.

He bowed his head and listened to the calming, rhythmic collision of perpetual waves. But not calming enough to quell the storm brewing in him. The old saying about taking the good with the bad came to him, causing some of his euphoria to dissipate. Louise was safe, but Argyle was still out there. And with a massive vendetta to satisfy.

Manny turned the corner of the dimly lit deck and looked at where the shadow-drenched lifeboats rested in silence. They looked like helmets of giant, long-extinct warriors.

His feet were on auto pilot, and the slow saunter stopped at lifeboat sixteen.

He closed his eyes and concentrated on bringing Liz's laugh alive, just one more time. For a brief, exhilarating second, he thought he heard it. Then it was gone in a blink. He made a silent vow. He would see Argyle in chains or a casket. He preferred the casket.

Going back to Deck Six, he used the master key he still had to let himself in Lexy and Mike's room. By then, the sun's early morning gold was tiptoeing into the cabin. He was almost overpowered with the sense of death. He shuddered, stood straight, and renewed his vow.

****

Manny and Louise were greeted at the door of their modest ranch in South Lansing by Louise's brother, a rambunctious black Lab, and an even more energetic teenager. (How was it possible to be more enthusiastic than a black Lab?) It was good to be home. Really good.

"What'd ya bring me? Like, I've got to know. Now," demanded Jennifer.

Sampson picked up on her excitement and let loose an ear-splitting bark.

Eyes twinkling, Louise hauled a jewelry case from her bag and handed it to her daughter. The diamond studded set of moon and star earrings caused Jennifer to squeal again. The earrings were her favorite all-time shapes—at least for this month.

"Manny?"

"Louise?" he mocked, turning her way.

He felt his legs go weak. Three black rose petals lay in his wife's hand.

"It was in my bag. I . . . I . . . I don't know how . . ."

Underneath the petals was a one-line note, neatly printed in black ink. "One never knows, detective."

Pulling his wife and daughter close, he crushed the petals in his hand.

Thank you so much for reading my book!!
Please go to www.rickmurcer.com to talk me.

****

CPSIA information can be obtained
at www.ICGtesting.com
Printed in the USA
LVOW10s1835200617
538750LV00010B/702/P